He lower

And as he turned and started to move away, Megan parted her lips. "Nicholas," she groaned softly, torn at the thought of his leaving.

He halted, his shoulders tensing. Then he slowly swiveled around.

She wet her dry lips, realizing he was not going to return to her. She would have to go to him. He was leaving the decision solely up to her. Expelling a shaky breath, she took a step forward. Hope sparked in his eyes. And that was her undoing. With a squeak, she flew into his arms. "Oh, Nicholas," she sighed, feeling him shudder. Then she lifted her head. "Kiss me," she insisted, raising her hands to thread her fingers through his cool, soft hair.

He closed his eyes and wagged his head from side to side, as though fighting some inward war. His jaw tightened, and Megan knew he was going to refuse her. Then he opened his eyes, eyes aflame with a fierce emotion she couldn't identify. And instead of pushing her away, he lowered his head and pressed his lips to hers.

She could not believe what she was doing. But somehow, being nestled in this man's arms, having his lips pressed against hers, felt right. With some inner certainty she new she belonged to Nicholas. Even as a child she knew. She had always belonged to Nicholas.

Then an irate voice from the doorway startled her, making her gasp.

"Get your bloody hands off of my sister."

Praise for INNOCENCE LOST

"The relationship between main characters Megan and Nicholas swings between tempestuous and tender, and their love scenes couldn't be hotter. With a splendid blend of romance, adventure, and drama this romance novel must be in the hands and on the shelves of the most discriminating romance reader."

~*Camille Cline, former Tor/Forge editor*

Innocence Lost

by

Tiffany Green

This is a work of fiction. Names, characters, places, and incidents are either the product of the author's imagination or are used fictitiously, and any resemblance to actual persons living or dead, business establishments, events, or locales, is entirely coincidental.

Innocence Lost

COPYRIGHT © 2009 by Tiffany Green

All rights reserved. No part of this book may be used or reproduced in any manner whatsoever without written permission of the author or The Wild Rose Press except in the case of brief quotations embodied in critical articles or reviews.
Contact Information: info@thewildrosepress.com

Cover Art by *Nicola Martinez*
The Wild Rose Press
PO Box 708
Adams Basin, NY 14410-0708
Visit us at www.thewildrosepress.com

Publishing History
First English Tea Rose Edition, 2009
PRINT ISBN 1-60154-623-8

Published in the United States of America

Dedication

To Father. I couldn't have done it without you.

PROLOGUE

Claremont Estate, England
November 21, 1813

On silent feet, drunk with giddiness, Lady Megan Westland padded across the room while the candle's flame danced from her candlestick. The thought of seeing him again shot strange lightning bolts up and down her body. Anticipation grew with each step. Her knees trembled. Thank goodness Julian wasn't here to see her. Her brother would box her ears.

She halted a foot away from him and lifted the candle. Golden light poured over his face. She found him wearing the devil's own grin with his light-brown hair spilling past his collar—somewhat disheveled—and he looked every bit the rogue his mother claimed he was.

With a pounding heart, Megan took a small step forward. Her eyes swept over him and heat flooded her cheeks. "Hello, Your Grace." She glanced back up. My God! He was too handsome. "You're looking well today." She paused and ran her tongue over dry lips, wondering how his mouth would feel against hers. Her breath caught. A girl of ten and three shouldn't think such thoughts, she knew, but she didn't care. She would do anything, *anything*, for a kiss from this man. This beautiful man. Why, she would even part with her beloved new pony, Aramis.

Her thoughts returned to why he rarely visited Claremont. Megan knew her brother's presence seven short miles away had kept His Grace in

London. "I wish you and Julian didn't hate each other so—" Megan halted when a noise sounded behind her. She spun around, aghast to find the door creeping open and light inching across the dark parquet floor, revealing the other portraits within the gallery. In a rush, she blew out her candle and darted behind the curtains covering the windows to her right.

Clamping her bottom lip between her teeth, trying to ignore the smoke rising from the candlewick, Megan strained to hear over the pulse hammering in her ears.

"What are you doing, Moll?"

"I thought I heard someone, Ruth."

Megan held her breath.

"Heard someone? In here?" Ruth chuckled. "Not unless these portraits can talk, you didn't. Come on, we don't have time for such nonsense. We've got work to do."

"I know I heard—" The door closed, muffling the last of the maid's sentence.

Megan released her constricted breath and crept out from behind the damask fabric. Tiptoeing toward the door, she gave in to one last glimpse of him. Her steps faltered. A stream of pale November light had escaped the curtains she'd disturbed and illuminated his portrait.

"Good bye, my love," she whispered to his motionless face, then hurried from the room, hoping her mother and the dowager duchess hadn't been concerned with the length of her absence.

CHAPTER 1

Claremont Estate, England
March 3, 1818

With a twinge of guilt, Lady Megan pulled on the riding breeches. She had taken the poor stable lad's pants. *Again.* But she'd had no choice. Her maid, Lucy, had found the pair she'd hidden in an old trunk in her dressing room, and there hadn't been time to bribe someone into purchasing another pair for her.

Megan loved to ride above all else. Oh, she knew it was quite unconventional for a duke's daughter to ride astride wearing breeches. According to her parents, society would think her mad. A raving loon ready for room and board at the asylum. But the exhilaration of racing across the meadow in the warm sun after a long winter was pure heaven.

After she'd stuffed the large shirt into the borrowed pants, Megan pinned a wool cap over the chignon Lucy had constructed earlier. She had no wish to have anyone notice her long black hair and report those findings to her father. Megan shivered. Father would be none too pleased.

Reaching for her horse, Aramis, Megan halted when a woeful nicker reached her ears. She turned to the last stall. "What is it, Titan?"

Her brother's horse whinnied softly. She could swear the big brute was begging her. "All right." She laughed, opening the stall. "I shall take you."

Titan danced around as she located the saddle. "It's a terrible shame Julian doesn't come home and ride you more often." The horse nodded his agreement.

With a chuckle, she tightened the leather strap and scrambled into the saddle. After she patted the sleek, black neck, they flew from the stables toward the pink and gold sky, ready for an adventure.

****

He leaned against a tree and watched her race away. She was wearing those deplorable clothes again. When she became his wife, he would make damn certain that never happened. His ring glistened as he opened his snuffbox and took a pinch. Why Lady Megan wanted to dress in breeches and ride astride a horse instead of wearing the finest silks, he would never know. She could damn well afford thousands of the finest gowns.

The man reached for his handkerchief, his hand brushing against the note he would deliver. The first part of his plan was about to begin. The plan that would solve all his problems. The plan that would make him rich and make Megan his wife.

Birds squawked overhead, then flew away. He gave the enormous estate of Kenbrook one last frown, then turned and walked further into the woods.

****

"Your Grace, it is urgent I speak with you," Higgins insisted, his words muted by the thick oak door.

Nicholas frowned and cracked open an eye. His bed curtains hadn't even been tied back. "What time is it?" he croaked, his voice rusty with sleep.

"Almost seven o'clock, Your Grace."

"'S too bloody early. Go away." He turned onto his side. Perhaps if he went right back to sleep, his dream would pick up where it had left—

"It's your new stallion, Your Grace. It is missing."

Nicholas popped open his eyes. "Missing?" He lifted his head. Throwing back the coverlet, he rose from the bed and swore when his feet connected with the cold floor. When he reached the door, he swung it open. "What in the bloody hell do you mean my new stallion is missing?" He'd had great pleasure in beating Huntington to the purchase, and now it was gone?

"My apologies, Your Grace." Higgins made a small bow. "The groom found the stall unlatched, and the horse gone just a few minutes ago. He has already assembled some men for the search."

"I don't believe this." It had taken Nicholas months to locate the animal and a great deal of blunt to secure it. And now some thief had ventured onto his estate and taken it right out from under him. His mood darkened. His mother was in residence. In fact, she resided here most of the time. If thieves had set their sights on the estate, she could be harmed. He turned toward his dressing room. "Summon my valet and prepare me a horse. I am going to find the stallion and catch this thief." And the bloody scoundrel would wish he had never stepped one foot on Claremont.

An hour later, Nicholas halted his horse within a copse of trees several feet from the stream's bank and glanced around. Damnation! He'd lost the trail. The horse must have gone into the stream.

The sound of galloping hooves caught his attention. A black horse raced by, kicking up small clods of mud. A young lad, he deduced, espying the rider's shabby breeches and boots, was crouched over the horse's withers.

The bloody scoundrel was making away with his missing stallion!

Fortunately, the thief was speeding toward the main road. Nicholas knew he could overtake him by cutting through the woods.

Without further consideration, he flanked his horse.

****

Racing along the path, Megan watched the forest blur into streaks of brown, grey and green. The rising sun expunged the late winter air of its frosty bite and she closed her eyes, inhaling the spicy mélange of pine, horseflesh, and rich, damp earth.

Something darted into their path. Titan came to an unsettling halt and reared up. Her eyes flew open and she groped for something to hold on to, but she toppled head over bum from the saddle, and landed facedown in a puddle of cold, sticky sludge.

Stunned, she lifted her head and forced air into her lungs.

Flattening her palms against the bottom of the marshy pit, Megan hefted herself out. She cursed the snow for melting into these dreadful mud holes as she sat on a nearby tuft of brown winter grass. After wiping the muck from her eyes, she glanced about, wondering what had caused Titan's fright.

The puddle lay to her left, and to her right stood two black Hessians, polished to a near blinding shine. Apprehension raced down her spine as a large hand descended and gripped her arm like a manacle.

"Now I've caught you," the man growled and hauled her to her feet.

"Release me at once," Megan demanded, tugging at her arm. Fear and anger swelled in equal measures. They stood midway between the seven-mile distance separating the Kenbrook and Claremont mansions. No one would hear if she screamed for help.

Tipping her head up, Megan started to issue another demand for freedom when mud dripped into her eyes, blinding her. "Blast," she hissed, blinking furiously. It burned like the devil. And wiping her eyes with her muddy hands would only make things worse. This thought came at the same time she realized the man hadn't let her go. She struggled.

"Cease your squirming, scamp, and tell me where this horse came from."

"I'll not tell you anything." She continued to pull and twist, certain she'd have bruises for a month. "Now let me go." Tears leaked from her stinging eyes.

"You shall not be released until you tell me exactly where you got this horse." His deep voice thundered with impatience.

She opened her mouth to inform the blasted man that this was her brother's horse, and they were standing on her father's land, but she thought better of it. She had no idea who this man was or what his intentions were. What if he abducted her? Or worse? She swallowed hard. No one was around to stop him. With renewed determination, she fought even harder.

"What the hell...? Cease your struggling at once," the man barked. "You're getting mud everywhere." As if to verify his statement, a glob of mud plopped right on those shiny boots.

"You have no business with me." A loud rip sounded in her coat's shoulder seam.

"The hell I don't. You stole my horse."

"What?" She squinted up at his blurry face in disbelief.

"Don't act innocent, little thief, admit you—"

"Thief? Thief?" she sputtered, then kicked the man square in his shin.

He grunted in pain, then issued a nasty-sounding growl. Oh hell, now she'd done it. Before she realized it, he was dragging her away. "What do you think you're doing?" she squeaked, unable to mask her fear.

He didn't answer. She blinked rapidly. The tears

helped wash her eyes, and they didn't sting quite so bad. Her vision began to clear, and she could make out the stream ahead. Now, if she could just escape this madman.

After several more steps, he halted. "All right, little thief, this is your last chance. Either you answer my questions, or I'll throw you in."

She went rigid. He was insane!

"Did you steal the horse alone, or had you assistance?"

"I didn't steal—" The man took a step toward the stream. "All right," she said, digging her heels into the marshy ground, "I shall tell what you wish to hear." When he stopped and turned, she continued. "I run with a menacing band of cutthroats," she lied. "Indeed, they wouldn't think twice about carving your liver out with a spoon and eating it for dinner." She paused and turned toward the forest, pretending to scan the greenery. "They're surrounding us this very moment. You really ought to release me. Perhaps I can convince them to spare you." She faced his tall, blurry form once again and prayed he would believe her.

The man expelled a long sigh. "My patience is running thin, scamp. Just admit you stole the horse from my estate, and I might not send for the magistrate."

Megan pulled at her arm, testing his hold. Blast! She might as well have been clapped in iron. "And where, pray, is your estate?"

"Three miles from across the stream," he said, nodding east.

With an unmannerly snort, she shook her head. "Impossible, that estate belongs to the Duke of Claremont."

Clamping his hands around her upper arms, the man leaned down and snarled, "It is not impossible since *I am* the Duke of Claremont." While Megan's stunned brain absorbed those words, the blasted man lifted her off the ground and pitched her into the stream.

And that was terribly unfortunate. She couldn't swim.

Frigid water engulfed her and pulled her down. Thousands of icy needles pierced her skin. Unable to withhold her panic, Megan flung her arms about in a desperate attempt to rise to the surface. She kicked her legs, all the while thanking God she had swiped the stable lad's pants. A dress and petticoats would have pulled her straight down. Then again, she probably wouldn't be in this mess if she had worn a dress. Her head bobbed up once. She opened her mouth to scream, but swallowed water instead. Something pulled at her foot and down she went again. The more she struggled to rise, the lower she sank. Frantic, she peeled away her thick coat. But it didn't help.

Oh, God, she was drowning. Her lungs burned.

Then an arm slipped around her waist. She was lifted out of the water, choking and gasping, and set down on the coarse grass. The air she'd thought warm earlier sliced a frosty path through her skin and turned her bones to ice. Shivering, she wiped the wet strands of hair from her eyes, realizing her cap and hairpins were gone. She lifted her head. Her vision cleared, and she swallowed hard. Dear God, he was even more handsome than his portrait in the gallery at Claremont. Then it occurred to her that the duke might recognize her. She turned away. Oh, no, he mustn't recognize her, not looking like this!

"You're a...a girl!"

Nicholas stumbled back a step. With the mud cleansed away, he discovered that this was no boy, but a young woman, closer to twenty years of age than ten. A stunning young woman. Below her gracefully arched brows were thick, black lashes, spiked with droplets of water, drawing attention to exquisite amethyst eyes. Her skin, a creamy peach without blemish, made his fingers itch to caress the silky texture. And her lips were...

He frowned, noticing her trembling, blue-tinged lips. Then he realized her entire body was trembling.

"Take your clothes off," he ordered, then gritted his teeth against the visions those words evoked. His eyes moved down the pale column of her throat, settling on the generous mounds quivering from the cold. He couldn't ignore what was plainly visible beneath the soaked white shirt plastered against her chest. Definitely closer to twenty than ten.

"I beg your p-pardon?" she gasped after a lengthy pause, anger building on her face.

No way in bloody hell was he going to repeat those words. He turned to his horse. "You will catch your death if you aren't warm and dry soon."

"And wh-whose fault w-would that b-be?"

Nicholas sighed and turned back. It took a great deal of strength to keep his eyes from straying down. "Do not place the blame upon my shoulders, lady," he said, tapping his chest with his fingertips. "You should have answered my questions."

"Well you d-didn't have to th-throw m-m-me into the s-stream." Sarcasm laced her words, even through chattering teeth.

He swung around. "Nor did I have to dive in and rescue you," he said over his shoulder, then hurried to his horse. Why the hell hadn't he realized she was a girl?

"W-What are you d-doing?"

"I have a spare set of garments," he explained without bothering to glance at the brazen little temptress. He rummaged through his saddlebag.

"I'll n-not take them."

Stifling a groan, Nicholas turned and folded his arms over his chest. "You must get warm and dry."

He also needed her covered. Fast. Seeing her breasts in such a revealing way made him crazed.

"S-So must y-you." That unselfish response surprised him. Then he noticed the water droplets dripping from the ends of his hair, and the chill sinking deep into his skin. "I h-have a b-blanket," she added and nodded toward the other horse.

Nicholas recalled his mission of finding his lost stallion. The saddle. Why hadn't he paid any attention to that earlier? He shuffled closer and found that it didn't belong to him. Although crafted of the finest materials, obviously the saddle of a very wealthy gentleman, it wasn't his. For the first time, doubt crept up on him. He removed the blanket and turned to the beauty shivering on the grass several yards away. She looked helpless and fragile. Could she really be a horse thief?

With the thick wool in his hands, feeling like a foolish dunderhead, Nicholas approached her. She needed to get warm; his questions could wait.

Kneeling before her, he unfolded the blanket and spread it across her trembling shoulders. She lifted a thankful gaze and favored him with a smile. God's breath, she was stunning. A fresh scent of jasmine rose up from her damp hair to tease his senses. He went still. Transfixed. A man under a spell. The desire flared within him to kiss her and heat her cold lips until they turned hot and pink. Nicholas could not escape the temptation.

Megan had been shivering so long and hard, her stomach muscles began to cramp. And she could feel her wet hair growing stiff. So when the duke spread the blanket over her shoulders, bringing a bit of relief from the cold, she smiled. As she watched his eyes grow dark and heavy-lidded, however, her smile dissolved. He lowered his head, and her breath lodged in her throat. She sat frozen, startled to realize he meant to kiss her, and unable to move away.

When his lips settled over hers, sweet, sweet warmth flowed into her, expelling the brutal cold. Her pulse roared in her ears, eclipsing all sound, and her insides melted down to her toes. How many times in the gallery at Claremont had she dreamed of his kiss? A hundred? A thousand?

His tongue brushed against her lips and Megan gasped, stunned by the lightning-bolt sensation. As he swept the interior of her mouth with his velvety probe, pleasure cascaded in waves throughout her body.

She heard him moan at the same time his arms came around her. He pulled her to him, his coat grazing the firm, sensitive peaks under her thin shirt and chemise. Never had anything felt so exquisite. His hold tightened around her, his tongue delved deeper, and she was lost in the intimacy of her first kiss.

When the duke lifted his mouth from hers, disappointment jabbed her in the stomach. If her bones hadn't turned to jelly, she would have pulled him back to her.

"Tell me your name," he said, his breath a warm caress against her lips.

As she formed the sound of her name, Megan wrenched her eyes open, realizing what she was about to reveal. What was she doing with this man? Nicholas Bradshaw, the Duke of Claremont, her brother's enemy. She shouldn't be here with him...in the forest...alone...attired most inappropriately...kissing him!

Dear God, this man had the power to ruin her. With just a few details of what had happened today, she would be ostracized from society. Completely and forever.

Her parents would be devastated.

She shot to her feet, the blanket pooling to the

ground. "I must go." The duke's gaze lowered from her face and settled at a spot below her neck. She glanced down and gasped, wrapping her arms around her body. Oh, good Lord! She had no idea how revealing a wet white shirt could be. If she didn't leave this second, she would die of mortification. "I must go."

"You are not going anywhere."

She gasped. "You, sir, have no—"

"The horse," he nodded to where Titan was nipping at some grass. "Where did you get him?" His voice sounded funny, a little raspy.

She was about to tell the blasted man the truth when she recalled one important detail. The Duke of Claremont was no friend of Julian's. "The horse does not belong to you."

He cocked a brow. "He looks just like the one stolen from my stables earlier."

She shook. From anger. From the cold. Mostly from anger. He was never this mulish in her daydreams. "Your Grace, I assure you, this horse does not belong to you." She tried to keep from sounding cross, but found it difficult with a clenched jaw.

"Then who does it belong to?" He folded his arms, that damn brow rising even higher.

"This is absurd." She shook her head and stepped in Titan's direction.

The duke blocked her path. "You are not going anywhere, lady."

Megan found the heat of his body surprisingly alluring. She had the strange urge to move into his arms. How ridiculous. He had just pitched her into the stream. And then kissed her!

He lifted his hand and grazed her cheek with his fingertips. That strange expression once again crossed his face. His words stopped her from batting his hand away. "You are so beautiful."

Tears threatened. Blasted, silly tears. Megan had waited so long to hear those words. *So are you,* she wanted to say. Almost said. But her throat clogged as memories and feelings swirled within her. Memories of standing before his portrait at Claremont and pretending to hear those words from him. Of her smiling and batting her eyelashes, playing the coy debutante. Of him professing his love and proposing marriage in a single breath. For years, she had envisioned the scenes in her head. Although it had been months since she last visited his portrait, she could recall every detail. She lifted her gaze to his. The same shade of blue. Then they grew dark and heavy-lidded. He started to lower his head. He meant to kiss her. Again!

A thought wheedled to the surface. Her brother hated this man. She could not be caught with him! Using every ounce of strength she possessed, Megan ran to Titan. Paying no heed to the duke shouting for her to return, she raced from the meadow. Escaping him would be easy this time. But not the next. Not when she was about to be launched into society.

Dear God, how would she escape ruination?

****

Nicholas watched her go, her taste still on his lips. Even fifteen rounds at Gentleman Jackson's had never left him so disoriented. When he pulled her out of the stream and found her to be female, he'd been speechless. Her wet clothes clung to her body, revealing curves that would drive a saint mad with want. Other than pure lust, he hadn't the faintest idea what made him kiss her. And what a kiss. He licked his lips and closed his eyes. She tasted like strawberries.

He ran to his horse. He would find her. Mad, yes. Crazy, definitely. Insane, probably. But something compelled him to go after her. He jumped on his horse and it sprang forward.

She had disappeared in the thicket of trees opposite the main road, and after an hour of searching, he decided to return to his estate. His hands tightened on the reins and he gnashed his teeth together. How the deuce she had managed to escape him, he would never know. She must be an accomplished rider to have out-maneuvered him. But that just brought about more questions. With one last sweep of his surroundings, he turned his horse around. He intended to have some answers.

CHAPTER 2

Nicholas halted his horse before the red brick townhouse in Bond Street, London, and sighed in resignation. He prayed that after calling here on his mistress Angela, he'd forget the mystery woman's stunning violet eyes.

At least he knew of a certainty she wasn't a horse thief. On his way back to Claremont, he'd found his missing stallion munching on some winter grass. He felt like such an ass. If he could just find her and apologize...

The searing kiss they shared forced its way into his mind. He could still feel her breasts pressed against his chest, could still taste her honeyed lips as his mouth settled over hers. He groaned and mopped a hand down his face. Why was it so difficult to forget the bloody little chit? And why couldn't he find her?

Shaking his head, he marched up the steps. The housekeeper greeted him at the door and informed him that Angela was in the garden having tea. He walked through the elegant house and spotted the voluptuous redhead sipping out of a dainty teacup.

She beamed when she noticed him. Her green eyes lit up. "Nicky! You're finally back. How was the country? Dreadfully boring, I'm sure," she replied before giving him the opportunity to answer.

"Hello, Angela." Nicholas sank into the chair opposite her. Angela didn't affect him like she usually did. He sighed and rubbed his eyes with two fingers. That beauty sitting upon a tuft of brown grass, shivering and looking entirely too tempting filled his mind. He remembered how her eyes had grown soft and dazed when he kissed her, and how silky her skin felt against his fingertips. Damn! Why couldn't he get the nymph out of his mind? And why did he feel so desperate to see her again?

A loud crash sounded. He jolted upright and focused on fiery green eyes, set in a beet-red face with pinched lips that dipped down at the corners. Angela's teacup, saucer and teapot lay in a thousand shards of milky glass at his feet. "Are you finally back, Your Grace, or are you still up in the clouds with the birds?" she screeched at him.

With a long glare, Nicholas conveyed a silent reminder that he did not put up with such impertinence. "What were you saying?" he asked.

She swallowed and looked down. "I-I'm sorry, Nicky. Would you like some tea?"

He stared at the smashed pot and shook his head. "I think not." Watching her sullen expression for a few moments, he groaned inwardly. He would require Angela to achieve a much better mood in order to drive the chit from his mind. "You look lovely. Is that a new gown?"

She brightened. "Why yes, it is," she purred, pushing her bosom further out from her gown's low-cut bust line. She stood and sauntered to his lap, wrapping her arms around his neck. "Let's go upstairs, Nicky, and I'll show you the other goodies you purchased for me. Then I'll thoroughly thank you for each and every one," she added, rubbing her bottom over his groin.

Closing his eyes, not at all surprised when that violet-eyed nymph appeared, he nearly growled in frustration as he scooped his mistress into his arms and carried her upstairs.

Once in the bedroom, he brought his lips down onto Angela's. All thoughts of that razor-tongued temptress had to be exorcised from his mind. But the longer he kept his eyes closed, the stronger his memory of her became. Blurred details sharpened into vivid splendor and fantasy became reality. It wasn't Angela's soft lips he devoured, but *hers*. "Tell me your name," he whispered and opened his eyes. Seeing Angela, he frowned, his body going soft.

Fury sprang into her eyes, and he knew she had felt his response. He rolled off the bed and began to straighten his clothes. He really had been bewitched. What in hell would he do now?

"Who is she?" Angela demanded. "The one you thought you were with?"

"That's none of your concern," he snarled, turning to the door.

"Have it your way, Nicholas. I'm leaving."

He nodded without breaking his stride and left.

****

A few days later, Megan flew into the house, knowing she had little time to change out of her riding habit. Her parents expected her for tea at precisely four o'clock. She turned to the gigantic clock in the hall and made a face. Six blasted minutes!

Spinning toward the stairs, she prepared to bolt up to her bedchamber when she noticed the dowager Duchess of Claremont exiting the drawing room. Something in the lady's expression halted Megan. Worry. Had something happened to her son?

The thought made Megan's heart lurch. Nicholas! She pressed a hand to her chest and began in the lady's direction. "Has something happened, Your Grace?"

"Come, dear," she insisted, linking arms with Megan, "we have something to discuss."

Nervous, Megan walked into the drawing room. She glanced around the empty chamber and frowned. "Where are my parents?"

The dowager patted her hand. "That is one of

the things I wished to discuss with you, my dear." She turned to the sofa. "Here, let us have a seat."

Her uneasiness grew, but she refrained from asking the thousand questions swirling around in her head until tea was served. She took the cup and sipped, not at all tasting the contents. "Where are my parents, Your Grace?" she asked again.

The cup in the dowager's hand trembled before she lowered it to the table. "I received a note just before they departed from the estate this morning."

"Departed? Where did they go? And why?"

The dowager duchess hesitated. "London, though I have no idea why."

"The note didn't say?"

The dowager moved her head from side to side, her perfectly arranged twist glistening silvery-gold in the nearby window's light. "No." She pulled out a piece of ivory vellum from her drawstring purse and held it out. "I received this from your parents this morning."

Megan took the note and began to read.

Dearest Genny,

A most important matter has arisen and calls for our immediate attention. There is no time to explain now. Expect another note with more details once we arrive in London. While we are away, please take care of Megan. Knowing our daughter is in your care will ease our troubled hearts.
Respectfully,
Joseph and Margaret
The Duke and Duchess of Kenbrook

Lifting her head, Megan asked, "What important matter, Your Grace?"

"Mrs. Finch told me that your parents received an urgent missive just after the morning meal and departed soon after, though she had no idea what the missive stated. I hoped you knew."

Megan shook her head, regret for once again sneaking away to ride lying heavy in her bosom. "I'm afraid I have no knowledge of it, Your Grace." She dropped her gaze back to the note in her hands. What terrible thing had occurred to make her parents rush off to London? Had something happened to one of their friends?

A knock sounded, pulling her from her thoughts, and she turned as the dowager invited the caller to enter.

The head housekeeper, Mrs. Finch, rushed inside. "My lady, Your Grace, pardon me, but there is a man to see Lady Megan. He says it's very important, something about a burned carriage," she explained, wringing her hands together.

Megan gasped.

A moment's pause. "Send him in," the dowager whispered, rising from the sofa.

With her legs turned to jelly, Megan struggled to her feet. That burned carriage was not a Kenbrook carriage. It was not. It was not.

An old man, garbed in soiled, threadbare clothing, shuffled into the room. His eyes darted around as he neared. "G'day, ladies, sorry ter be bargin' in on ye. Name's Grover."

"Do you have important news about a carriage?" the dowager prompted, her voice a little stronger. Megan's throat clogged with fear.

He nodded. "Yes, well, I seen smoke 'bout five miles back. An' off the road, there be a carriage afire. But I got a real good look at the crest on the door."

"Are you saying the door held this emblem?" the dowager asked, pointing her collapsed fan to the spot above the room's fireplace.

Grover's rheumy eyes grew round as they focused on the solid gold shield of the Kenbrook crest. It contained thousands of precious stones that formed a large cross with a griffin on either side. He wouldn't stop staring at the priceless shield and the dowager had to clear her throat several times before the man looked back at her. She repeated the question twice more before he responded.

Panic tore a fiery path through Megan's insides. Her hands wouldn't stop shaking. She pressed them together and kept trying to convince herself that the burned carriage did not belong to her parents. But they were missing. She swallowed back a sob. Please. Please let her parents be all right.

"Yes'm, that be it," he confirmed with a nod, then swung his stunned gaze back to the glittering buckler.

"Oh, no," Megan gasped. She took a step but her foot caught on the Persian rug and she fell. She heard the crack of her head against the floor just as pain exploded in her skull. A loud roar filled her ears. Her limbs grew heavy. Then everything went black.

****

When Megan rose to consciousness, she had no idea how much time had passed. She focused on the painted ceiling and realized she lay on the bed in her chambers. The right side of her head pounded, so she let her eyes slide shut and remained motionless, waiting for the ache to pass. Then she heard the dowager duchess speak. The words sounded muffled, as though she had water in her ears.

"And you're absolutely certain, Dr. Benson, that Lady Megan will be all right?"

"Rest assured, Your Grace, she shall be fine. Just see that she consumes three drops of laudanum in water at bedtime each night for a sennight."

"Yes, I'll see to that."

"I also advise that Lady Megan be moved from the country as soon as possible. I've just been informed that five Kenbrook servants are infected with the influenza spreading through the countryside."

The dowager sighed. "Yes, I fear you are right. As you know, Claremont is infected as well. My brother Charles, who arrived three days ago, is now showing signs of fever. I could not possibly expose Megan to that." There was a brief pause. "Would it be prudent to move her with such an injury, doctor?"

"Lady Megan should be well enough to travel tomorrow, Your Grace. In fact, I have a need to go to London at that time to purchase more medicine..."

Sleep tugged at Megan, lulling her into the darkness hovering at the edge of her consciousness. Then she thought of her parents. And the burned carriage. With a gasp, she opened her eyes. "Mother...Father..." she cried, struggling to rise from the bed.

The dowager rushed to her side, placing a hand on her shoulder. "Shhh, dearest. The footmen I sent to the carriage informed me there was no one inside."

The vice around her heart loosened. "Oh, thank goodness." She slid back down onto her pillows. Her head pounded something awful. She took several deep breaths, and the terrible ache eased enough to speak. "You're sending me away?" she asked with a fleeting glance at the doctor.

"Yes, dear, to keep you from contracting influenza."

"Where am I to go?"

The dowager perched on the edge of the bed. Leaning forward, she removed a lock of hair that had fallen into Megan's face. "London."

"London?" she repeated, a funny tickle developing in the pit of her stomach. Then she recalled that her parents had gone there. "Yes. I could look for my par—"

Blue eyes turned stern. "No, dearest, Nicholas

shall locate your parents."

Megan felt her jaw drop open. "Your son?"

"The very same. After I pen him a note explaining the situation, I am most confident he shall find your parents."

The memory of the duke's searing kiss exploded in her mind. Heat rushed over her cheeks. "I-I cannot possibly stay with your son, Your Grace," she stammered, aghast at the very idea. Well...aghast and intrigued.

The dowager patted her hand. "Years ago, before my husband died, your father had certain guardianship documents prepared. The documents decreed that in the event your parents and brother were unable to care for you, the Duke of Claremont would become your guardian."

She didn't want to hear about guardians and documents. "Once Julian becomes aware that Mother and Father are missing, he is certain to make haste in his return."

"I have no doubt of that, dear, but your brother is currently at sea. It could take weeks for a message to reach him. Since Nicholas is now the Duke of Claremont, he is your legal guardian until your brother or parents return."

She cut her eyes back to the dowager. Of course, since his father's death years ago, his only son was the duke.

Fear surged at the thought of facing him again. But her parents needed to be found, even if it meant her ruination. Her parents could be out there somewhere, hurt. They needed to be found at whatever cost. She bit her lip. Would His Grace truly ruin her once he learned she was the Duke of Kenbrook's daughter? And Julian's sister, she thought, recalling the enmity between them. She dashed the wetness from her cheeks knowing she would take the risk. Any risk.

Before she could change her mind, Megan agreed to go to London.

To be in the care of the Duke of Claremont. Her brother's enemy.

The very man who had believed a lie instead of his one-time best friend.

CHAPTER 3

Nicholas glanced about the dark-paneled room, trying to remember the damned clock's whereabouts. God's truth, he knew White's as well as his own townhouse. But his senses grew foggier by the moment. Since leaving the faro table some while ago, he'd been keeping company with the gin decanter.

He could no longer deny the truth. That violet-eyed wench had him twisted in knots.

A snuffbox in the shape of a woman's leg appeared beneath his nose. He grimaced as the strong odor of Macouba laced in brandy assailed him. He shook his head. "Curse your eyes, Jeremy. Are you trying to make me ill?"

His friend chuckled. "I'd rather be offering you a fine cigar. Unfortunately, snuff is the only form of tobacco allowed here. Try some, Nick, it's not half bad."

"Be damned, Jeremy, put that bloody thing away," he insisted when his stomach flipped over.

Jeremy took the seat beside him and nodded for his usual whiskey. "I have a few things to discuss with you, Nick, but you look quite dull in the eye. Perhaps I should wait."

He welcomed anything that would take his mind from *that girl*. "I am not so fuddled." He swiveled his head and focused on Jeremy. "What is it?"

His friend sipped from his glass, then set it aside. "I was at Brooks's last week while you were at Claremont and watched Stenwick lose a wager."

He hiked his brow. "I presume that means something."

"That wager lightened his purse by two thousand pounds."

Nicholas whistled through his teeth. "Surely that gave him the blue devils for a time."

"Nick, I saw the books. He hasn't paid a single debt in over four months." Jeremy paused and lowered his voice. "I believe your uncle may be in a quandary."

He snorted doubtfully. "It's more likely his daft secretary misplaced the duns as he does Charles's invitations. The man is a complete imbecile." He took a gulp of his drink. "Moreover, if Charles were in need of blunt, he'd speak to me of it."

"You are probably right. I've seen his secretary."

As Nicholas raised his drink to his lips, he felt Jeremy's gaze on him. He turned and found his friend watching him in careful contemplation. "What. Have I a bit of muck on my nose?"

"I just realized that you've been imbibing gin."

"Meaning...?"

Jeremy grinned. "You guzzle the ghastly stuff only when you're troubled, Nick." His grin widened. "Perhaps you need to initiate in a bit of amorous congress to help ease your disquietude," he said and wagged his brows.

"Good Lord, Jeremy." He glared at his friend. "The lack of copulation is not my difficulty."

"I daresay, Nick, you've been at sixes and sevens since you and that barracuda, Angela, parted company. What else am I to believe? Not to worry, old man, I know the perfect replacement," he boasted. "Which happens to be the other thing I wished to discuss with you."

Sighing, Nicholas lifted his gaze to heaven, beseeching God for patience with his friend. "I am done with mistresses. By God, they're more trouble than wives." He drained his glass, then lifted his hand and requested another.

"And you being such an expert on wives," his friend replied dryly. "Aren't you even the least bit curious about the, um, lady?"

"No."

"She's very beautiful. And young."

Nicholas glared at his so-called friend. "Then you take her."

"I already have three mistresses and cannot afford another." Jeremy blew out a sigh. "But I am tempted. This one is quite the go. So what say you?"

"I am not interested."

Jeremy looked stunned. "Surely, you don't actually miss that jealous, red-headed twit."

"Absolutely not," he snorted. "In fact, I should have rid myself of Angela much sooner."

"Then what is plaguing you, old friend?"

He hesitated, reluctant to divulge any information about the brazen beauty he'd met. But he had to confide in someone. Her memory ate away at his soul. "When I went to Claremont, I met someone," he said quietly into his glass. His friend listened. "I cannot banish her from my mind, no matter how hard I try." He gulped down the remainder of his gin and nodded for a refill.

Jeremy's softly spoken question broke the thick silence. "What happened?"

He lifted the fresh drink to his lips. "We conversed for a while and then she disappeared." He took a generous gulp.

"Where did you meet? On your estate?"

Feeling sufficiently numbed, he turned and studied his bemused friend for a moment before he answered. "We met by a small stream on the property's border. She's the most beautiful lady I've ever met. She was young, probably under twenty. She is absolutely stunning, Jeremy."

"Who is she?"

He grimaced. "I don't know. She left before I

could even get a first name."

"Why don't you describe her in detail? Maybe I can help identify her for you."

He shook his head. "You haven't met her."

"How can you be certain?"

Releasing a long sigh, he wished he'd never started the conversation. "Because she's a commoner."

Jeremy choked on his drink. "Be damned, she's one of your tenants?"

"No."

"Then a tenant of Kenbrook's?"

"Perhaps." He frowned. "I just wish I knew how to find her."

"And, my friend, what would you do if you did find her?"

He opened his mouth, then snapped it closed it with a click of his teeth. "Bloody hell. You're supposed to be helping."

"I am trying, Nick, but you're making things rather difficult."

"Oh? And how are you helping?"

A smile spread across Jeremy's face in slow degrees. "I've already explained, old chap. There is a young, beautiful damsel eager to expunge all of your unhappiness. Take my word for it, you shan't be disappointed."

"I don't want her," he grated out. He couldn't just come right out and tell Jeremy what had happened with Angela. How his body had refused to respond. What if this was a permanent condition? He gulped down more of his drink.

Leaning back in his chair, Jeremy crossed his arms over his chest. "But you wouldn't hesitate to bed that gorgeous country girl."

He didn't bother to deny it. His body only responded when he thought of her. Blast it all to hell. He drained his drink and rose unsteadily. "I'm leaving now."

"Take care, Nick," his friend said as he brought his glass to his lips.

With a curt nod, Nicholas left the gentleman's club, choosing to ignore the chuckle behind him.

After maneuvering his befuddled body into his carriage, he leaned his head back to ride the rest of the short journey in a blessed drunken haze. As the vehicle lumbered down the vacant, cobbled street, he did not allow sleep to pull him under. It would be near impossible to heave him from the carriage, and he didn't relish the idea of slumbering within the cold, cramped interior.

He felt the turn, then the smooth halt a few seconds later. The door swung out and he pried his eyes open. Exiting the high vehicle proved more difficult than entering. He stumbled as he stepped to the ground, then caught himself before swearing out loud. He shook his head when the footman offered assistance, then straightened his spine and walked carefully up the front steps. "Damned gin," he mumbled.

One of the twin oak doors opened, and his impeccably dressed butler stood to the side, waiting for him to enter. "Good evening, Your Grace," the man said with a bow.

"Carson." He hurried past, in no mood to palaver.

"Your Grace," Carson called to his retreating back.

He sighed heavily but continued his unsteady trek toward the stairs. "Whatever it is can wait until morning."

"But this note, Your Grace, is of utmost importance," the man insisted as he followed. "And your ward—"

Nicholas spun around so fast, Carson nearly ran into him. "My *what?*"

The butler held out an envelope, unfazed by the outburst. "The lady said this note will explain—"

"Lady?" he interrupted, lowering his gaze to the envelope. "Tell me, Carson, is the lady young and beautiful?"

"Oh, indeed, Your Grace."

Swearing inwardly, he vowed to get even with Jeremy. His friend should know better than to bring a girl like that into his family's home. He shuddered to think what his mother would say if she were to learn of this.

He swiveled around. "Worry not, Carson, I know what is going on."

"What about this note, Your Grace?"

Undoubtedly a ruse to gain entrance, he guessed as he took the envelope and dismissed Carson for the night.

Espying the thin strip of light glowing beneath one of the guestroom doors, he slowed his steps. "Wait until I see you next, Jeremy," he hissed, shoving the envelope into his coat pocket. Turning the silver knob, he slipped soundlessly into the room. The lamp's rosy glow spilled over the bed and he saw thick, raven hair lying in slight disarray over the snowy pillow slip. He sucked in a breath, his thoughts turning to another with the same color hair. But it couldn't be.

He pushed away from the closed door and shuffled forward. He caught the faint scent of jasmine and his heart leapt. It couldn't be. But his body refused to listen to his mind as need swelled within him.

She moaned and turned over. Nicholas halted, his eyes riveted to her face. It was her! But when…how…? He shook his head. It didn't matter, he decided, stripping the cravat from his neck.

His mind spun with images of their entwined bodies, and his shaft swelled at the thought. He moved to the bed, wondering why she had traveled all this distance for him. His doubt eased when he recalled those hideous garments she'd been wearing the day they met. Certainly, she had come for one reason alone. To be his mistress.

"Your Grace."

With a jolt, his gaze flew from her breast outlined in the thin white material to her face.

She stared up at him.

As the gin's numbing effects began to diminish, he felt his doubt return. What if he was wrong about the reason she'd come?

"I'm glad you're here," she sighed, closing her eyes.

Slumping in relief, for a lady glad to see him in her bedroom meant only one thing, he moved to the edge of the bed and sat. "And why, nymph, are you glad I'm here?" He had to hear the words.

"Because I need your help," she answered softly, opening her eyes to reveal a glimpse of desperation.

He nodded. "You have it."

"Thank you," she whispered, lifting her hand to his face. "I was afraid you wouldn't."

As her petal-soft fingertips grazed his cheek, he groaned. Then, unable to stand another second without tasting her, he lowered his head. "I am your servant."

She murmured something incoherent just before their lips met and he could swear lightning exploded within him.

It took only moments to shed his shirt and waistcoat. He refused to break contact, afraid the magic would end. He kicked his boots away, then worked the buttons at the front of his pantaloons. Dear God in heaven, she was to be his.

She groaned and he knew he could wait no longer. He moved one of his hands down her side and gripped a fistful of her night rail, then raised it up to her waist.

Her hands fluttered to his shoulders as he settled over her and he could taste the tanginess of her arousal on his tongue.

CHAPTER 4

The dream had returned. Nearly every night since sharing that searing kiss by the stream, Megan had dreamed of the duke. His lips on hers, his hands holding her tenderly. A difference weaved its way into her mind. Tonight, Nicholas kissed her in a way she never before experienced. These kisses held power and magic. These kisses possessed her. And his hands...she gasped as a hand closed around her breast. He halted, and she opened her eyes. That face. That incredibly handsome face that had been branded into her memory since childhood. She reached up and touched his cheek.

"Am I moving too fast?" he whispered, his brows puckered.

"Your Grace—"

"Nicholas. You must call me Nicholas."

"Nicholas," she breathed, saying his Christian name out loud. That one little word brought such a rush of joy. She had imagined saying his name many times, even practiced in the mirror. But saying his name to his face brought her to the brink of tears.

He lowered his head and nuzzled her neck. "And what shall I call you?"

"You know my name is Megan." She slid her eyes shut as tiny sparks of excitement skittered down to her toes.

"Megan." He kissed just behind her ear, sliding his mouth over to her cheek. "Megan," he said again, his lips finding hers.

A longing gripped her. It mounted and surged, swelled and bloomed. She had no power to fight whatever it was. From somewhere deep within her, her core was aflame and throbbing with desperate need. She had never before felt this way. And with each second, it grew worse.

His tongue moved over the seam of her lips and her thoughts scattered. She opened her mouth and allowed the delicious exploration. She couldn't think. Wrapping her arms around his neck, she kissed him back with all the feelings she had for him. All the years she yearned for him, all the hopes and dreams she had for a future with him. Nothing else mattered but Nicholas. Her Nicholas.

****

Nicholas nearly exploded. Megan drove him mad with need. Megan. Her fingers combed the back of his hair and he groaned. Another few seconds of this and he wouldn't be able to control himself.

"Megan," he lifted his head, "are you ready, love?"

Her eyes swept up, dazed. Filled with passion. He swallowed. "Are you ready?" he repeated.

"Please." She wiggled beneath him. "I need..."

"I know." He kissed her deeply. Hungrily. He could wait no longer. He slid into her taut heat, not at all expecting to pierce the thin barrier of her maidenhead. But when he felt the breach and heard her gasp, he knew exactly what he had done.

Lifting his head, he gazed down at her. His chest pinched when he saw the pain in her eyes. "Oh, God, are you all right? Why didn't you tell me?"

She blinked several times, the pain receding from her eyes. "What?" she whispered in a strangled gargle.

Possessiveness welled up within him and his confusion vanished. No one had ever touched her. And no one would. He held her face between his palms, his gaze delving into hers. "You are mine, Megan. Mine alone." He traced the tip of his right forefinger down her smooth cheek. "And I don't think I could ever let you go. Do you understand what I am saying?"

Her brows puckered and she shook her head slowly.

He closed his eyes, fighting for control, fighting the fierce need to keep her safe. "I want you to stay with me. Always," he insisted, opening his eyes.

She looked strangely at him, her features softening. He swallowed. His heart pounded in his chest. He could hold her forever.

****

Megan stirred and opened her eyes. Her head felt like it was full of wool as she tried focusing on the fuzzy images dancing before her. She frowned. Laudanum caused these uncomfortable effects and she'd take no more of the horrid stuff. The throb from the lump above her temple was hardly noticeable anyway.

Gradually, her vision sharpened. She gazed around the lovely peach room and threw back the bed covers. Cool air met bare skin. Shocked, she remained still for several seconds, then glanced down. Her eyes widened in disbelieving horror. She wore not a stitch of clothing and the area between her legs throbbed . Then she sighted the smear of blood on the pristine sheet beneath her. Nausea churned within her stomach. Dear God, what had happened to her?

Images flickered in her mind, dreamlike. She watched the duke settle over her, his heavy body pressing hers into the bed, filling her...

In a desperate attempt to force the pictures from her mind, she squeezed her eyes shut. Clutching the sheet to her chest she groaned, humiliation spreading over her. With sickening dread, she knew what had transpired.

Then she remembered some of his words. She

opened her eyes. He had told her she belonged to him and that he wanted her with him. Always.

Her panic diminished. Her fingers loosened from the sheet. Truly, those words could only mean one thing. She would become his wife.

How many times had she dreamed of this? How many times had she stood before his portrait in the Claremont gallery and imagined him professing his undying love, then asking for her hand in marriage?

She had always wanted that. Hadn't she? She bit her lip, feeling a spurt of disloyalty toward Julian. How would her brother react? She blanched, not at all liking the images that question evoked.

Glancing at the delicate mantle clock across the room, she noticed the time and pulled a face. How in the devil did it get so late? Moving to the edge of the bed, she noticed a slip of paper on the pillow beside her. Her heart skipped a beat. It had to be from Nicholas. A love letter, perhaps? Eager to read his honeyed words, she snatched up the note.

My darling,
I cannot thank you enough for the wonderful gift you have given me, as well as for accepting my offer.
Please forgive my need for this hasty letter, but I must leave instructions for you to follow. I promise all will be explained later.
First, do not be frightened, I will be with you soon. Gather any possessions you have, along with the coin I left on the bureau, and hire a hackney to No. 17 Bond Street.
I will come to you as quickly as I can.
Once you arrive, Mae will see to your every need.
Forever,
Nicholas

She wrinkled her brows. That didn't sound like any limerick of love. But the reason for the letter soon dawned. Since they were to be married, Nicholas might not be her guardian. Perhaps it was now improper for her to remain in his house without a chaperone. Some of Society's rules were ridiculous, but her parents would wish her to adhere to them. With a gusty sigh, she exited the bed and placed the note within her drawstring purse. She used the water in the bowl beside the bed for a quick wash, then retrieved her clothing and dressed, choosing a simple gown that buttoned up the front. She usually dressed herself, having sneaked to and from the estate on many occasions for an early morning ride, and had many gowns made to get on and off with ease.

Her hair, she found a few minutes later, was another matter. Her maid had been called away just as they were about to depart for London. But Lucy's mother had become very ill and needed assistance much more than Megan did.

After stepping into the rose-colored slippers that matched her gown, she left the room and walked down the stairs. The butler, identified by his black attire instead of Claremont's usual livery of burgundy and gold, passed and halted when he noticed her. She had spoken briefly to him when she arrived, she recalled.

"Can I be of some assistance, my lady?" he asked as his eyes darted to her valise.

"Yes. It seems I am in need of a hackney. Would you hail one for me?"

"Yes, of course, my lady," he answered, unable to mask the confusion from his features.

In the hack, Megan clutched her wrist bag, Nicholas's note crinkling within. She chewed her lower lip, wishing she'd had the chance to discuss her parents with him before leaving. Her stomach grumbled. She'd eaten little since her parents' disappearance, but now that she would have

Nicholas's help finding them, the burden lightened.

As she rapped on the white painted door, she guessed that he had sent her to the mother of one of his friends. A duenna. She hoped he would arrive soon because she wished him to begin the search for her parents immediately.

The door opened. "Can I help you?" the silver-haired housekeeper asked.

Megan nodded. "I have arrived at the request of His Grace, the Duke of Claremont. He and I are—"

"Please, do come inside," the woman interrupted kindly, excitement dancing within her dark eyes.

She marveled at the woman's manner until she realized that His Grace must have forwarded a message.

The housekeeper led her into an attractive pale green salon. She eased onto the green silk sofa, tamping down a surge of disquiet. How would the dowager duchess react to her son's sudden betrothal?

"Would you care for a spot of chocolate, miss?"

Ignoring the improper address as her stomach rumbled, she gave a weak smile. "Yes, that would be grand."

A few minutes later, the housekeeper placed a large tray of delicious-looking sweet rolls and a steamy cup of chocolate before her, then quit the room humming a cheery tune. She ate two of the tasty rolls and wondered about her hostess. Probably still abed, she concluded when she recalled what her mother had told her of the strange hours of the season. She wrinkled her nose, unable to imagine everyone socializing until dawn and then sleeping until noon. She rose with the sun no matter what hour she retired. Her nanny had once called it a curse.

The housekeeper returned as she was finishing the last of her chocolate. "That was delicious. Thank you..."

"Please, call me Mae," the housekeeper supplied.

She smiled her appreciation. "Thank you, Mae." Then she remembered the name from the note the duke had left. Odd that he would mention the housekeeper instead of her employer. "When will your mistress be rising? I would very much like to meet her."

Mae drew her brows. "His Grace, the Duke of Claremont, is my employer."

Her smile slipped. "I beg your pardon?"

"The Duke of Claremont is my employer," the lady repeated. "You did mention him at your arrival." Her eyes narrowed. "Have you any proof he sent you?"

Feeling dazed, she retrieved the note from her purse, hoping the woman wouldn't guess 'the gift' she'd given. She watched Mae's skepticism melt away almost at once. "This is His Grace's signature. You had me alarmed, dearie." But before the cloud of confusion lifted, the woman continued. "Do forgive me, but I must be careful. I refuse to serve another spoiled brim like His Grace's last paramour. I am ever so glad to be rid of that one." She lifted the sterling server and walked to the door.

Megan stared at the housekeeper for several seconds. Paramour? She closed her eyes and tried to recall the meaning of the word. She stood, grabbed her valise, and hurried after the housekeeper. "What is a paramour?"

Mae's face remained blank for several seconds. "Oh, dear," she whispered, her hand flitting to her bosom. "Well...it's...that is...uh... It's when a man gives a woman a comfortable means to live in exchange for..."

Her heart sank. Nothing good was going to come from Mae's next words. Megan's dreams were about to be dashed into a million little pieces. The palms of her hands grew wet and a sick knot of dread churned low in her belly. "In exchange for what?" she prodded, her mouth dry.

"Bedding her," Mae answered softly.

She felt the color drain from her face. "There seems to be a misunderstanding. You see, I'm positive His Grace has asked me here and not as his—his paramour," she babbled, nearly choking on the last word.

The older woman shook her head. "I'm sorry miss, but there can be no other reason you're here. This house, you see, is used for that purpose alone."

Her stomach rolled over. Nicholas—her Nicholas—couldn't have meant for her to become his—his…

"Are you all right, miss?" Mae hovered near.

Megan clamped a hand over her mouth and ran from the house. She had to get out or be sick all over Mae. Dear God. She stumbled through the front door and took slow, deep breaths. Walk. Just walk. Sounds buzzed in her ears. She looked down at the valise she held in her white-knuckled grip. She quickened her pace. Get away. Coming to the end of the street, she looked around. Nothing looked familiar. A hack. Just call a hack and get away. She forced her hand up.

"Where to, m'lady?"

"Just get me away from here."

Megan settled back in the seat and closed her eyes. She tried to reason that Mae was wrong. But the more she pondered the duke's instructions, the more she began to realize *she* was wrong. Since their engagement had not been announced, she should have been allowed to stay in Nicholas's family home. Indeed, the simplest arrangement would have been to keep the engagement a secret until his mother's arrival.

Anger ignited somewhere deep within her and

mounted with each turn of the hack wheel. She popped her eyes open. Before she could change her mind, she called out to the jarvey an address. She needed some answers.

The hack stopped. Fury raged through her veins, heating her blood to the point of boiling, but she'd not unleash it yet. Not until she heard the revolting omission spill from the duke's own lips.

"Please wait here. I shall not be long," she instructed the jarvey. She climbed from the hired coach and marched to the structure in front of her. The door opened, but she spoke before she allowed the butler a word. "I insist upon seeing His Grace at once, it is urgent," she ordered calmly, though her insides seethed with indignation.

"I am sorry, my lady, but His Grace has not left his chambers," the man said with a hint of astonishment.

But she had already proceeded through the door and to the stairs before the butler finished speaking. The devil himself would not stop her now. No, she would not leave until she had answers. Then the Duke of Claremont could go hang. Certain which rooms belonged to the duke, she threw open the polished mahogany doors and marched forward. She rushed beyond the sitting room and into the dim bedroom, noting that the bed curtains had been tied back. Her steps faltered when she saw his nude form tangled in the white sheet and rumpled burgundy coverlet, but her anger propelled her on .

Straightening her spine, she turned to the butler, who had been sputtering behind her since she walked through the front door. "Leave us," she ordered in the exact tone her father used when demanding obedience. He quickly bowed and left, closing the doors on his way out.

****

Nicholas started at the sound of that clipped

command and pried open his eyes. Had sand been poured into them? An unpleasant tempo beat in his temples. He grimaced. Damned gin.

"What, exactly, is going on, Your Grace?"

The joy he felt at seeing his nymph standing there fled when he realized that she hadn't followed his instructions. "Didn't you receive my letter?" He sat gingerly up against the pillows.

Her eyes narrowed. "I went to that little house and met Mae, who informed me that I am to be your new paramour. Is that true?"

"Now, sweet—"

"Is that what you intended of me?" she interrupted. "Is that what you meant last night when you said that I would always remain with you?"

"Yes." He sighed. Leaving her a note had been a bit tactless.

"I gave you my innocence," she said, her voice turning ragged. "I thought—" She stopped and clamped her mouth shut.

He went still. "What? That I'd marry you?" She lowered her eyes, but not before he saw the answer in them. That was exactly what she'd thought. Rather, what she had hoped to gain. So, that was the game. She would rather be a duchess than a mistress.

He had been betrayed.

"Yes." She lifted her head and speared him with a look of pure fire. "But that assumption was obviously made in error. Good day, Your Grace." She spun around, heading for the door.

"Wait a minute. Where do you think you are going?"

She halted. "Worry not, Your Grace, I won't bother you again."

"Wait."

But she was already gone.

Disgusted, he rose from the bed and summoned his valet. When he was dressed, he lumbered down the stairs and called to Carson.

The man materialized at his side. "Yes, Your Grace?"

"Have my horse readied and brought around."

"Right away, Your Grace," the man said with a bow.

"Wait, don't send for the horse just yet. I have some questions."

"Yes, Your Grace?"

"The, uh, lady that was here. Did she give you her name last evening?"

Carson's brows rose. "Of course. She said her name is Lady Megan, and that she is your ward."

"And you believed her?"

"I had no reason not to, Your Grace. She had a note from your mother the duchess."

Nicholas crossed his arms over his chest. "You read this note?"

"Of course not, sir. The note was addressed to you." Carson paused. "I did give the note to you."

Nicholas did recall something about shoving a note into his pocket. He nodded. "Come, Carson." He went back up the stairs to his bedroom and summoned his valet. "Where is the coat I had on last night?"

"Here, Your Grace. I found it on the floor."

Nicholas checked each pocket twice. "It's not here. Carson, look on the floor. Maybe it fell out."

"I do not see it, Your Grace."

Handing the crumpled coat back to his valet, Nicholas turned to the doorway. The same door that *Lady* Megan had entered earlier. No doubt, she had come back for the note—an obvious ruse to gain entry into his home, hoping to dupe him. Damn! He wished he had read the letter when he had the chance. Perhaps then he would have seen through her scheme sooner, and last night would have never happened.

"Would you still like me to summon your horse, sir?"

Nicholas turned to his window. Did he still want to find her? No, not since he knew the truth. Not since he couldn't think straight in her presence. "No, Carson, I don't think I will need my horse after all."

CHAPTER 5

"That...that—" Megan picked up a flower vase in her family's London townhouse and sent it sailing across the room, "—beast." The vase struck the wall and splintered into shards, the cluster of lilies going everywhere. She looked for something else to throw. To destroy. Spotting the perfume vials, she marched forward and grabbed two. "Damn him, how dare he treat me with such—" One vial smashed just to the left of a window, "—utter disrespect!" She sent the other vial after the first, ignoring the smell of jasmine hanging heavy in the air. "And to think I spent my whole life mooning after him." She clenched her fist, itching for something else to smash. As she marched toward the table with a horse figurine, a knock sounded at the door.

"Lady Megan? Are you all right, child?"

"Fine, Wentworth. I'm just fine."

"Sounds like Napoleon's army marching through your room."

She held the heavy porcelain in her hands, eyeing the bay windows at the far end.

"May I enter, please?"

With a sigh, she replaced the figurine. "Yes."

Wentworth hastened forward, not at all showing his eighty-plus years. He looked severe. "Is something amiss, my lady?"

"Besides my parents missing, you mean?"

He glanced around at the broken glass, upturned tables, and pillow feathers littering the floor. "This is not the work of grief, my dear." His all-knowing, all-seeing gaze swiveled back to her. "This is fury."

Megan crossed her arms. That scoundrel…that cad…that wretch of a man had taken advantage of her. She had been under the influence of laudanum, and his black soul had—she curtailed the thought quickly, knowing her cheeks were glowing red.

"Would you like to talk about it, child?"

Megan shook her head. "Goodness, no." She needed to talk about something else. She arranged the stuffed cockatoo Julian had given her to regain her composure. "Have you received any word of my parents yet?"

His features softened. "Not in the twenty minutes since I sent the messages out, no."

Her shoulders drooped as the fury drained out of her, leaving her weak. Since her arrival here earlier, she had informed Wentworth about her parents and the burned carriage, asked him to send messages to the friends of her parents for any word on their whereabouts, and then taken refuge to her room. Damn Nicholas for not helping her when she needed him. He could search for her parents and make inquiries. She, on the other hand, was limited by Society's ridiculous rules and couldn't go looking for her parents on her own. Unlike the Duke of Claremont, who could do anything he damn well pleased. Tears stung the backs of her eyes. The Duke of Claremont did to what he damn well pleased. Even at her expense.

"Are you all right, child? You look as white as a marble statue." He stepped forward. "Shall I send for the doctor?"

Blinking back her tears, Megan shook her head. "No, I'm just tired." Her temples pounded and her throat burned. A strange lethargy had sneaked up on her suddenly. She looked around her once-pretty room and sighed. The maids would be none too happy about cleaning this mess.

"What you need is some rest. Come, let me prepare one of the guestrooms for you."

"No, thank you. I think I just need some fresh air." The heavy smell of jasmine made her head throb. A ride on one of her horses would be better, but she would have to settle for a walk. Maybe that would energize her. "I won't be long."

****

"This had bloody well better be a matter of life and death, Carson," Nicholas said as he slammed the front door. He had been about to spar with Lord Marshley at Gentleman Jackson's when he received the urgent message to return home.

Carson held out an envelope. "The note has been found, Your Grace."

He took a step toward his butler. "That's why you summoned me here? I thought the matter was urgent."

"It is. Look." Carson turned the envelope over, revealing the Claremont signet clearly impressed in the red wax.

The bottom of his stomach fell away. "What is this?"

"The note the lady claimed came from the dowager duchess, Your Grace."

"Where did it come from?"

"Stella found it." Carson paused and lowered his voice. "Under the bed in the guestroom the lady used. When I saw the signet, I knew I had to summon you at once."

Bombarded with confusion, he broke the seal and unfolded the missive. His heart skipped a beat when he saw his mother's tiny, looping script swim before his eyes on the bright paper.

Darling Nicholas,

This letter must come as a surprise, however it is extremely important. Your Uncle Charles has arrived ill (do not be concerned, it is not serious), and I must remain here, or I would see to this urgent matter personally.

My dearest friends, the Duke and Duchess of Kenbrook, are missing. They departed days ago on a mysterious trip to London, but told no one their reason for doing so. Then their empty carriage was found near here, ruined by fire.

Their daughter is distraught with worry and wishes her parents found. I would keep her here, but Influenza is spreading at both Claremont and Kenbrook. Therefore, I am sending her to you, but not without reason. Years ago, your father was pronounced her guardian in the event that her parents and brother were unable to care for her. Since your father's death, that position has fallen upon you. You are her legal guardian until the duke and duchess or their son return.

Because Megan is only ten and eight, she must be protected by someone I trust and who will be able to help find her parents.

Take care of her, darling. She is a very special young lady.

Mother

Nicholas read the letter three times before he looked up. The paper slipped from his fingers and fluttered to the floor. His cluttered thoughts sharpened on one thing: Megan was not some gold-digging harlot, but the Duke of Kenbrook's daughter. By God, he had completely forgotten that Kenbrook had a daughter, having not visited Kenbrook in nine years.

Lady Megan. His heart twisted in agony. He shook his head a couple of times before he became aware of Carson addressing him.

"Are you all right, Your Grace?"

He focused on his butler's concerned face. "Yes.

Carson, have my carriage brought to the front." His voice came out in a coarse whisper.

"Right away, Your Grace."

Nicholas rode the whole way to the Kenbrook townhouse, torturing himself by replaying every second that he wronged Megan. Every second he hurt her. Oh, God, had he really thought she was a...His mother's words rushed to his mind. *Because Megan is only ten and eight, she must be protected by someone I trust...She must be protected by someone I trust. She must be protected. Someone I trust. Protected.*

He squeezed his eyes shut as searing self-contempt crushed his chest. He prayed his heart would explode before he had to face Megan with a completely inadequate apology. Looking into her beautiful eyes and seeing the loathing that he deserved would be torture.

The carriage came to a halt. He staggered to the door, pausing a minute to gather his courage, then banged on the door.

"Your Grace! My, this has been a month for surprises. Please, come in. Would you care for some tea?" Wentworth held the door open.

He glanced down at the ancient butler, amazed that the old chap still remembered him. "No, thank you, Wentworth. I would like a word with Lady Megan. Is she in residence?"

"She returned from a walk a short time ago, Your Grace. But I believe she may be indisposed."

The man's rheumy eyes looked worried. "Which room is she occupying?" he demanded.

Wentworth didn't hesitate. "Left hall, extreme end on the left."

He took the steps two at a time. He hastened through the sitting room toward her bedroom. He swung the door open with a bang and his eyes flew to the crumpled body on the floor two feet from the bed.

"Oh, no!" he choked. He turned and found Wentworth hovering near the door. "Summon a doctor immediately," he ordered. Gently, he gathered her in his arms. She burned with fever and her skin had a deathly wan look. Carefully, he laid her on the bed. She didn't rouse. He used the nearby washbowl to cool her fevered cheeks. His hands shook. *Please, God, let her be all right.*

Just as he covered her shivering body with a thick, warm blanket, the doctor arrived and hurried to her bedside. The man told Nicholas to leave.

Like a caged tiger, he paced the sitting room. Time slowed to an agonizing degree. After what seemed like hours, the door opened. He jerked around, and his heart sank at the doctor's grave expression. "How is she?"

The large man sighed and removed his spectacles. "Not good, Your Grace," he answered sadly as he scrubbed the two pieces of glass with a handkerchief.

He swallowed the lump in his throat. "Explain what you mean."

"The young lady is very ill, indeed. She has quite a high fever. It's no doubt the Influenza."

Every word struck Nicholas like a stake to his heart. "She isn't going to die, is she?"

The doctor smiled in understanding. "She has a great advantage in being young, Your Grace. The fever does have me concerned. It must be broken with cool compresses. However, if it doesn't linger overmuch, she should recover nicely."

"Thank you, doctor. I shall make certain she receives the proper care."

The doctor placed his hand on Nicholas's shoulder and gave him a slight squeeze. "Good. I'll be nearby in case you should need me, Your Grace."

Nicholas remained at Megan's side every minute

for the rest of the day and during the long night. Since he couldn't sleep, he sat in the chair beside the bed and spoke softly to her. While he focused on her pallid, drawn features, he recited stories of his childhood mishaps and his world travels. Even when his voice had grown coarse from overuse, he continued.

At daybreak, after he'd recited several of his most notorious boxing contests, he paused to run his fingers over her flaming cheek. He bowed his head and sighed. He couldn't lose her. Not now. Not when he had just found her. "Megan, I do not know if you can hear me. You didn't deserve any of the misery I gave you. Not one second of it. I was wrong, love, so very wrong." He remained in her room for two days and nights. He had come downstairs only twice, for the two brief meetings with the investigators he'd hired to locate her parents. He refused to allow anyone else to tend to her. On the third day, pink fingers streaked the morning-grey sky and birds were beginning their primordial song. He shuffled away from the window with a sigh and slumped on the chair beside the bed, his mind numb from lack of sleep. He longed for his bed, but he would not leave. Not until she woke. He propped an elbow up on the chair's wooden arm, rested a beard-rough cheek in his hand, and stretched his legs out before him. Suffused with exhaustion, both physical and emotional, he closed his eyes.

Something jogged him to full consciousness. He stretched his arms above his head and yawned heavily, then rubbed his hand over his face to measure the length of growing stubble. He blinked a couple of times and glanced at Megan. She was still and pale, except for the red stain growing on her cheeks. He felt her skin, the heat startling him. Alarmed, he reached for the water basin and found it empty. He jumped to his feet and went to the door.

The doctor had arrived. He could hear the man's muffled words through the oak.

"Has Lady Megan come to yet?"

"No, doctor." Wentworth lowered his voice. Nicholas had to strain to hear. "Do you think she will recover?"

"These things are hard to predict. But I do know the longer she remains unconscious, the more serious this becomes."

Nicholas placed a hand on the cold wood, trying to deny what the doctor was saying. Megan could die? Fear, unlike anything he had ever known, rose up from within and threatened to choke him. It clawed at his throat and took his breath away. Megan couldn't die. By God, he would not let that happen.

Wrenching the door open, he startled Wentworth and the doctor. He pressed the water basin into the butler's hands. "I need water." He turned to the doctor. "And Megan is not going to die. Understood?"

****

Brightness manifested behind her eyelids and Megan struggled to lift them. Slowly, she focused on the sunlight pouring through the windows. *Her* windows. She was in her bedroom in London.

Swallowing the dust that had accumulated in her raw, burning throat, she turned her heavy head and spied the duke asleep on a chair beside the bed. He looked awful. Dark blue smudges lay under his closed eyelids. His clothes were wrinkled, his hair a disheveled oily mass, and he desperately needed to shave.

Snippets of memory tickled her mind. She recalled him speaking lovingly to her, cooling her fevered forehead. She heard tears in his voice as he apologized for what had happened between them.

The door opened, drawing her attention. A

portly man with small oval spectacles walked into the room carrying a large, black leather satchel. She watched the duke open his tired eyes, then rise when he became aware of the man. When he glanced in her direction, his features stiffened in surprise, then grew contrite.

"Well, Your Grace, it looks as though our little lady has finally returned to us," the man said. He walked to the bed wearing a warm smile. "Hello, my dear, I am Dr. Kellerman. How are you feeling?"

She parted her cracked lips and swallowed a couple of times before she tried to say she felt better.

The doctor shook his head. "That's all right, my lady, you mustn't strain yourself. I'll do the talking." He sat on the chair the duke had vacated and raised her wrist as he spoke of the fine spring morning.

She kept her attention on Dr. Kellerman, even though she was aware of Nicholas hovering at the foot of the bed.

"You must receive plenty of rest, Lady Westland." The doctor hefted a giant brown bottle from his bag. "And take a large spoonful of this restorative tonic three times every day until it has been fully consumed. I will also leave some laudanum in case you are uncomfortable and need sleep."

Goodness, no, she would never take that dirty old laundry water again. Unable to resist, she looked at the duke, but his guarded eyes made it difficult to discern his thoughts. When the doctor began speaking, she focused back on him.

"His Grace has been quite worried about you, my dear. You are most fortunate to have such a concerned guardian," he said. "I will continue to monitor your condition every day for the next couple of days. But it looks as though you will fully recover. Now, get some rest. And fear not, my lady, His Grace shan't allow any untoward thing to happen to you."

The large man rose and bade them a good day, then vacated the room.

She shifted her gaze back to Nicholas.

He sighed, then shuffled back to his seat. "What I have done to you is beyond any measure of forgiveness." He paused and cleared his throat. "What happened between us..." He shook his head. "I know there is absolutely nothing I can do that would atone for my actions, but please..." He stopped and closed his eyes. "Oh, God, Meg, I am so very sorry." He shot to his feet and fled the room.

****

Nicholas stayed away long enough to gulp down some gin. He hung his head as he headed back up the stairs. He felt the pulse at his neck begin to race as he entered the room. Dread filled him. She would probably insist that he be hung, drawn and quartered. He bloody well deserved it. "Can I... Do you need anything?" he asked.

When she looked at him, tears filled her eyes. "Find my parents," she whispered.

His insides shook so badly, he thought everything within would break into a million pieces. She was actually asking him for help. *Him.* Humbled, he blinked his stinging eyes. He would find her parents. By God, he'd do whatever it took to regain her affection. "I promise you, Megan, they shall be found. I have already hired dozens of investigators."

Her eyes brightened. "What have you learned, Your Grace?"

"Wentworth has confirmed that your parents were in residence for only one night, then departed at dawn the following morning. Unfortunately, he has no idea where they've gone."

She picked at the lace on her sleeve. "Wentworth said he heard Father tell Mother that Sims would deliver a note explaining everything to me. That's why the carriage had been returning to the estate."

He nodded. "And then they hired a hack and departed one way, Sims, the other."

"That's right. Have you learned anything else, Your Grace?"

Your Grace. For the first time in his life, he detested the title. "You know my name. Please, call me that."

She smoothed a wrinkle from the bedspread. "I would prefer not to, Your Grace."

That stung. He wanted to make amends. Hell, he wanted more than that.

"Your Grace?" Her amethyst gaze lifted, and he felt a kick square in the gut. God, how he wanted her. More than simple lust. He wanted to protect her. A fine mess he'd made of that. Not only had he propositioned Kenbrook's only daughter to becoming his mistress, he had taken her maidenhead.

"Your Grace?"

He shook his head. "What did you say?"

"Have you learned anything else?"

He cleared his throat, trying to focus on the matter at hand. "Some of the men I've hired are searching for the missing coachman, Sims, while the rest are combing the city for your parents." He leaned a bit closer. "Megan, they shall be found."

The silence stretched out. One minute became two, then three. Every second seemed to pull them farther apart. "Meg, about what happened—"

"Don't, Your Grace," she interrupted. "I don't ever want to think of it, much less discuss it." She closed her eyes as if speaking had exhausted her. "If her mother has recovered, I would like my maid, Lucy, to be brought from the estate. Would you send a coach and driver?"

"Yes, of course. Is there anything else I can do for you?"

She opened her eyes and looked straight into

his. "Yes. Go home and get some sleep, Your Grace. You look like hell."

****

He ground his teeth. Things hadn't gone as planned. Megan should have been in his possession by now. He knew exactly what had gone wrong. She was brought to London instead of Claremont. Damn it! He twisted the ring on his little finger. The plan would have to be reworked. Just a setback.

With a sigh, he sat down at the secretary and began scribbling a note. Perhaps having Megan in London could work to his advantage. He pursed his lips. He scratched out some words, growing more satisfied that the altered plan might work out even better. After sealing the note, he leaned back in his chair, satisfied.

****

Megan tossed and turned. She knew that she would never rest the two hours each day that the good doctor insisted. Groaning in frustration, she bounced from the bed and began to restore some order to the tangled mass of her hair. Then she rang the pull for Lucy to help her dress.

"Here, my lady, let me," the maid said, seeing her struggle with her hair.

Lucy was an angel, she thought with an inward smile. She used to detest all of the attention the maid showered on her. But after dressing herself for a short time, she felt grateful to have the attentive lady's maid with her. And in the two weeks since Lucy's arrival in London, she was actually glad to have her maid care for her instead of the duke. Indeed, she refused the remorse bubbling within, reminding her how he had wiped her forehead with cool water and fed her spoonfuls of broth.

After Lucy had arranged her hair, Megan went downstairs.

"My lady, the Duke of Claremont requests a

meeting with you," Wentworth announced. "He's waiting in the parlor."

A groan slipped from her lips. She knew a confrontation would eventually occur. The stubborn man had returned with luggage and his valet a short time after she'd told him to leave. Although she would never admit it, she ached to know what was happening with the investigation. True to his word, the Duke was working feverishly with the investigators to locate her parents.

She frowned, not wanting to feel pleased with the man. The door to the parlor opened and the duke stepped out. He looked exceptionally fine in a crisp white shirt with a grey waistcoat, charcoal pantaloons, and polished black Hessians. A large pear-shaped diamond sparkled brilliantly in the center of his snowy cravat. Her gaze moved up to his freshly shaven face. Goodness, the man could still take her breath away. Her frown deepened.

She watched his eyes skitter over her before he cleared his throat. "May I have a word with you please, my lady?" he asked in a gentle voice.

She thought of her parents and nodded. Her acquiescence most certainly had nothing at all to do with wanting to be near him.

She clasped her hands together and followed the duke into the parlor. "What have you learned of my parents, Your Grace?"

His shoulders drooped. "Will you not call me Nicholas?"

"No."

"Stubborn girl," she heard him grumble as he went to the sideboard and poured some amber liquid into a tumbler.

"My parents, if you please."

"The investigators are still looking for them." He tossed back the contents.

"Then why did you wish to see me?"

His eyes fused with hers, rooting her to the spot. He took a step in her direction, then stopped and shook his head. "Can you not guess, Megan?"

Her body tensed. "Guess what, Your Grace?"

He opened his mouth to say something, then must have thought better of it. Instead, he turned back to the liquor tray. "Why did you not tell me who you were when we first met?" He finished pouring his drink and turned.

Caught off guard, she examined the cream silk shawl tossed over her arms. "A lady doesn't dress as a stable lad," she said, then lifted her head. "I was afraid you'd ruin me if you learned my identity."

His brows shot up. "Why would I do that?"

She hesitated, wondering how he would react to her answer. "Because Julian is my brother."

The glass halted midway to his lips. His eyes darkened and he clenched his jaw. After a moment, he sipped his drink, the anger receding. "Why were you dressed as a stable lad?"

Her cheeks warmed. How many daughters of a duke would ride a horse dressed as a stable lad? She tossed her head back and squared her shoulders. "In order to gain maximum speed, one must ride astride. As you are aware, Your Grace, unmentionables happen to be the best garments for the job."

"I see." He lowered his eyes and she knew he was remembering her in those tight, wet garments. Her entire body went warm. Clearing her throat, she asked, "Have you any more questions, or may I be excused?"

He nodded. "I do have another question, my lady. When I recalled that Joseph had a daughter, I thought that she—that you were named after your mother."

"I am. Megan is my familiar name."

He lowered the empty tumbler on the nearest table and approached her. "Call me Nicholas."

Standing so close, feeling the heat of his body, inhaling his unique scent of sandalwood, she could hardly think. "You know I cannot call you that. 'Tis not proper."

"Yes, it is."

She shook her head, unable to speak, as a thought dawned. She was partially responsible for what had happened. Indeed, if she hadn't kept her identity from the duke at the stream, none of it would have come to pass. "So, you didn't know who I was the night we..." She swallowed hard, unable to finish.

His gaze roved over her face, settling on her lips. "No."

"Then h-how did you finally learn my identity?" she asked, needing a distraction.

"Carson gave me this." He extracted a folded note from his pocket. "It must have fallen from my coat and slipped under the bed that night." His eyes darkened, and she knew he recalled what had happened between them. "If I had just read it before..." He stopped talking.

Megan forced her eyes from his to the paper he held. Agony sliced through her tattered heart at the reminder that her parents were still missing. She wrapped her shawl around her trembling body and turned away. Misery crashed down on her like the pounding surf on a stormy shore. Something terrible must have happened to them. They would never say away this long without contacting her. Pain swelled in her chest. Not unless they... She refused to finish the thought.

Light and cautious hands turned her around. She tipped her head back and found blazing eyes full of guilty pain. His hands trembled as they cupped her cheeks, then his thumbs gently swiped at tears she hadn't been aware of shedding.

"I promise you, Meg, your parents will be

found," he rasped. His voice held tenderness.

Her grief lessened. But as he started to move away, she knew a moment of panic. Their relationship had changed. The way he wiped all expression from his face proved it. He had pulled away from her, physically and emotionally. As soon as his mother arrived, she knew with utter certainty he would be out of her life forever.

He lowered his hands and took a step back. "Nicholas," she groaned softly, torn at the thought of his leaving. She wet her dry lips, realizing he would not return to her. She would have to go to him. He was leaving the decision solely up to her. Expelling a shaky breath, she took a step forward. Hope sparked in his eyes. With a squeak, she flew into his arms. "Oh, Nicholas," she sighed, feeling him shudder. Then she lifted her head. "Kiss me," she insisted, raising her hands to thread her fingers through his cool, soft hair.

He closed his eyes and wagged his head from side to side, as though fighting some inward war. His jaw tightened, and Megan thought he might refuse her. Then he opened his eyes, eyes aflame with a fierce emotion she couldn't identify. And instead of pushing her away, he lowered his head and pressed his lips to hers.

Her thoughts scattered and sharpened on one thing. She belonged to Nicholas. Even as a child she knew. She had always belonged to Nicholas.

"Get your bloody hands off of my sister," said an irate voice from the doorway.

CHAPTER 6

Megan gasped and pulled away from Nicholas. "Julian!" She threw herself into his arms. Her brother was home. He would find her parents. "Oh, Jules, thank God you're here," she sobbed against his chest.

"Just what in the hell have you done to my sister, Claremont?" her brother asked with venom dripping from each syllable.

She cringed and lifted her head. "Julian, please. Mother and Father are missing. That's why I sent you the urgent missive to come here." She nodded to the letter he clutched in his fist.

He glanced down, his frown deepening. "What do you mean, they're missing?"

"They departed for London last month. I don't know why. Their carriage was found a few days later about five miles from the estate, empty and... Oh God, Julian, it was destroyed by fire. I came here to look for them."

His brows shot up. "You came alone?"

She nodded, stepping from his arms.

Julian scowled. "Megan, any one of a hundred terrible things could have befallen you. Young ladies of quality do not travel alone, nor do they permit a man," he paused to glower at Nicholas, "to be alone with them."

She felt the sting from those words down to her toes, but she refused to show it. "Under normal circumstances, I agree. However, I had to find Mother and Father." Then she realized that Julian hadn't remembered the terms of her guardianship.

She would tell him later.

"Pray tell, how were you to conduct the search? And don't you dare inform me that you planned to do it alone."

She turned to Nicholas.

"Oh, no." Her brother shook his head. "He is not involved in this. In fact, Claremont, you may leave now," he ordered.

"I am already involved in this," Nicholas said, crossing his arms.

Dread filled Megan as she watched fury leap into her brother's eyes.

"Absolutely not," Julian snapped. "And never again shall you be allowed any contact with my sister."

Nicholas shook his head. "You don't understand—"

"No, you don't understand," her brother interrupted, his voice rising. "Megan is my responsibility; she will have nothing to do with you."

Anger flared into Nicholas's eyes. "That's quite impossible now," he shouted back, uncurling his arms. When he took a menacing step toward Julian, Megan gasped.

"You have absolutely no rights where my sister is concerned," Julian roared.

"Yes, I do." Nicholas balled his hands into fists.

"Julian. Nicholas. Please," she implored.

Both men ignored her. They stood a hand span apart, eye-to-eye, equal in height and strength. Dear God, they would kill each other.

"What makes you think you have any rights where my sister is concerned?" Julian demanded.

"Because I'm going to marry her," Nicholas bellowed.

She gasped and Julian lunged forward, his eyes glittering with murder. "You bloody bastard!" He swung his fist.

Nicholas ducked, but before he could retaliate, she wedged between them. She spread her trembling arms to keep them separated. "Stop it. Both of you," she ordered, looking from one menacing face to the other. She turned to Nicholas. "Julian and I must form a stratagem to locate our parents. I think you should leave now."

"You heard her, Claremont. Get out." Her brother placed protective hands on her shoulders. The gesture made it clear just who was in charge of her.

Nicholas shifted his eyes down to her. She held her breath, watching the fury drain from his expression. "I'll leave," he said, "but the investigators I have hired to locate your parents—"

"I do not require your help, Claremont. You've done enough," her brother sneered. "Besides, I am quite capable of locating my parents."

Nicholas clenched his jaw, but his eyes didn't lift from hers. "My investigators shall keep searching," he vowed softly. Then he left.

Once they were alone, Julian turned her to face him with a hard stare. "Start from the very beginning, dear sister, and don't you dare omit a thing," he said, leading her to the Queen Anne sofa.

She omitted quite a lot, except that Nicholas had been her guardian. He'd learn of it from any one of the servants, anyway.

The explosion occurred just as the words tumbled from her lips. "I bloody well don't believe it!"

She clamped her hands onto his rock-solid arm and repeated what the dowager duchess had explained about her guardianship. She added that the dowager had promised to arrive as soon as her brother, Lord Stenwick, was well enough to travel. She summarized what had been gleaned of their parents' disappearance, hoping his thoughts would center on them and not on Nicholas.

He shot to his feet. "I must leave for a short time," he said.

"Where are you going?"

"To begin the search for Mother and Father," he answered as he pulled the door open and walked through.

****

Nicholas paced his study. Be damned, why couldn't he have seen that Megan wasn't some commoner at the stream? She had refined speech and aristocratic features.

A jolt of awareness shot through him, and he came to an abrupt stop. The beautiful little nymph would be his wife. The way she reacted to him earlier left little doubt that he just needed a bit more time to convince her of it.

He chuckled. For many years, he'd fought hard against being ensnared into marriage, much to his mother's consternation. And now he wished for nothing above marriage to Megan. After pouring himself a whisky and settling into the comfortable leather chair behind his desk, he raised the glass into the air to celebrate his good fortune. But just as he brought the drink to his lips, a disquieting thought nettled its way into his mind, something—rather *someone* who would ruin his chances with Megan. He lowered the crystal tumbler onto the polished wood with a bang, sloshing a goodly portion of the amber liquid over his hand. Megan's brother. According to the guardianship papers he had found within his father's repository in the study, Julian was named above the Duke of Claremont as Megan's custodian in the event that both of her parents were unable to care for her. As long as Julian remained her guardian, Nicholas knew that he would never be allowed to marry her.

Damn him. He would not permit the man to

take another love from him.

Then he realized that Julian was but Megan's temporary guardian. Her father would certainly return. Joseph Westland's strength and cunning were as vast as his wealth. And upon hearing the truth, he was bound to agree to the marriage.

That was, Nicholas thought, if Megan's father didn't kill him first.

****

Megan watched Julian take a deep sigh. His guarded expression sent chills through her.

"Moppet, I feel that I must inform you of something."

She gripped his hands. Tears glazed her eyes and stung her nose. "Oh, Julian, Mother and Father..."

He shook his head. "No, no, I have hired many investigators to locate them. Our parents will soon be found."

She slumped with relief.

"I wish to speak to you regarding Claremont," Julian continued. "Take heed, Megan. I know why he seems enamored of you and has proposed marriage."

Heat bloomed in her cheeks. "Julian, please." She made a careful study of the row of pearl buttons at the end of her gown's long sleeves.

"I am a man, dear heart, and understand the workings of men rather well."

She sighed and raised her head. She might as well have this done with. "Very well, why does the duke seem enamored of me?"

His eyes went as dark as thunder clouds. "Revenge."

"What?"

"He still holds me responsible for a transgression I never committed," Julian explained calmly.

"Are you referring to that incident with Emily

Wakefield?"

"How did you—" He halted and shook his head. "Yes. And now Claremont is using you for his revenge."

"Julian, that is absurd. His Grace had no idea I was your sister when we first met," she said without thought.

He tensed. "How is that possible when you indicated that his mother had sent you to him?"

She cursed her blunder. Knowing she had no alternative, she confessed to the accidental encounter with Nicholas at the stream and his belief that she was a commoner. She didn't dare elaborate, but made the entire affair seem brief and trivial.

Julian chuckled humorlessly. "I daresay, dear sister, he knew who you were."

"How could he have known? I was but a child when he last saw me," she pointed out.

"How many young ladies with dark hair and violet eyes are there on our estate? Or in all of Europe, for that matter?"

She closed her eyes and allowed her head to fall back against the sofa. Could Julian be right? Had Nicholas only pretended not to know who she was? Oh, dear Christ! If he had known and still taken her virginity…

"Are you all right, Moppet?" Julian asked softly.

Her stomach began to churn with denial. She bit her lip, refusing to believe Nicholas would use her in that way.

"But he couldn't have known I would arrive in London," she added, desperately wishing to believe that Nicholas hadn't acted out of some sort of sick retribution.

"Your arrival in London, I am certain, was pure coincidence. He would have returned to the country had you not fallen into his lap."

She winced at her brother's words.

"Oh, dearest, I apologize. Pray, forgive me," he begged, placing an arm around her shoulders. "The time at sea must have addled my brain, as well as impeded my manners."

****

An hour after his sister had pleaded fatigue, Julian undressed in his room when he recalled a conversation he'd had with his parents last fall. His mother insisted Megan was too lonely and decided that she would debut this spring, much to his father's consternation. He grimaced. He now had the great pleasure of seeing her launched.

Bloody hell! He hadn't the stomach for endless fetes and galas, balls, soirées and those devious little chits out to sink their meat hooks into him. But he must endure it. His parents would expect it of him.

Sleep eluded him, but by morning, he'd arrived at two decisions. First, he would see that Claremont had no further contact with his sister. Second, he would chaperone Megan to the various balls and parties that he deemed necessary. Once she was exposed to the many gentlemen anxious to be near her, she'd forget Claremont's very existence.

He was certain that Megan's inexperience drew her to the first handsome man to profess a few honeyed words. Within a couple of weeks of her coming-out, his sister would be wise enough to realize her naiveté. In fact, he'd wager a goodly sum she'd be betrothed to another by mid-season.

The question of his parents' whereabouts also besieged his mind during the night. He reasoned that they were not being held for ransom since there was no demand for payment. He couldn't imagine why they'd left in such haste, since they had already planned Megan's debut. And where the deuce had the driver, Sims, vanished to?

****

The next morning, Megan stifled a yawn as she

came down to breakfast. She'd thought of pleading a stomachache, but Julian would probably send for the doctor and she would no doubt have to spend a week abed. She shuddered at the very idea.

When she entered the breakfast room, Julian watched her closely, his silver-grey eyes narrowed above the paper he held out before him. She filled her plate and sat, hoping he would go back to his reading.

No such luck.

"You look tired this morning."

Megan picked up her fork. "I'm fine, Julian."

The silence stretched out for several minutes. Megan moved the scrambled eggs around her plate, trying to think of something, anything other than Nicholas.

"I am quite certain it's dead. Feel free to eat it."

"I'm really not hungry."

"Well, I know something that will cheer you."

She looked up sharply. "What?"

"I am taking you to the finest *modiste* in London today," Julian said as he folded his paper and set it aside.

"For what?"

His brows sprang up. Good Lord, Julian had actually thought she would be pleased with this bit of news? "For your presentation into Society."

She shook her head. "But I'm not going."

"Of course you are."

"How can I attend those galas knowing that Mother and Father could be stranded somewhere, starving to death?" The tears that sprang to her eyes were mostly real. She gave a sniff for good measure. Truly, she had no desire to be out in Society, around so many people all the time.

Julian rubbed each temple with his first two fingers. "Look, Megan, Mother and Father had already planned your coming-out and would want you to go. You know that upon their return, they will demand every detail of every party you attended. And if they return before the season is out, they will expect you to be ready. Either way, Moppet, we must have you fitted right away."

Megan opened her mouth to argue, but Julian was right, curse him. Mother and Father would expect her not to sit about and mourn their absence. But what had happened with Nicholas made her heart ache. How could she go out and have a good time when she was sure to see him? How could she act like nothing had happened between them?

Her brother rose from his seat and walked around Father's empty chair. He knelt beside her, taking her hands in his. "Don't fret, little one. They will be home soon, I assure you." He kissed her forehead and brought her to her feet. She squelched a groan when he informed her that they would depart in a quarter of an hour. She would rather clean the privy every day for a year than get fitted for clothes she didn't want in order to attend a Season she didn't want. How would she get through this?

****

The journey to Madam Devereux's House of Fashion in Berkeley Square took an eternity as carriages, coaches and wagons crowded the street. But Megan didn't mind that half as much as being pinched, poked, and prodded by a dozen French women fitting her for what seemed a hundred gowns of varying styles and fabrics.

Julian paid a blasted fortune to have her dressed to the nines by the start of the season. Indeed, Madame Devereux was already aghast at having to fit another few gowns into her busy schedule when her brother withdrew that exorbitant block of notes from his pocket and insisted on an entire trousseau. Seeing this, though, the French woman plastered a smile across her painted lips and accepted.

As another pin found its mark in her flesh, she grimaced and vowed to get even with her dear brother. If he disliked balls and galas before, he'd certainly loathe them by the end of the Season.

That thought almost made her chuckle.

Finally, after four hours of torture, Julian assisted her back into the carriage. The return to the townhouse would be slower, she noted with a sigh, seeing even more wagons and people in the street than when they'd set out this morning.

She hadn't realized she'd fallen asleep until she roused when the carriage halted. Between the hectic day and lack of sleep the night before, exhaustion found her. The restorative tonic wasn't so restorative either. A footman assisted her from the tall vehicle.

As she reached the front door, she heard her name. Spinning around, she noticed Nicholas leading his horse toward them. "I would like to speak to you," he stated.

Recalling the conversation with Julian last evening, she tamped back her burst of joy and lifted her chin. "There is nothing you have to say, Your Grace, that I wish to hear."

His eyes widened a fraction. "Meg?"

"Don't you dare call me that," she said as the impact of his betrayal rushed back into her tattered heart.

He shook his head. "Why are you acting this way? Yesterday—"

"I learned the truth behind your intentions, Your Grace."

"I told you to stay away, Claremont," Julian said from behind her. "Megan, go into the house."

Nicholas lifted his gaze to her brother. A look of comprehension, then cold disdain slid onto his face. "I have news of your parents," he said.

CHAPTER 7

Megan clapped a hand over her mouth. If she learned her parents had died, she would be sick.

Her brother glared murderously at Nicholas. "If this is one of your pathetic attempts—"

"Shut up, Julian, and mark me well," Nicholas interrupted. "I know where they are, and why they left."

Her brother marched forward, stabbing a finger at Nicholas. "How is it that the infantry I have working on this haven't found a trace of their whereabouts, yet you have solved the entire matter?"

"They probably aren't searching hard enough, or in the right direction. Quit being a stubborn ass, and allow me to explain."

Megan slid her arm through her brother's bent elbow and tugged. "Julian, please," she implored. "If he does have information about Mother and Father, we must listen."

A muscle leaped in Julian's jaw. "By God, Claremont, if I find this doesn't signify, I'll flog you until the fires of Hades nip at your heels." Julian spun her around and led her into the house. "Go upstairs, dear sister, and lie down. We've had a busy day, and I know how tired you are."

She shook her head, all traces of her earlier exhaustion vanished. "I will hear what is said about Mother and Father."

"I'll not have you near that, that—"

"Julian," she interrupted, "I want to hear what he has to say." Gripping her hands together, she glanced at Nicholas. Her heart raced. She turned away, lest Julian got suspicious, and closed her eyes. Her brother could never know how deeply she felt for Nicholas. No one could ever know.

After several seconds, Julian heaved a sigh. He turned to Nicholas, standing in the doorway beside Wentworth. "Follow me, Claremont."

She hesitated as she entered the study. Nicholas stood beside one of the leather wingback chairs before the desk, waiting for her. His brow cocked, and his eyes dared her to take the seat beside him. She bit her lip, torn between wanting to fly into his arms and wanting to box his ears. Sit beside him, indeed! She pressed her lips together and marched toward the sofa beyond, ignoring the spurt of hurt in his eyes.

"Well, what of your news?" Julian asked from behind Father's massive oak desk.

Nicholas sat. "Your parents left aboard the *Wind Song* the day after they arrived here, heading to America."

She froze stiff as a walking stick. *America?* She felt faint. Her gazed snapped to her brother to gauge his reaction.

Julian leaned back in his chair and crossed his arms. "Why would they do that? And pray, how did you learn of it?"

"I concluded that the duke and duchess would not have left Megan behind unless they felt you were in severe distress." He shrugged. "I went to Kenbrook Shipping and learned from the attendant, Benny Wells, that Joseph had requested your schedule and the swiftest clipper available. He and your mother set sail immediately."

Relief struck her a precipitous blow and Megan took a deep breath. The vise around her heart lessened. She glanced at her brother, grateful to see his white-knuckled grip around the razor-sharp letter opener had loosened.

Julian leaned forward. "My schedule would have indicated that I was to arrive soon. Why didn't they wait?"

"Mr. Wells said he pointed out that very fact, but Joseph acknowledged the possession of a message to the contrary."

"Does Benny know who penned the message?"

Nicholas shook his head. "Your father didn't say."

Julian remained silent for several seconds, then his expression cleared. "It must have been the missive they received before leaving Kenbrook. Obviously made in error."

"Julian," Megan asked, relieved beyond measure that her parents had been located, "wouldn't you have encountered the *Wind Song* on your return from America?"

He glanced up and nodded. "Perhaps, but we altered our course. My first mate wished to make a stop at a port in the Caribbean." Julian turned back to Nicholas, his face tightening in displeasure. "Anything else, Claremont?"

Nicholas cleared his throat. "Not regarding your parents, no."

A knock sounded just as Julian started to speak. "Enter," he snapped.

"Forgive the intrusion, my lord, but the Duchess of Claremont and Earl of Stenwick have arrived and are waiting in the gold salon," Wentworth announced.

Megan's heart pounded as she left the study. She walked beside her brother but felt Nicholas's eyes on her. She could feel the heat of his body, could smell his spicy scent. She closed her eyes and breathed him in. Flashes of their entwined bodies filled her head, his lips on hers, his hand over her bare breast. She pressed a hand over her mouth to keep from gasping and prayed her face wasn't as red as a cherry. Oh, God, what had she done?

Two footmen opened the doors as they approached. The dowager duchess started when she saw them approach. Nicholas's young uncle, Charles, sat frozen with two fingers buried in his ornate snuffbox, gaping at them. Not every day Nicholas and Julian stood together.

"Mother, Charles, I am surprised by your arrival," Nicholas confessed. He embraced his mother, then shook his uncle's hand.

"Carson informed us where to find you. And—" She glanced at Julian, "—saints be praised, you and Julian are in the same room." Her voice rang with pleasure. "Julian, I'm so pleased to see you! When did you arrive?"

"I have been back for two days, Your Grace," her brother responded with a bow.

Megan turned to the tall, blond man beside the dowager. His blue eyes resembled his nephew's, but his hair was lighter and his frame much less powerful. "Are you feeling better, my lord?"

Lord Stenwick nodded. "Indeed, my lady, I feel much more the thing."

"I have some news," the dowager announced. "The missing coachman, Sims, has been located. It seems that vagabonds burned the carriage, then knocked the poor man unconscious. Sims woke five days later in a peasant couple's home, confused and disoriented. Only yesterday was he able to recall his mission and make the journey to Kenbrook. And here—" The dowager handed Julian a slip of paper, "—is the note written from Joseph requesting my assistance in Megan's debut."

"May I?" Megan asked, reaching for the note. "The letter says nothing," she said after examining the brief missive. "We learned more from your son."

"What does Megan mean?" the dowager asked.

Nicholas recounted his discussion with Mr. Wells, then Julian's conclusion that the missive had been made in error. Megan had to turn away when she realized how she stared. Dear Lord, at this rate, Julian would learn everything. Her feelings for Nicholas and what happened between them.

The dowager looked relieved. "At least we know that they are all right."

"Quite so. And someone was surely in a blunder regarding Julian. Probably a case of mistaken identity," Lord Stenwick reasoned.

"But what to do now?" the dowager asked. "My dearest friends are still at sea looking for Julian."

"I'll send the *Sweet Siren* after them," her brother answered. The tension in Megan's shoulders eased. Her parents would be home soon.

"Thank goodness." The dowager nodded. "When will you leave?"

"I merely intend to send my ship, madam, not board it. I must stay with Megan."

The lady smiled and shook her head. "You needn't worry about Megan. Nicholas and I will take excellent care of her."

"Your son will have nothing to do with my sister, Your Grace," he retorted in a low, acrimonious voice.

Megan cringed, close to tears. Not see Nicholas? She pressed her lips together and willed the wetness gathering in her eyes away.

The dowager looked startled. "Yes, of course. If that is your wish."

****

Nicholas cursed the fates that had brought his mother so soon. He longed to stay with Megan, but he'd departed the Kenbrook house with his mother and uncle. Every step further away from her tore at him.

"Please come in, Mother. Will you and Charles be staying the night?" he asked as Carson opened the front door.

"I don't know, Nicholas. It shall depend on how long it takes you to explain what you've done." With an I-know-you've-misbehaved expression, she took her brother's arm and entered the townhouse.

Nicholas winced, then followed them inside. Of a sudden, he knew how King Louis felt as he walked to the guillotine.

He sat beside his mother on the sofa as Charles took the seat opposite, and waited until Carson left the drawing room. He told them about his encounter with Megan at the stream and mistaking her for a commoner. Then he explained his shock at finding the same girl occupying one of his guestrooms over a sennight later, and his belief that she'd lied about being his ward.

His mother gasped. "Oh, Nicholas, please tell me you didn't have Megan removed from your house?"

"No, Mother. That's not quite what happened."

"Then, darling, what did you do?"

"I kissed her...and...well...it just happened," he sputtered.

Her smile slipped. "*What* just happened?"

Charles coughed, and Nicholas was certain it wasn't because of his recent illness.

He sighed, feeling as if he were still in short coats about to receive a good trimming from his mother. Only the lack of short coats had changed.

His mother cleared her throat. A warning, that. It was time to finish his confession. "We, uh, that is... she..."

Her hand flew to her throat and her eyes grew large and round. "Oh, Nicholas. Surely you didn't seduce that sweet, young girl?"

"She didn't stop..." He trailed off at his mother's scathing glare.

"Megan was taking laudanum to relieve the pain from a fall and to ease the distress of her parents' sudden departure." She sighed hard. "Dear Christ, Nicholas, I am certain the poor darling was sedated at the time."

He bowed his head in humiliation. He was a cad, a rakehell. Worse than Jeremy, if such a thing existed. What kind of gentleman ruined a lady? Not just any lady. The Duke of Kenbrook's only daughter. God, he felt sick. "I had no idea," he admitted to the tips of his polished Hessians. With a sigh, he straightened and fused his gaze with his mother's. "My brain was swimming in gin, madam," he said with remorse. "And I truly thought she was a commoner."

Her eyes flashed. "So that validated your behavior?"

"No," he answered, rubbing his sore neck. Be damned, he thought Megan had been fully aware of her actions. God, if only he had known.

The clock rang out the hour, sounding more like a death knell in the strained silence. Nicholas shifted in his seat and waited. He waited for her to come to the only conclusion left to him.

"Nicholas, you do realize that you must marry the girl."

"It's not I who oppose marriage, Mother."

"I understand why Megan would resist. I trust you need only to convince her that your proposal is genuine and not out of obligation."

He gave his head a small shake, wondering how the deuce his mother knew. He shouldn't be surprised. She could always guess what he was feeling. "Mother, it's not that simple. There is a tremendous factor opposing this union, not including Megan."

"And what is that?"

"Julian."

She clanked her cup hard against the saucer. "Oh, dear."

****

Megan stood before her sitting room windows viewing the decorative garden suffused in moonlight, thinking of Nicholas. Again. Would she ever get him out of her mind? A slight rap sounded and she turned, relieved to focus her attention elsewhere. "Enter."

"Moppet, why haven't you retired? It's late. Another sleepless night will do you no good."

She ignored Julian's question. "Where have you been? I didn't think you would be gone so long."

"I wanted to have Stuart Williams depart after Mother and Father on the morrow."

She closed her eyes in relief. "Oh, Jules, that's wonderful." As soon as her parents returned, she'd convince them that she had no need to cut a dash amongst the *ton*—rather, she would like to remain at Kenbrook. She was certain she could persuade her father with ease. Her mother would be difficult. And Megan needed to keep what had happened with Nicholas a secret from her parents at all costs. She clenched her hands together. That would be the hardest feat of all. She desperately wanted to exorcise all feeling for Nicholas, but her feelings could not be plucked away like chicken feathers.

"My clipper is under repair and cannot leave right now," Julian said. "However, I have sent another ship after them. Mother and Father will return before long, my darling sister."

"They must come home soon, Julian. They must," she whispered. She couldn't stand the thought of having to stay in London to attend those ridiculous socials. And she'd never have the ability to respond indifferently in Nicholas's presence. She pressed a hand to her stomach. The mere thought made her sick.

Julian gathered her in his arms and tucked her under his chin. "All things resolve as they should,

Moppet."

She heaved a sigh against his silk shirt. "Let us return to Kenbrook, Julian. Truly, I have no desire for a season."

Her brother gave a short laugh. "Now, dearest, think of what Society would believe if we returned without you being betrothed. Everyone would be convinced you had bad teeth or somesuch," he teased.

Megan frowned. "I do not wish to marry."

"Ever?"

She pulled out of his embrace. "Ever," she said.

"Megan..."

She backed away, clenching her hands into fists. "Don't you dare tell me that that is what a lady is supposed to do, Julian, or I swear I'll knock a few teeth out of your head."

He grinned.

"Damn it, Julian, I'm serious."

"A lady ought not to swear."

"Ohhh, go to Bath!"

"I'm just trying to help you," Julian said with laughter in his eyes.

"If you really wanted to help me," she said, "we would leave for Kenbrook at first light."

He sighed and shook his head. "Mother and Father wish you here. Besides, I am certain you will have a grand time and make many friends."

"I'd rather go home," she grumbled.

The teasing light dwindled from Julian's eyes and a frown came to his lips. "Has something happened?" he asked in a low, lethal tone.

She smoothed her dress. "Of course not."

Julian studied her for several seconds. She wanted to squirm. *He must not find out. He must not.* "Then we are agreed?"

Taking a deep breath, she nodded. She had no choice. "Good, now get some rest." Julian walked to the door. "I'm taking you to Drury Lane and then to dinner at Clarendon's tomorrow."

As the door closed, she turned back to the windows. How was she going to attend all those...? Her thoughts halted as a large shape moved in the garden below. She squinted at the silvery tree trunks and the large bench below. Nothing moved. Had someone been out there?

After a few more minutes of scanning the moonlit garden, she turned away. She must have imagined it.

CHAPTER 8

Megan's knees wobbled as she entered the drawing room. "Hello, Your Grace."

"Hello, dear. I pray I'm not intruding?" the dowager asked.

"Not at all," she answered. "How is Lord Charles?"

"Much better, indeed. The cough has completely left him now."

"That is wonderful. Would you like some tea?"

The dowager nodded. The honey-colored strands of her neat twist glimmered with the regal movement. Megan wished one day she'd be that elegant. "That would be most welcome. Have you any news of your parents?"

"As a matter of fact, I do," she replied as she engaged the pull to signal for refreshments. She explained what Julian had told her the previous evening.

"I daresay, I am grateful to know they shall return soon."

The tea arrived and she poured a cup for each of them, aching to inquire about Nicholas. But she found the strength to withhold the words. Why did he always have to weave into her thoughts? She did not wish to love him.

Her hand hovered over her teacup. Love him?

"How are you, my dear?"

A tremor went through her and she took a sip of tea to hide her reaction. "I am doing very well, thank you," she said as her gaze lowered to the string of pearls around the duchess' neck.

"I am truly glad to hear that. Megan, I've also come to extend an invitation. Nicholas and I would like you and Julian to dine with us tonight."

Oh, how Megan wanted to say yes. But Julian would never agree. She signed. "I apologize, Your Grace, but I must decline. Julian and I are having dinner out after we attend the theater this evening."

Disappointment flitted into the dowager's eyes. "Perhaps another time?"

"Of course."

Megan watched the dowager leave, her heart heavy. She and Nicholas would never be together. Not only were he and Julian enemies, Megan would never be elegant and stylish. She was not at all what a duchess should be. She liked to ride horses, not serve cucumber sandwiches in the drawing room. She turned from the window, swiping the tears from her cheeks. She had no future with him.

****

He gulped down his drink. Megan's brother shouldn't have arrived so soon! He slammed his glass on the table. This destroyed his plan. Closing his eyes, he wondered how he would keep the creditors away this week. They were banging on his door at all hours.

With a sigh, he poured another drink and settled in the chair before his desk. He glared at the stack of unpaid bills and took out some paper. One more time, the plan had to be altered. He wouldn't be able to take Megan with her brother so near. He drained his glass. He was running short of time. Kenbrook would be back soon.

****

That evening, Nicholas sat in his plush, red velvet theater seat, cursing his foul luck. He should not have halted at Jeremy's house earlier. An enormous mistake, that. Jeremy's sister was there and had invited herself when she learned that he was attending the theater alone. Phyllis Longwell Granger was an attractive widow, two years younger than he and a diligent flirt. Not even her brief marriage had stopped her from pursuing him. But Nicholas never felt any interest in her. Especially since he'd discovered Megan. And he would have no one else.

He anxiously waited for Megan's appearance, but the chattering magpie seated next to him kept interrupting. He gnashed his teeth when she spoke again.

"I adore Shakespeare. It was good of you to invite me," Phyllis cooed as she touched his leg for the third time in as many minutes.

"Yes, well, I'm glad you were available to come on such short notice." He doubted she would pick up on the sarcasm.

She didn't. "Actually, Nicky," she whispered loudly, "I cancelled Lord Bradbury's invitation for this evening in order to attend with you." She smiled up at him in bald suggestion. He sighed inwardly, wishing he'd never brought the chit along.

Phyllis opened her mouth to speak yet again, but stopped on a gasp. Similar noises sounded from others within the theater. After several seconds of total silence, loud chattering broke out. The hairs on the back of his neck rose and his stomach tumbled over. Most of the audience was focused on the Kenbrook box with eyes raised and mouths agape. When he found Megan standing there, his heart stopped in his chest. He couldn't breathe. Although he had glimpsed her beauty many times before, he never saw her like this. Dressed in a shimmering silver and amethyst evening gown, she was more than exquisite. Even from this distance he could see her pearly skin unmarred by a single flaw. Her shining, raven-black hair had been arranged in several barrel curls at the back of her head. His eyes shifted to her lips and he felt a jolt of lust so poignant it hurt. How he wished to kiss those full, cherry lips until he no longer craved the sweetness of her taste. Until he no longer wanted to feel her silky skin or hear the sound of her voice in his ear. Until he closed his eyes and wasn't haunted by visions of her.

"Isn't that Marquess of Amersleigh, Lord Julian Westland? But who is the girl?"

Hearing the jealousy in Phyllis's voice, he wrenched his gaze away and cleared his throat. "Yes, that's Amersleigh, and he's escorting his sister, Lady Megan."

"Oh, that's right. I had heard that she was to be launched this season, but I must say, I hadn't realized she was so..."

"Absolutely exquisite," he finished, unable to prevent the words from slipping past his lips.

She turned to him, fury sparking in her hazel eyes. "I just saw Marian Billingsly." A blatant lie, he knew. "Since there is time before curtain rise, I must say hello. I'll return shortly."

"Phyllis..." Nicholas wanted to apologize for being rude, but she was already gone.

****

Megan could not keep from trembling. Everyone was staring at her. She fumbled with her fan, not at all certain what to do with the blasted thing. Oh, how she wished she had paid more attention to instruction. Her mind had no doubt been filled with sneaking from the house to ride Aramis. She gave up trying to open the fan and smoothed out a wrinkle in her dress. She chanced a peek at the audience. Thousands of eyes still on her. How she wished she were in breeches riding one of her horses rather than wearing a mountain of silk and having everyone gawk at her so.

"If I didn't know any better, Moppet," Julian

said from his seat beside her, "I would think you were the one appearing on stage tonight. Why the nerves, love?"

"Everyone is staring at me, Julian," she whispered.

He chuckled and shook his head. "Oh, sweetling, do you not realize how beautiful you are?"

"Fair, perhaps, but not beautiful." Julian started to laugh, and she demanded, "What's so amusing?"

He wiped his eyes. "I find it difficult to believe that you look into a mirror every day, yet miss your own reflection. Dear sister, you are by far the loveliest lady here. Probably anywhere. And these poor souls are seeing that for themselves."

"Oh, Jules, you're biased." She dismissed his compliment with a wave of her hand.

A knock sounded, and the doorman announced a visitor.

She rose as an attractive man about Julian's age, with dark hair and eyes, entered the small chamber. He wore a wide smile.

"Julian, it's been a while, how are you?" His twinkling eyes slid to her. "And who is your beautiful companion?"

"Hello, Michael. I was just thinking that you or Jeremy would be the first to dash up here," Julian said as he shook his friend's hand.

Michael laughed. "Jeremy isn't here. But I daresay, he will be regretting that decision on the morrow."

Julian made the introduction. "This lovely lady is my dear sister, Lady Megan Westland. Megan, this is an old friend of mine, Lord Michael Farrell, the Earl of Bentwood."

"Sister?" the earl asked in surprise. "It is indeed a pleasure, my lady." He scooped up her hand and settled a kiss on her satin-clad knuckles.

His hand was warm in hers. Megan watched

him place a kiss on her glove, expecting to feel something. No, nothing. Would Nicholas be the only one to ever evoke her feelings? "As it is for me, my lord."

Another knock sounded, and soon people filled the tiny box. Megan was pressed against the wall, finding it difficult to draw in air. The noise was unbearable. Strange men grabbed her hand and kissed her knuckles. The room grew stifling hot. She had to escape. "Julian. I feel a few pins coming loose," she lied, her voice soft so the others couldn't hear. "I must visit the ladies' retiring room. I'll return in a few minutes."

"Give me another moment, and I'll escort you," he replied.

"It's just down the hall. I shan't be overlong, really," she insisted.

He glanced around, then turned back to her. "As you will, Megan, but hurry back."

"I will."

She slipped from the box with a sigh of relief and began to walk down the empty corridor. After several steps, someone grabbed her from behind and hauled her into the adjacent box. She spun around to face her abductor—about to release a tirade sure to leave mortal wounds—but stopped short when she saw—

"Nicholas," she rasped in surprise.

"Hello, Meg. By God, you look lovely."

His husky voice weakened her knees. She stumbled back a step. "Release me at once, Your Grace," she demanded, seeing that he was leaning against the only door out.

"I shall in another moment. Just let me look at you."

She glanced about the vacant box, noticing all but one lamp extinguished and the front curtain lowered. At least no one would see them alone together. Alone. Together. She swallowed hard. "Is this your box?"

He shook his head. "It belongs to Jeremy Longwell, the Marquess of Fielding. And worry not, he isn't to attend tonight. Forgive me, love, but I had to see you again."

She crossed her arms to expel the sensations his nearness caused. Indeed, she did not like desiring a kiss from the very man she was trying not to love. "You have two minutes, Your Grace."

He pursed his lips. "My name is Nicholas."

"One minute, fifty seconds." She paused. "Your Grace."

He sighed. "I am truly sorry for the despicable things I said and did to you. My actions were beyond horrid." He paused and closed his eyes briefly. "Sweet Meg, I truly wished I had known you were Kenbrook's daughter."

She had to grit her teeth to keep from reaching out to him. "I am finding it difficult to believe that you didn't recognize me, Your Grace," she admonished. "I know you saw me as a child."

"Truly, I'd forgotten Julian had a sister," he answered without hesitation.

Megan snorted in disbelief and looked away.

He took a step forward and nudged her chin to face him. "It's true. I've spent years trying to forget anything and everything about Julian Westland. And that included a shy little sister who refused to stay in the room long enough for me to get a proper look." His finger traced her brow, then moved over her cheek and stopped when he reached her lips.

She shivered, afraid he would kiss her, afraid he wouldn't. The air charged between them. All she had to do was move forward. His eyes begged for the kiss.

She took a hasty step back and his hand fell away. She couldn't think when he touched her. "Are you denying that you used me to get even with Julian for what you believe he did to Emily Wakefield?" She tried desperately to hold on to the anger seeping away.

His breath caught. "Is that what Julian has made you to believe? My God, Megan, no wonder you're so bloody upset."

"Are you denying it?"

"Of course, I deny it. That is the most absurd thing I've ever heard," he spat out.

Megan bit her lip. Could she have been wrong? "It's not so absurd when you think about it," she said quietly.

"Meg, I am telling you the truth." He looked steadily into her eyes. Then, without warning, he pulled her into his arms and dropped his mouth down over hers.

Surprise kept her still for a second, then she began to struggle. She continued to resist until his sliding lips melted her. Her willpower evaporated. Nothing mattered but the taste of him and the feel of his velvety tongue gliding against hers. She had to respond or die of longing.

She released the handfuls of his black coat and wound her arms around his neck. She melted against him and returned his scorching kisses. Her breasts pressed against his solid chest. She ached for him to touch her bare skin. For him to pull off the blasted gown she wore and have his way with her.

He lifted his head, his eyes intense. "Meg, you are everything to me, and I could never use you as Julian has suggested. If that were true, why do I still want you so desperately? Why haven't I discarded you? Why can't I remove you from my mind? My heart?" He lowered his head to capture her mouth again, but an impatient knock sounded behind them.

"Nicky, are you in there? The play is about to

begin."

He cursed under his breath.

"Nicky?" Megan mouthed as anger bloomed within her chest. If she was all he thought about, then why was a woman outside that door waiting for him? And calling him Nicky?

"Nicky, darling, where are you?" After several seconds, the woman stomped away.

"You filthy swine! I cannot believe I almost trusted you," she hissed.

As she moved toward the door, he grabbed her arm and spun her around. "I have never lied to you, Megan. Phyllis is a friend who invited herself along tonight. That is all."

"Let me go."

"Never," he replied before kissing her again.

Incensed, Megan drew back and slapped him. She jerked away from the duke and yanked open the door. She flew from the room and didn't stop until she reached her family's box.

"There you are, Moppet. I was about to come looking for you," her brother said. His brows crashed together. "Are you all right?"

"Yes, I'm fine." She paused, trying to catch her breath. "I had to hurry because I didn't wish to miss the opening."

He studied her a moment, then said, "I hope you don't mind, but Michael will be joining us tonight."

She widened her smile when she noticed the earl. Everyone else had departed. "Of course I don't mind." Taking her seat between the two men, she tried hard to squelch Nicholas and his searing kiss from her mind. As the curtain on stage rose, the actors drew her attention in their colorful and elaborate costumes. And soon, the fascinating dialogue of *A Midsummer Night's Dream* enthralled her.

Julian wanted to leave after the intermission,

but she wouldn't hear of it. She wished to stay and experience every minute of her first theater. However, when the play ended and everyone crowded in the foyer, she realized the wisdom in her brother's desire to leave sooner. Many halted them for an introduction. The crowd swelled in her direction. She shuffled back a few steps. Nicholas could be in there somewhere.

"You look tired, sweet. Shall we leave?" Julian asked after dozens of introductions.

She halted mid-yawn. "I'm sorry."

His eyes softened. "Don't apologize, Moppet. Michael, we must take our leave."

The earl's face fell. "So soon?"

"My sister is not used to keeping such late hours."

"I understand. However, I have one request before you go. Could I be permitted the first dance at Huntington's masque?"

"Why, Michael," Julian joked, "I could not possibly accept. No doubt, you'd step all over my toes."

She smothered a laugh.

With a chuckle, her brother turned to her. "What do you think, Moppet? Do you want to dance with this old cad?"

"It would be a pleasure, Lord Bentwood," she answered, then smiled.

His frown melted into a saucy grin. "Believe me, Lady Westland, the pleasure will be entirely mine," he said, and bade them farewell.

Thank goodness Julian had decided to return her home instead of having dinner at the opulent hotel. How did these people keep such late hours? Then she recalled that they usually didn't rise until after noon. She shook her head. Mornings were the best time of day.

The horses trotted along the cobblestones in a

soothing rhythm. She relaxed against the seat and closed her eyes. What a long day. The clip-clop and gentle sway of the carriage lulled her to sleep. Sounds fell away.

The coachman shouted out. The horses whinnied in fright and surged forward in an uncontrolled frenzy through the streets.

She screamed in alarm and fell against the back of the carriage. A loud buzz sounded in her ears. Julian helped her straighten, and she nodded when he asked if she were unharmed. The vehicle jostled dangerously, and her fear mounted. Julian tightened his grip on her with one hand, and grabbed the leather strap above the window with the other. She glanced out. The lit street lamps sped by, almost blurring together. Dear God, they were going to crash!

Just as her brother released her and started to crawl out of the window, a lone rider pulled alongside the horses. The man leaned over and managed to grab the reins. He spoke soothingly to the animals until they slowed, then stopped.

Julian opened the carriage door with a bang and flew out. "Are you all right, Megan?"

She pressed a hand to her thundering heart and nodded.

He helped her down. She followed her brother toward their savior as the man dismounted.

"My most heartfelt thanks, sir. How may I repay you? Just name the price, and it is yours," Julian said to the gentleman's back.

The man turned slowly and said, "Permission to marry your sister will do quite nicely."

"Nicholas," she gasped, relieved beyond measure to see him standing there.

He stepped forward, his brows drawn. "Are you all right, love?" he asked, cupping her cheek in the palm of his right hand.

She wanted to crawl into his arms and stay there forever.

"Take your bloody hands off of my sister, Claremont."

Nicholas lifted his head, anger building in his eyes. She took a quick step back so his hand fell away.

A groan sounded from the driver's seat of the carriage. Julian turned and scrambled up to the seat. "Perkins, are you all right? My God, you're bleeding, man."

"Bleeding?" she repeated. "How bad is it, Julian?"

"He's got a nasty wound on his head. Can you hear me, Perkins?"

Nicholas climbed the other side. "Grab him carefully under the arms, Julian," he directed, lifting Perkins by the legs. "Now let's get him down."

They lowered the injured coachman to the ground, and she swallowed at the sight of so much blood covering the man's face.

The poor fellow winced. "Just be still, you'll be all right," Julian said.

Julian removed his handkerchief and placed it over the man's injury, but blood quickly drenched the fabric. She gripped her hands together. As her brother reached into his pocket for another handkerchief, Nicholas held out a pristine piece of white linen. "Here, use this," he said. "I'll fetch a doctor."

He turned to her, his eyes troubled. "Will you be all right?"

"Yes. Now do hurry. Perkins looks dreadful," she replied in a hushed tone so that the man wouldn't hear her. But as she glanced back at the dear old coachman, she noticed that he had already lost consciousness.

Nicholas gave a curt nod, then jumped onto his

horse.

Megan watched him leave. Nicholas had saved them. She drew her shawl tightly around her shoulders. He had risked his own life for theirs. Her heart flooded with joy. Nicholas had saved her and Julian and Perkins.

But how did he just happen on them like that? That meant Nicholas had been following them. But why? Her heart leaped. Could he actually care about her?

She looked back in the direction he had gone. *Please, let the answer be yes.*

****

After assisting Julian with the injured servant, Nicholas glanced around the hall, wondering where Megan had gone. He had to see her again, to try and convince her that—

"Go home now, Claremont," Julian said, joining him in the hallway.

"No. We need to discuss my betrothal to Megan. I am most serious about marrying her."

Julian stood silent for a moment, his silver-grey eyes assessing, calculating. "We shall discuss this in the study."

Nicholas followed Julian into the room. Settling into the butter-soft leather, he watched his former friend take the seat behind the desk. What was the man up to?

"I know not what sort of callous game you're playing with my sister, Claremont, but I do not like it," Julian snarled into the silence.

Nicholas splayed his hands on the polished desk and leaned forward. Looking steadily into those hostile eyes, he said, "This is no game, Julian. I mean to marry her."

"The hell you say. Perhaps you mean to commit to a betrothal, then leave her at the altar once your wedding day arrives," Julian said, his voice rising.

"Or, more accurately, you wish to get her with child, then leave her like you thought I did years ago to Emily Wakefield."

He balled his hands into fists. "Damn you, Julian, is it so difficult to believe that this has nothing whatever to do with Emily?" He took a deep breath, reining in the fury trying to overtake him, and lowered his voice. "This is not some sort of game or plan for revenge."

Julian did not respond for several minutes. Nicholas could read nothing in the man's expression but anger. Finally, Julian leaned back in his chair and crossed his arms. "From what I have learned tonight, Megan will have no difficulty finding a husband. In fact, there were seven offers this evening alone."

It took every ounce of strength he possessed not to rise up out of his chair and lunge across the desk. "Curse your black soul, Julian. You cannot do this," he said.

Julian's brow cocked up. "I daresay I can, Claremont. I am her guardian. Megan hasn't given me any indication she wishes to marry you."

As Nicholas listened, his grip tightened on the chair arms.

"In fact," the scoundrel continued, his lips pulling into a grin, "I think Bentwood has captured her attention."

A bloody lie, Nicholas thought.

Julian leaned back in his chair. Nicholas caught a glimpse of disappointment. So, that was the bastard's game. Nicholas relaxed, his fingers throbbing from having dug into the leather so long. Julian had wanted him to lunge forward, had been waiting for him. Well, he'd restrain the urge to rearrange Julian's face even if it killed him.

"I have an idea. One that may solve everything," Julian said.

"I'm listening," he prompted.

"Leave Megan completely alone until she decides on a husband."

"What?" he roared. He could no more stop the sun from rising in the morn.

"You heard me. Do not attempt to see or talk to her, by any means. And if the two of you were meant to be together, you will."

"If I do stay away from her, and she chooses to marry me, you will allow it?"

"Yes." Julian answered with reluctance, as if it pained him.

"There is something else." He leaned forward. He would walk the fires of hell if it meant he could marry Megan, but this agreement had to be fair.

"And what would that be?"

"Quit trying to turn her against me," he bellowed.

"I've only spoken the truth to her."

He grunted. "No, just what you believe is the truth. You must allow her to discern things for herself."

After several seconds of silent deliberation, Julian nodded. "Now, do you agree to these terms?"

"Not just yet, Amersleigh." He frantically worked his mind for any advantages.

Julian heaved a sigh. "Now what?"

He chewed his lip. *Think, man, think.* His heart knocked so hard against his chest that he could hardly form a thought. "If she desires to see me, I will not refuse her," he said.

After a lengthy hesitation, Julian said, "Fine, but she is to know nothing at all of this agreement, or it is ended. I wish to be certain her decision is genuine. Do we have an understanding?"

The door opened and Megan walked into the room, stemming Julian's words. Nicholas rose from his chair and feasted his eyes on her loveliness, wanting to pull her into his arms and kiss her senseless. What was it about this young woman that he could not live without?

"I thought you had retired for the evening, Megan," Julian said.

Megan's heart quivered at the sight of Nicholas standing there dressed in evening black, looking far more handsome that he ought. Those intense feelings she'd harbored for him since finding his portrait all those years ago rushed back. Forcing her gaze away, she turned to her brother, realizing that he and Nicholas had been speaking without exchanging a round of punches. Incredible. Then she recalled her brother's words. "I was assisting Dr. Kellerman."

"How is Perkins?" her brother asked, rounding the desk to stand before her.

She cleared her throat, suddenly gone dry. "He needed to be stitched, but is doing much better."

"Did he regain consciousness? Was he able to explain what had happened?"

"Perkins said a man darted across the road, scaring the horses. When they reared up, he hit his head."

"A man? Did Perkins recognize him?"

"No. It was too dark," Megan said.

Nicholas stepped forward. "Lady Megan, may I have a word with you?"

She opened her mouth, but Julian answered first. "No, Claremont, you may not. Now leave here before I have you forcefully removed."

Nicholas took another step forward, his blue eyes snapping with fury.

Megan's heart thundered with alarm. She eased into the narrow distance separating the two men. "Cease this madness, both of you." She turned to Nicholas. "I think it would be best if you left now."

He lowered his gaze, the rage subsiding from his features. "Please, I must speak with you first, Meg," he implored softly. "It is important."

"I won't have it, Claremont," her brother barked.

Noticing a glimmer in Nicholas's eyes, something almost beseeching, she turned to her brother. "Give us a few minutes to talk, Jules."

Julian threw up his hands. "All right, a few minutes. But that is all." He glanced over her head and addressed Nicholas. "And you will not lay one finger on my sister. I will be right outside that door. All she has to do is make one questionable sound and I'll be on you in a trice." He strode from the room with military stiffness.

Warily, she turned back to Nicholas.

"Thank you, Meg," he said, moving toward her.

She took a step back to distance her body from his. "Whatever you have to say, do it fast," she said as her bottom hit against the desk.

"I wish you to be my wife." He advanced another step so that he stood mere inches from her. "We must marry."

"That is close enough," she snapped.

Must. He didn't want to marry her. He merely felt obligated. Oh, God, why couldn't he love her? She wanted that above anything. But his cold arrangement had nothing to do with love. She squared her shoulders. "So," she sneered, trying to bury her pain, "your proposal has changed from mistress to wife?"

He jerked back as though he'd been struck. "Megan, I have apologized. What more can I do? Name anything and it shall be done."

Just love me as much as I love you. Her gaze skidded away to focus on the leather-bound books behind him. "There is nothing you can do."

"Will you at least allow me to try?" He paused to graze her cheek with his fingertips. "Say you'll marry me, Meg," he insisted.

As his warm skin sent tingling sparks through her body, pooling in the pit of her stomach, confusion enveloped her. She wanted desperately to take what he offered, but she held back. Being a duchess meant being the perfect lady, like her mother. Megan was not the perfect lady. She was anything but the perfect lady.

The door crashed open, jarring Megan from the spell Nicholas had woven around her. "Good night, Claremont," Julian said.

"Let me know what you decide." Nicholas held her gaze for a moment, then spun around and was gone.

Megan stared at the empty doorway for several seconds. Could it be possible he truly wanted to marry her, even with all her faults? She bit her lip, tamping back her soaring hopes. Nicholas's future words and actions would reveal his true feelings. And since she knew with last week's menses that she didn't carry his child, there was no rush to the altar.

There was plenty of time for him to prove the sincerity of his proposal. If, indeed, he was sincere at all.

CHAPTER 9

One week after the carriage incident, Megan plodded into the dining room. She'd had another sleepless night, identical to the six before. Not even the beautiful new gowns that arrived daily from the fashion house had improved her mood. And it was all Nicholas's fault, curse him.

Just seven short days ago, he'd been adamant about her becoming his wife, and now...nothing. She hadn't heard one blasted word from the man. He hadn't even bothered to pen a note.

She sighed and moved to the sideboard. Without filling her plate from the extensive fare offered, she poured a cup of tea from the silver pot and sat in her chair. Unaware of Julian's steel-grey eyes watching her from above his paper, she wrapped her chilled hands around the hot teacup and stared into the dark, steamy liquid.

"Megan, you must eat or none of your new gowns will fit," Julian said as he folded his newspaper and set it aside.

"I'll eat when I'm hungry. How is Perkins this morning?"

He sighed. "He is angry that I won't allow him to return to work until his stitches come out in a couple of days."

"Good," she breathed, grateful the dear man was almost recovered. She glanced down and watched the steam rise from her cup. "I think I'll take a stroll in the park today." Anything to keep from dwelling on Nicholas.

"I'm sorry, Moppet, but I must go to the dock

and inspect the clipper's progress."

"Julian, will you please stop calling me that? I am not a child."

He raised his brows at her request, but didn't agree to it. "I shan't be overlong. Eat something," he said instead, then kissed her forehead and departed.

She abhorred the idea of spending another day alone dwelling on that insufferable man. How she wished she could ride her horses. Then she recalled that Julian didn't say she couldn't go, just that *he* couldn't. She told Wentworth to have the carriage brought around.

She held her face up to the sunshine after she alighted from the vehicle, followed by her maid disguised as a duenna. It was necessary that Society not realize Lucy's identity since a maid was not a proper escort. But she refused to remain indoors another day. She needed a distraction from Nicholas like she needed air.

Walking along the path to the park, she smiled in admiration of the colorful flowers in bloom. They reminded her of her mother's gardens at Kenbrook, and a wave of sadness threatened her. She shook her head, forcing back the looming depression. Today, she decided, she would not be sad.

Unaware of the many appreciative male eyes that followed her, she sat on a bench to watch a group of children play. Her maid took the seat beside her and began to chatter about their lovely surroundings.

"What a lovely rose garden, my lady. Oh, look at the statue. Is that marble?"

She groaned inwardly. If only she could have a few moments to herself... "Lucy, didn't you say just yesterday how you needed to visit the apothecary and find a treatment for your mother's swelling?"

"Oh, yes, my lady."

She kept her eyes fixed on the children. "Well

then, why don't you go now? I'll remain here and wait for you."

"But Lady Megan, I could not possibly leave you alone."

She smiled in reassurance. "I shall be quite safe. Look at all the children. Were it not safe, would they be allowed to play thus?" She waved a hand toward them as they rolled upon the grass and tackled one another.

"I guess not," her maid answered.

"I am certain you shan't be but a few minutes. Have Hanson escort you in the carriage."

"Are you sure, my lady?"

"Yes, Lucy, now off with you. I shall be perfectly safe during your short absence."

"Well...all right. And thank you, Lady Megan," Lucy said breathlessly, her excitement at being taken somewhere in the grand ducal conveyance evident. Servants were rarely allowed the use of such vehicles.

"Would you mind if I took the seat beside you?" asked a voice.

She looked up to find a pretty girl standing before the bench. "Please do," she answered.

The girl sat, trying a little too hard to be ladylike. "I'm Evelyn Thornton, but everyone calls me Evie. And you must be Megan Westland," Evie said as she opened her parasol against the bright sun.

"Why, yes I am. How did you know?"

"Everyone has been talking about you," Evie answered. She laughed. "You certainly made an impression at the theater, from what I hear."

She felt her cheeks grow warm. "I did?"

"Absolutely. My brother, Ash, was there and couldn't stop talking about you. I had no idea how accurate he was in his description. My dear, you are stunning," Evie said, her soft brown eyes swimming with merriment.

Megan ducked her head, a little embarrassed. "Thank you." Megan learned that Evie celebrated her twentieth birthday two months ago. Her only sibling was her brother, Ash, older by six years. Upon the sudden death of their father five years ago, he became the Earl of Ashton and her guardian.

"Why aren't you married, Evie?"

Pain filled Evie's liquid brown eyes. "I was betrothed once, but he cried off," she answered.

Crossing her arms, Megan expelled an indignant huff. "Well, in my opinion, he was a damn fool."

When Evie spun around sharply, Megan popped a hand over her mouth. She prayed she hadn't offended her new friend with her bluntness. She was ever driving her parents crazed with her unladylike ways.

Evie threw her head back and laughed.

Megan removed her hand, pleased and a little surprised by Evie's laughter. Then she joined in and they laughed so long, tears streamed down their faces.

"Oh, my, I haven't laughed this hard in...I don't think I have ever laughed this hard," Evie said as she wiped the tears from her cheeks.

"I haven't either." Then she sobered, recalling why she had no cause for laughter lately.

Evie's hand moved over hers. "What is it?"

She found herself telling of her parents' hasty departure, which still caused her great concern. But she said nothing of Nicholas.

"That's terrible, Megan. Well, it's no wonder I can feel your sadness. However, they shall be here soon," her friend said in a soothing tone.

"Yes, soon," she repeated, and a shiver ran through her. Her parents could learn what had happened between her and Nicholas. Especially after Julian's mention of the marriage offer.

With a sigh, she chose a more cheerful topic. "Are you attending Almack's tomorrow?"

Evie looked aghast for a moment, then shook her head.

"Why not?" she asked.

"I did not receive a voucher," her new friend answered while smoothing non-existent wrinkles from her dress.

She drew her brows together. "I don't understand."

After a moment of silence, Evie looked up. Tears glistened in her eyes. "I am not acceptable."

"Why? Because of your broken betrothal?"

"Yes," Evie whispered, her gaze skidding away.

"Well then, it will be my pleasure to turn down Lady Jersey's invitation. I suddenly find Almack's not acceptable."

With a gasp, Evie swiveled back around. "Oh, Megan, I didn't mean for you…"

Smiling, she patted Evie's hand. "I know you didn't."

Evie's eyes filled with more tears. "That's the nicest thing anyone has ever done for me," she said and pulled a frilly piece of linen from her bag. She gave a sniff and scrubbed the wetness from her cheeks. Then she straightened and asked, "What about Huntington's masque? Are you attending that?"

"Are you?"

Evie nodded. "Is your brother escorting you?"

"Yes. And who might your escort be for the night?"

"Usually, I would say Aunt Agnes. But I have a feeling that my brother will suddenly be delighted to perform the task."

They chatted for a while longer before she heard Evie exclaim that she had left her aunt asleep in the carriage and needed to return for her.

"Would you like to come?" Evie invited.

Megan shook her head with reluctance. "No, I'm waiting for my, uh, duenna to return with the carriage. You go. I'll see you at Huntington's," she replied, then bade good day to her new friend.

After Evie's departure, she realized how late it was. With growing alarm, she thought that Lucy should have returned quite a long time ago. Hours must have passed.

Standing, she fretted about whether to stay and wait or search for the carriage. Something terrible must have happened.

After retrieving some coins from her small wrist bag, she hired a hackney to convey her to the apothecary. When she found the shop closed for the day, she had the jarvey take her to the townhouse, her heart racing. But the carriage hadn't returned, nor was her brother back from the shipyard.

Julian would know what to do.

The jarvey squinted at her. "Yer sure ye be wantin' ter go there, miss?"

"Yes, and I would like to arrive before Christmas, please."

The driver shrugged and whistled at his horse. The wheels crunched over the road and they made their way through the streets of London much slower than she wanted. Megan resisted the urge to yell out at the driver. She should not advertise the fact she was unescorted.

The air thickened with a horrific stench at the same time she noticed the dingy buildings. The only things holding up some of the dilapidated structures were light feet and heavy prayer.

Children stood at either side of the street, shoeless and wearing filthy rags. Large, haunted eyes stared blankly from little faces streaked with dirt and grime. The adults were in no better condition. Pity welled up within her and she swallowed tears. She would speak to her father about this.

A few minutes later, the hackney stopped and the driver announced, "'Ere ye are, miss."

"C-could you wait here, please? I'm just going to get my brother," she asked with a measure of desperation. She handed him more coins to sweeten her request.

The driver looked around, taking in the rough atmosphere, then back to her and sighed heavily. He shifted in his seat. "Don't be long, miss," he warned.

"Thank you. I shan't," she promised, turning toward the row of large ships anchored nearby.

When she found her brother's clipper, she eyed the narrow boarding plank. Thoughts of her maid snuffed the urge to turn back. Taking a deep breath, she began to climb the unsteady board.

The piercing cry of a gull startled her. Her foot slipped, and she gasped. By God's grace she managed to keep upright. Giving the bothersome bird a good frown, she continued up the plank until she reached the deck.

"I say, miss. Ye ain't supposed t' be 'ere."

She spun around, plastering a hand over her thundering heart. Seeing a boy, she closed her eyes momentarily. "Oh, you frightened me," she breathed.

"Are ye lost?" the boy asked as he stared up at her.

She smiled, her pulse no longer exploding in her temples. "That depends. What ship is this?"

"The *Sweet Siren*," the boy confirmed with a puffed-out chest.

"Then I'm not lost. I need to see your commander. It is urgent."

"Right-o, miss," he said as he spun on his heel and ran to the steps leading below deck.

Within moments, he returned with someone other than her brother. The man walked toward her with a surprised expression and roved his eyes over her face several times before he spoke. "I'm sorry, my lady, but the Master—our captain—has already departed. I am Stuart Williams, the second-in-command of this ship." He gave a bow. "Can I be of some assistance to you?"

Her shoulders drooped. "No, thank you, Mr. Williams. It's Julian I need. Do you know if he left straightway for home?"

"I haven't a clue, my lady," he answered. His sky blue eyes held an unspoken question.

"Then I am sorry to have disturbed you."

"Believe me, my lady, you didn't disturb me." A smile grew on his lips.

As she began to return the smile, she remembered the jarvey. "I must leave. My driver said he wouldn't wait long."

"Are you sure I can't help you, Miss..." He trailed off and lifted his eyebrows.

"Oh, forgive my rudeness, Mr. Williams. I am Megan Westland, Julian's sister," she replied and held out her hand.

Surprise flared in his eyes. "I had no idea that the master has such a lovely sister," he said, taking her hand. He bowed over her gloved knuckles.

"Thank you, Mr. Williams, but I really must go now." She turned and began the journey back to the hackney, praying the driver hadn't left. As she walked amongst the squalor, she pulled a lavender-scented handkerchief from her bag and held it to her nose.

The sun began to dip into the western waters as she took the last few steps to the waiting vehicle. Thank God it hadn't moved. Just as she placed a foot on the steps, she noticed the empty driver seat. A strong arm pulled her against a body as big and stiff as a tree trunk. She shrieked. His other hand clamped over her mouth, and a retch-provoking smell hit her. Dear God, he probably hadn't taken a bath in months.

"Yer not to make a sound," the big oak grumbled into her ear with rancid-ale breath.

She nodded. She doubted she could scream again since her furiously beating heart was in her throat.

The large man looked around, then shuffled them into the dark alley behind him. She thrashed and tried to cry out. No use with his filthy hand clamped over her mouth. Her heart surged up her throat. Oh, God, oh God! She dug her heels into the ground, but he dragged her along. Using all her strength, she fought for freedom. He squeezed. The pain made stars dance before her eyes.

As they approached the shadows between the two buildings, the large man whispered into her ear. "Now, 'old still an' do as I says. I'm takin' me 'and away, so don't go makin' no noise."

She nodded, and the oaf removed his hand. But as he tried to lift her skirt, she gnashed her heel onto his boot and threw her elbow into his bloated paunch.

The man grunted in pain, then wrapped his arms around her. "'Old still or t'will 'urt all tha more," he hissed into her ear.

Megan prayed as hot fat tears coursed down her cheeks. Dear God, why did she ever leave the safety of her home? Why did she come to the docks? She shivered, imagining the big oaf dumping her into the water after having his way with her. Hot bile rose up her throat.

A crack rent the silence and she was freed of his suffocating grasp. She spun around and saw the large brute stagger. His face contorted with pain and he shook his head. He blinked several times and then focused on her.

She shivered at the look of rage in those black,

beady eyes. Taking a step back, she plastered her back against the dingy brick wall behind her. The man's fingers curled like talons, and he began to stalk toward her. She squeezed her eyes shut and turned away, unable to bear the thought of what was to come next.

Another loud crack sounded, followed by a heavy thud. She slowly opened her eyes. The large man lay on the ground. She turned to the alley's entrance. Was she being rescued or merely captured by another ruffian? She could detect nothing above the outline of a man standing there.

Her rescuer stepped forward. "Are you all right, Lady Megan?"

She sagged against the filthy wall and tried to calm her trembling. "Oh, Mr. Williams, however did you find me?"

He moved closer and steadied her with an arm around her shoulders. "I knew you weren't safe in this area, so I followed you." He eyed the filthy man. "Now, let's get you home. Can you walk?"

She leaned heavily against him, feeling weak. "I believe so, thank you," she whispered.

The sky darkened a shade with each passing minute; it became difficult to see. They arrived at the hired hackney, and she gasped when she saw the crumpled form hunched over the driver's seat.

Mr. Williams stepped onto the coach and examined the old man. "He will have a nasty ache in his head when he arouses, but he should be fine," he announced as he stepped down.

"Oh, thank heavens."

"I'll help you inside and take you home, my lady."

"Thank you."

They had gone some distance when she began to settle her trembling. When the vehicle turned onto Upper Brook Street, she heard a familiar voice roar over the clip-clop of the horse's hooves.

"Where is she?" Julian bellowed.

She jerked upright. "Mr. Williams, please stop," she implored, then scampered down from the hackney without assistance.

****

"What are you talking about?" Nicholas asked when his surprise at seeing Julian arrive at his townhouse had abated.

"You know exactly what I am talking about. Megan. Where is she?"

He tensed. "Megan is missing?" Fear doused his entire body. A movement beyond Julian's right shoulder caught his attention, and he looked up. Recognizing the disheveled little body, he rushed down the steps and scooped her into his arms, noticing her dirty, torn gown. A large, grungy handprint covered her mouth and chin. Dismay made his head spin. Most of the pins had come out of her hair, causing the thick tresses to pour over her shoulders and down her back in a tangled black mass. She shook like a leaf in a gale.

He held her tenderly against his hammering heart. "Meg, are you all right? What happened, love?" he asked when he could locate his voice, then kissed her forehead and cheek.

"My God, Moppet," Julian breathed as he approached.

"She's had quite a scare, Master."

Julian's head snapped up. "Stuart, what are you doing here?"

"I was bringing your sister home, sir. She came to the dock looking for you, but a large bloke took her into an alley. I had to hit him over the head with a piece of plank to get her away from him."

Nicholas looked back down at Megan and felt a violent jolt of wrath for her attacker burn a path through his body. "Did the man hurt you, love?" he asked.

"No. Mr. Williams arrived in time," she responded in a small, shaky voice.

"It's late. Give Megan to me, Claremont, and I shall take her home," Julian ordered.

He shook his head. "I think she needs to lie down right away. She shouldn't be moved until a doctor examines her." He refused to let her go.

"The driver," she said, turning to Mr. Williams.

"The man must have knocked the jarvey out and waited for your sister to return," the seaman explained. He turned back to Megan, his eyes softening.

"Come, Meg, I'll have Carson bring in the driver and fetch a doctor for you both," Nicholas said, not liking the way the seaman looked at Megan.

"Absolutely not, Claremont," Julian said.

Nicholas tightened his hold on her and stepped away, shaking his head. Not yet.

He heard her sigh. "Nicholas, I am fine. Please, put me down. It is the driver who is hurt and needs a doctor."

"Are you sure, love?" God, how he missed her.

"Yes, I'm sure. Put me down," she insisted.

As he lowered her carefully to the ground, he couldn't resist a taste of her lips. It had been way too long.

"God's blood, man. Are you insane?" Julian hissed, glancing around. Before he realized it, Julian captured Megan's hand and stowed her within the hackney. He stood helpless as he watched the vehicle roll away, his heart torn from his chest.

****

Fury boiled behind Julian's eyes as he ushered Megan into their house. She knew it wasn't directed at her. Well, not yet, anyway. Once he realized she had gone out without him, he'd give her what for. She dreaded that little chat.

As Julian handed his coat to Wentworth, Lucy ran up to them. "Oh, Lady Megan, are you all right? I heard you went out looking for Hanson and me. We had a bit 'o trouble with one of the wheels, but you had already left the park when we finished repairing it." She paused, her teary eyes growing wide. "Look at your gown. What happened? I shouldn't have left you!"

She took a deep breath. At least Lucy hadn't been harmed. "It's nothing, Lucy. Would you prepare my bath and something to eat? I'll be up momentarily."

As she started for the stairs, Julian placed a hand on her shoulder. "I'd like a word."

Megan sighed and followed her brother into their father's study.

Julian glared at her for several seconds. "I told you not to go to the park without me."

"No, Julian, you said that you couldn't go."

He leaned back in his chair. "In the future, you are not to leave this house without me. Is that clear?"

Megan could not believe her ears. "You have no—"

"Father has given you too much freedom at the estate, but we are not at the estate. We are in London, where ladies go missing, never to be found." He paused to give her a good frown. "Next time, there might not be anyone around to assist you."

Megan couldn't force away the terrible images of being held in that alley. And what almost happened. Her anger fizzled away, leaving her weak and hollow.

"Now," Julian gentled his voice, "tell me exactly what happened."

****

After Megan left, Julian sat at his father's desk and sipped his brandy. A knock sounded. "Enter."

"My lord, Mr. Williams to see you," Wentworth announced.

He nodded. "Send him in."

Stuart entered the room a moment later, looking haggard. Julian gritted his teeth, knowing what his first mate would report. The man who attacked his sister had escaped. "Master," Stuart began uncomfortably. "When I returned to the alley, the man was gone. I've searched everywhere and cannot locate him."

"Do you have any clues as to the man's identity?"

Stuart shook his head. "Sorry, sir. I never got a proper look at his face. When I returned a little while ago with a lantern, I found nothing but a few spatters of blood."

Julian closed his eyes. He had hoped Stuart could give a better description than the one Megan had given him earlier. Hell, a 'foul-smelling brute with dark, greasy hair and a grungy beard who spoke incoherently' described almost every dock worker in England.

"Is there anything else I can do, Master?"

He glared at his first mate. "Just keep your eyes open," he snapped, feeling his body tremble with the effort to control his fury.

Stuart nodded. "Aye, sir," he said, then left.

He lifted his forgotten brandy from the desk. "Damn," he roared as he threw the crystal snifter into the fireplace.

CHAPTER 10

"I think we should cancel this evening."

Megan finished arranging the crown that went with her queen's costume. "Julian, you were the one who insisted I go."

"That was before you were..." He paused and sighed. "I think you should stay indoors until that man is found."

She frowned at his reflection in the large mirror before her. "I have been staying indoors for days, Julian, and quite frankly, I'm beginning to go mad. Besides, I'm looking forward to tonight. And," She turned to him with a smile, "I'll have my big brother protect me from all of the dangers a masque could bring."

He shook his head, a grin lurking at the corners of his mouth. "You are too clever for your own good, my sweet."

An hour later, she regretted her decision to go. Once Julian had guided her to the balustrade at the top of the stairs, she glanced down at the crowd and gasped. There seemed to be more people here than at the theater. A thousand eyes would be on her, staring, scrutinizing every step. What if she didn't hold her fan right? What if she tripped on the rug? What if she forgot the steps to a dance? Oh, Lord. This night would last forever.

"Lord Julian Westland, Marquess of Amersleigh, and Lady Megan Westland, son and daughter of the Duke and Duchess of Kenbrook," the under-butler announced.

A hush swept over the room, eerily similar to

the night of the theater. Clutching the stick of her golden mask, she held it firmly to her face as she began to descend the staircase with her brother. After a few steps, she realized that the clop of Julian's boot heels and the swish of her costume were the only things to disturb the room's thick silence. She trembled when they cleared the last step.

The hostess, the dowager Duchess of Huntington, greeted them. "Lord Amersleigh, how wonderful it is to see you again."

Julian bowed. "Indeed, Your Grace, it is always a pleasure to see you. I present my sister, Lady Megan Westland." He turned. "Megan, please make the acquaintance of Her Grace, Anne Claiborne, the dowager Duchess of Huntington."

She took away her mask and heard a rumble move through the crowd. She ignored it and curtsied low to the dowager duchess before Julian turned her attention to the three standing beside the regal, silver-haired lady.

"And this is His Grace, Daniel Claiborne, the Duke of Huntington."

She issued another graceful curtsy then held up her hand. "Your Grace."

His Grace blinked a couple of times, then gently captured her hand and bowed over it. "Lady Megan."

She turned when her brother continued the introductions.

"This is Huntington's younger brother, Lord Andrew. And this beautiful young lady is their sister, Lady Victoria," Julian said. Then he leaned down and spoke softly into her ear. "This is her come-out as well, Moppet."

Lady Victoria produced the most perfect curtsy to Julian, then turned and smiled true warmth. Megan smiled back, wondering how the girl could stay calm with so many people watching.

As the next guests were introduced, Julian led her into the bustling ballroom. She hoped she would have the opportunity to get to know Victoria Claiborne better. Perhaps they could become friends.

The crowed pooled around them as soon as they moved beyond the stairs. Megan grew more uncomfortable as Julian performed all of the introductions. It was difficult for her to remember which name went with which face. But a familiar voice had her smiling suddenly.

"Megan, hello. Or should I address you as Your Majesty tonight? You make a stunning queen, my dear. That costume is quite the go." Evie's voice.

Megan turned and beamed. "Evie, I am glad to see you again." She took note of the colorful wings sewn into the back of her friend's jade-green gown. "And what a splendid butterfly you are."

Evie's round, brown eyes sparkled with the compliment. "Why, thank you." She nodded, dislodging a few chestnut curls from their pins.

When a man cleared his throat, Evie rolled her eyes. "Lady Megan Westland, please make the acquaintance of my brother, Lord William Thornton, the Earl of Ashton. As you can see, he didn't have time to fetch a costume." Evie stated the last under her breath, then giggled.

Lord Ashton stood about six feet tall and surprisingly handsome, Megan noticed as he came forward and kissed her gloved hand. "I am pleased to finally meet you, my lady," he drawled, his dark eyes smoldering.

She extracted her hand. "I'm glad to meet you as well, Lord Ashton. Your sister has spoken a lot about you."

He leaned forward, a smile curving his lips. "I hope she lied and told you nothing but good things," he whispered.

Her brother's summons for another introduction

kept her from making a reply. The earl's open interest made her a little uncomfortable. There was no spark, no excitement like when she was around Nicholas. Nicholas. Just the thought of his name sent shivers down her body. She scanned the crowd, wondering if he could be out there somewhere.

She had a difficult time keeping account of all the new faces. Thankfully, Evie was with her. Her new friend seemed to have information on everyone.

When Julian summoned her yet again, Megan groaned to herself and politely left Evie and Victoria.

"Jeremy, meet my sister, Lady Megan Westland. Megan, this is Lord Jeremy Longwell, the Marquess of Fielding."

"Lord Fielding." She curtsied. All this curtsying was giving her a backache. Who invented such nonsense anyway?

"Oh, please call me Jeremy," he replied silkily. He brushed her knuckles with a kiss.

She removed her hand. Speaking a given name in public upon introductions would be scandalous. "Have you been acquainted with my brother long, my lord?"

"Only about twenty years, my lady."

Although quite attractive, with light brown hair, hazel eyes, and an alarming grin, he didn't do anything for her. Nicholas was the only man able to make her heart leap from just a glance and have her insides melt from one touch. But where the devil was he? She bit her lip, unable to deny her feelings any longer. He owned her heart. Perhaps he'd always owned her heart. And no one else would ever possess it. "Pray, you recall the first dance belongs to me," a deep voice announced in her right ear.

She turned in surprise and a little fright. The low rumble in her ear from behind reminded her of the beastly oaf who had her trapped in that rancid alley just days ago. With her heart pounding, she found it hard to speak.

"Are you all right, my lady?" asked Lord Bentwood.

"Yes, thank you. I'm sorry, but you frightened me so," she answered, unable to keep her voice steady.

Evie came forward. "Megan, what's wrong?"

She nodded, feeling silly for overreacting. "You haven't met my brother."

Evie shook her head. "I'm sorry, but Ash wishes to see me. I promise to return later."

As Evie scurried away, Megan noticed that her friend glanced over her shoulder with tears in her eyes, then disappeared into the crowd.

Swiveling around, Megan found the one that Evie had looked upon with such anguish and realized that Jeremy Longwell was the man who broke her friend's heart three years ago. And it seemed that the poor girl's heart had remained shattered ever since.

Megan thought again of Nicholas and began to scan the crowded room. Most of the men in attendance wore masks or dominoes with their costumes. Was he behind one of those disguises? Perhaps he had yet to arrive. Oh, she hoped so. She wanted to dance with him, even if it would anger Julian. Or maybe he'd decided not to attend. She gripped the sides of her gown, her heart aching. Perhaps he decided to wash his hands of her for good. No. *No!* That couldn't happen. She would always love Nicholas, and no other could take his place in her heart. Even time wouldn't lessen the love she felt, just like it hadn't for Evie.

As the first notes of the quadrille sounded, Lord Michael Farrell guided her onto the dance floor. Why did she ever agree to tonight? She didn't want to be here if Nicholas wasn't. She missed a step. Lord Farrell smiled to let her know it didn't matter, but her cheeks burned with mortification. Everyone was watching. She had to dismiss all thoughts of Nicholas in order to concentrate on the dance steps. Even if it killed her.

The second dance was a gavotte, and she found it belonged to Jeremy Longwell. She frowned at Julian. He didn't have to accept the rogue's offer. As Jeremy took her arm, she looked for signs of Evie in the crowd. She did not want to upset her friend. The blasted song droned on. Megan concentrated on the steps, biting her lip when she nearly faltered. *Concentrate, Megan.* Finally, the dance ended, and Jeremy escorted her back to Julian with obvious reluctance.

"Are you able to dance another?" Julian asked when they were alone.

She saw the Duke of Huntington watching them. "I think I'll rest after the next one." After all, how could she refuse a dance with their host?

"Excellent," Julian replied, looking pleased. Very pleased. She had a sinking suspicion, but no time to ponder on it. The Duke of Huntington was approaching.

"My lady, may I have this dance?"

She smiled. "It would be my pleasure, Your Grace." As the duke led her to the dance floor, she glanced over her shoulder. Julian wore his scheming expression—the one that she had learned over the years meant trouble.

So preoccupied was she by trying to figure out what Julian was up to, she almost didn't hear what the duke was saying. "Why haven't I met you before now, my lady?"

"This is my first season, Your Grace."

He chuckled. "Actually, I was thinking of the parks and shops that, for years, Victoria has had me escort her to. Surely this isn't your first visit to London?"

Her cheeks heated. Did he think her unconventional? She wondered how he would react if he knew she would rather race through the meadow on the back of a horse than shop in the finest London stores. "No, I've visited many times. But I love the country and do not venture here very often. I am most uncomfortable around a myriad of people, as you may have already guessed, Your Grace."

"Then I shall turn everyone but you out this very minute."

She almost choked in surprise, then realized he was jesting. "That would be most unfair." She tried to sound stern.

He grinned. "Not for me."

She grinned back, some of her nervousness diminishing. She rather liked His Grace. He produced none of the heart-pounding, toe-curling emotions Nicholas did, but he was very nice. Nicholas. She glanced around the room. Where could he be?

"What do you enjoy doing in the country?" he asked, moving them around another waltzing couple.

"I love to ride—"

"You like horses?"

She nodded. "Very much."

"Then I must invite you to see mine. There are many different breeds, but all are the most exquisite of their kind." He pulled her a bit closer, his face turning serious. "You could say that when I see an exquisite creature, I make certain it becomes my own."

It took several seconds for his meaning to sink in. Megan sucked in a breath and moved back a fraction. His brows rose. She could tell the duke wasn't used to a lady's reluctance. "Your sister seems very nice, Your Grace. I think we shall become good friends."

He smiled. "Torie said the exact same thing

about you," he said as the last notes of the waltz hung in the air.

As he escorted her back to her brother, she noticed quite a few gentlemen lined up behind Julian. They weren't all waiting to dance with her, were they? She rather hoped not. She fiddled with her fan, trying to think of some plausible excuse for leaving. Would Julian believe she had a headache?

"Would you like a rest, Moppet?"

Not caring if Prinny himself was next in line, she nodded. "Yes. My feet are about to fall off."

"Would you care for some refreshment, my lady?"

She glanced at the duke. "Why, yes, Your Grace, that would be wonderful."

Seeing a smile on her brother's face as the duke departed, she sighed. He was up to something, all right. She saw Evie a short distance away talking to Victoria, and recalled Julian was friends with Lord Fielding. "Jules, exactly what happened between Lord Fielding and Evelyn Thornton?"

"How on earth did you learn about that?" He held up his hands. "Never mind, I don't want to know," he said with a small chuckle.

"I cannot recall much since I was at sea," he continued, "but I think that their fathers had arranged the marriage without Jeremy's knowledge. When she told him, he was furious and decreed that the agreement was void since both fathers had died before she was of age. He further maintained that since no contract existed with her current guardian's signature, he wasn't obligated to marry her." He paused and cocked his brow. "The girl really should be grateful, though. Jeremy would make a terrible husband."

That was a blatant hint if ever she heard one. "Don't worry, brother dear, he will never be in consideration."

"Good. There are others much more suitable." He glanced at the Duke of Huntington as he spoke.

****

Nicholas cursed as he stumbled in the darkness. He waded through the bushes, groaning when his shoe landed in a mud hole, and sneaked closer to the window. He smacked his shin against the stone ledge and bit back a howl. No one could know what he was up to. After giving his throbbing shin a good rub, he glanced into the bustling ballroom. The musicians plucked away at their instruments and dancers in colorful costumes swished and twirled around the floor. He scanned the faces, hoping to find her. Maybe she wore a mask?

A couple exited the house. The girl giggled as the man whispered in her ear. Nicholas moved further into the bush. The moon cast enough light to reveal his location. He couldn't allow someone to see him. The pair walked down the path to the garden, oblivious of their surroundings. He released his breath and turned back to the window.

Where the deuce was she?

The musicians struck up a waltz and he saw Megan. One of Lord Marshley's punches to the gut would not have been as strong as what hit him at that moment. God, how he wanted to march into the house, grab her hand, and take her away. Certainly take her from all the admiring eyes glued to her.

He watched Huntington lead her to the dance floor. He gnashed his teeth. Did the bastard have to hold her so close? She said something Huntington found amusing and Nicholas had to glance away. His heart thundered in his chest and he had a hard time drawing breath. God, why couldn't that be him dancing with her? Of course, Julian had a great deal to do with that. But what of Megan? He watched her smile and he gripped a piece of brick. Had she already forgotten him?

Nicholas wanted to leave, but he couldn't. He had to stay and watch her. Thankfully, one of his footmen had a cousin who worked for Kenbrook and could inform him of every invitation Julian accepted. Nicholas pulled up his collar against the chilly air and continued to watch her. This would be a long night, he thought. One of many to come.

CHAPTER 11

On the carriage ride back to the townhouse, Megan gazed out into the darkness. Nicholas hadn't shown up. Her stomach clenched and she closed her eyes. Why did he stay away? Did he care nothing for her? Oh, why did she have to love him so?

Julian took her hands. "Did you have a good time tonight?"

"I had a grand time, Jules." She pulled her hands free.

"Then why are you so melancholy? Didn't the Duke of Huntington pay you enough attention?" he jeered.

She felt her cheeks bloom with color and nudged her brother's knee. "Julian, will you not tease me, please?"

"You know I can't resist, dear heart. But there is nary a finer man in all of England than Daniel Claiborne."

"He seems very nice," she agreed quietly.

From the corner of her eye, she watched her brother purse his lips and lean back against the seat. He folded his arms over his broad chest. "But he's not Nicholas Bradshaw."

Her eyes filled with tears. No, he wasn't. Her one true love would forever be Nicholas. "This isn't easy for me, Jules, but I am trying."

Julian cupped her cheek. "I know it isn't, sweet," he said as a tear slid from her eye and rolled down his hand. Then he pulled her close.

Although she loved her brother to distraction, she wished he wouldn't smother her so. She'd even grown to dislike his pet name for her. He treated her like a child and she detested that. He also hated Nicholas. Their mutual hatred must be the reason Nicholas stayed away. She squeezed her eyes shut. Or he had figured out she wasn't right for him after all. Had he given up on her?

****

The next two weeks were much the same for Megan. Invitation after invitation poured in and she attended the various galas with numb endurance.

Julian declared that she was "The Preeminent One of the Season," yet still insisted Daniel Claiborne was the best choice for her. Although she held a great fondness for Daniel, she didn't feel a massive flood of joy grip her whenever he was near, the way she did with Nicholas. With Nicholas, magic filled the air. The way he looked at her, the way he touched her made her forget the world existed. She would never have that with anyone else.

Squeezing her eyes shut, she tried to force her mind to think of something else. The miserable cur had forgotten her. She hadn't seen or heard from him in almost three weeks, since she was attacked at the dock. How would she ever get over him?

She opened her eyes and looked out the front parlor windows to find Upper Brook Street congested, as usual. Many came to the townhouse to see her, but Julian allowed only a few to speak to her. He was able to keep most of the suitors from her presence, but he couldn't check the traffic.

Turning from the windows, she sighed. How she longed to ride one of her horses instead of going mad with boredom.

"Pardon me, my lady, but Lord Julian would like to see you in the study," Wentworth announced from the doorway.

"You wanted to see me, Julian?" Megan asked as she entered the room.

"Yes. And I have some wonderful news, dear sister," he said.

"What is it?" she asked, unable to remember the last time she saw her brother so happy.

"First of all, the *Sweet Siren* will depart tomorrow to fetch our parents. They're probably on their way back, but I'll send the ship anyway."

"Oh, Julian, that's wonderful." She rounded the desk and threw her arms around his neck.

"But that's not all of the good news, sweetling," he announced when she released him. He lifted a large stack of papers from the desk. "I hold in my hands many offers for your hand in marriage, dear sister. It's time you made your choice."

Megan's stomach pooled down to her toes. Her knees went weak. She was going to swoon. She never swooned. Her breath came forth in choppy gasps. She turned and wrapped her arms around her middle to warm her suddenly chilled body. She couldn't marry someone. Unless that someone was Nicholas.

Julian's hand settled on her shoulder. "Wouldn't you even like to know who has proposed?" he asked. He chuckled. "Actually, it would be easier to name the few who haven't."

She gazed into the murkiness of the barren fireplace, eyes unfocused, and remembered Nicholas loving her. She saw the fervency in his eyes as he declared she would always be his, she saw his concern when the carriage nearly crashed, and she saw him hold her to his heart after the incident by the dock. Then she saw his complete absence from her life for the last three weeks.

She turned to her brother and held out her hands for the papers. She read the first one and shook her head. She refused the next as well. She read and refused dozens. Most of them, she barely remembered. Some, not at all.

She came finally to the last offer. She read it, then hastily looked at her brother. "Did you ask him to do this?"

She'd heard many rumors that the Duke of Huntington had no wish to marry yet. That was why she'd felt so comfortable around the man. She had thought it safe.

"Of course not. Daniel acted alone. The man is captivated by you, darling. Promise me you'll give his offer some serious consideration."

She sighed. "I promise." Although she didn't love Daniel, she held a great fondness for him. She supposed if she had to marry someone other than Nicholas, it would be the Duke of Huntington, Daniel Claiborne.

Megan fled the study before she burst into tears. How could she possibly consider marriage to anyone other than Nicholas?

She didn't sleep that night. By the time the sun rose, she had decided she needed to see Nicholas one last time before she made such a life-altering decision. She needed to hear the reason for his sudden absence from her life. She had to know if Julian was right about him. Just as she'd conjured up enough nerve to see Nicholas, she found Julian had other arrangements. At breakfast, he announced that the Duke of Huntington wished them to visit his country estate and view his prized horses.

"How long does he wish us to stay?" she asked, trying to sound nonchalant. Inside, she trembled. How would she get the chance to talk to Nicholas being that far away?

"I'm not sure. My guess would be a week. You'll love it, Moppet. It's almost as beautiful as our estate, and he has more horses." He raised his brows. "Did he, perchance, mention them to you?"

"Yes, I believe he did," she replied with a touch of sarcasm. "How far must we travel?"

"Not very. It's half a day's ride. I've already sent our acceptance, and we shall leave as soon as Daniel and Victoria arrive."

She jolted upright. "Torie is to come with us?"

"I thought you would like that idea," he said. "And I've another surprise for—" he began, but was interrupted when Wentworth announced visitors. "Ah, right on the mark. Come, Megan."

She followed her brother into the drawing room and smiled when she saw Evie and her brother, Ash, rise from the sofa.

"They are also coming with us," Julian explained.

Megan pulled Evie to aside when Julian and Lord Ashton began discussing a boxing tournament. "How did you know about this trip? I was just informed a minute ago."

Evie's eyes lit with excitement. "His Grace invited us last evening at Ellison's dinner. He asked us to meet here, so we could all travel together. Oh, Megan, the Duke of Huntington is absolutely wonderful. You're very lucky to have him pay you such attention."

"Not to mention his proposal for marriage," her brother added from behind them.

Evie gasped, and Megan groaned. She thought she heard another groan, and looked behind her brother. But Ash was studying a solid gold chess piece he'd lifted from the nearby board. She turned her attention back to her friend when Evie took her hand.

"Why didn't you tell me? That's splendid news. When is the wedding to be?"

She licked her lips, not liking how things were spinning out of control. "I-I haven't agreed yet, Evie."

"Why ever not?" Evie asked.

Megan rubbed at her temple. "This is the

greatest decision of my life. I must give it careful consideration."

The assemblage departed shortly after His Grace and Victoria's arrival. Megan rode with her two friends in the luxurious Huntington ducal carriage, and their servants and luggage followed in another carriage. The duke, Julian, and Lord Ashton rode their horses as front escort, while two postilions and six outriders completed the traveling army. Every step from London took Megan that much farther from Nicholas. She looked out the window and wondered if Nicholas missed her at all.

Megan sat in silence for a time, content to listen to Evie and Torie prattle about a variety of topics. But when a familiar name came up, she jolted upright.

"The Duke of Huntington is quite a catch," Evie said.

Torie shook her head. "Not as big a catch as the Duke of Claremont. He is so very handsome." Her features took on a dreamy look.

"Claremont is extremely handsome," Evie agreed. "Unfortunately, I haven't seen much of him this season."

Torie's shoulders drooped. "Indeed, that is a shame."

Evie chuckled. "Why, Victoria, I do believe you are smitten."

Megan turned away from her friends and looked out the window. She couldn't stand to hear any more. Listing to them go on about Nicholas didn't lighten her spirits one bit.

"Everyone is curious about Claremont's anomalous behavior," Torie said. "Several times he has attended a party, but retreats quite suddenly. Daniel believes he's still very angry with Lord Julian."

Evie nodded. "Ash spoke briefly with him last

Tuesday evening at Scofield's dinner party, but when he saw Lord Julian—"

Megan jerked her head around. "Nicholas was there?" Her body went cold and dread settled in the pit of her stomach.

Her friends exchanged startled looks. "Yes, but Ash said that he left as soon as he spied your brother," Evie answered.

"When?" she whispered.

"Just prior to the first bell," Evie said.

She closed her eyes and moaned. A dagger slipping between her ribs would not have been more painful.

"What is wrong, Megan?" Victoria asked.

She paid her friend little attention. Before the first bell at Scofield's dinner, she stood directly between Julian and Daniel. Nicholas would not have neglected seeing her. He didn't want to face her, she realized as a shudder went through her, nor did he wish to marry her any longer. The pain coursing through her intensified. Julian had been right about Nicholas all along. The dagger twisted and drove in to the hilt.

Squeezing her eyes shut, she forced back the pitiful lamentation hovering behind her lips. When she felt a hand on her shoulder, she opened tear-drenched eyes. Evie's concerned face swam before her.

"Are you all right?"

"Yes," she whispered, sounding unconvincing even to her own ears. She took the handkerchief Torie offered and wiped the tears from her eyes. After a calming breath, she turned to her friends. "I am fine, truly." She fought to form a smile.

Finally, Torie spoke. "Anytime you wish to talk, Megan, we're here for you." Evie nodded in agreement.

"Thank you," she replied, grateful they hadn't

pressed her for details.
****

Nicholas squared his shoulders, then nodded for the footman to open the doors. "Angela."

She lowered the handkerchief from her cheek and rushed forward. "Oh, Nicky, I need your help."

His anger receded at the naked desperation in her eyes. "What sort of assistance can I give you?"

"I-I need to return to the townhouse." She twisted the handkerchief in her hands. "Just for a little while," she added when he opened his mouth to object.

He closed his eyes. "What about the fortune I settled on you?"

"You know I'm no good with money."

He opened his mouth to object, but her next words stopped him cold. "Please, I cannot go back." The desperation in her eyes deepened to urgent fear. She grabbed his arm. "I cannot go back to my father. The horrible beatings." She choked on her words. "I would not survive a month."

The mantle clock ticked away the seconds. He focused back on beautiful, spoiled Angela and wanted to refuse her. Oh, Christ, how he wanted to refuse. He had Megan to think about. His sense of duty and obligation kept the refusal at bay. He would never allow a woman, even Angela, to return to such an abusive situation. His shoulders slumped. "If I am to help you, no one can know."

Her smile melted into confusion. "All right, if that is your wish."

"It is." He turned to the secretary and scribbled a note. "This will allow you back into the townhouse."

Angela reached up and brushed a kiss across his cheek. "Thank you, Nicholas."

He watched her leave the room and wondered if he had just made a terrible mistake.

In the hall, he stopped Carson with the instructions for Mae. Then he marched to his study where he'd left Jeremy upon Angela's arrival.

Jeremy looked up as Nicholas stormed inside. "Bad news?"

"In a manner of speaking," he said. Damn! He needed to see Megan.

"Well, I have some good news," Jeremy announced.

He halted to glare at his friend. The man's good humor darkened his mood. "And what might that be?"

Jeremy cracked a ridiculous, face-splitting grin. "I've met the most beautiful lady in the entire world. Nick, I think I'm finally in love."

"In lust, you mean," he said as he turned and studied the spine of a leather volume on the shelf behind him.

"Definitely that, too," Jeremy agreed. "But there's something special about her."

He slid the book back into place. "And just who is this lady that has managed to capture your heart?" He turned, stunned to find no trace of humor in Jeremy's eyes. Could England's most notorious rake really be in love?

"You would know if you went out more, Nick. But I'm damn glad that you don't or you would probably be just as besotted for her as everyone else. It worries me that Huntington has an eye on her, though," his friend said.

"Daniel Claiborne?" Nicholas knew that the man was avoiding the marriage mart just as fervently as he and Jeremy had been. And now Jeremy was speaking of matrimony? And Daniel...? A funny tickle developed in the pit of Nicholas's stomach.

"I know," Jeremy said, shaking his head. "I'm even awaiting approval before proposing to her. Eventually we must marry. It might as well be to someone as comely and desirable as she." An amused glint sprang into his eyes. "And I've heard that her dowry is hideously large."

The bad feeling worsened. "Who is she? The only family I know with a marriageable daughter so desirable and who could afford to give such…an…enormous…dowry…" He stopped speaking and eyed his friend. "What is her name?"

"Lady Megan Westland," Jeremy said.

Blinding fury suddenly took control. "She is mine," he growled.

Jeremy's eyes went wide. "But how… When?"

He spoke with clenched teeth. "The gorgeous country girl I met at Claremont."

"Good God, Nicholas, didn't you tell me at White's that the girl was a commoner?"

"I didn't know who she was at the time," he snarled.

"Well, then, why in the hell aren't you—"

"Julian," he interrupted.

His friend lifted his drink and gulped it back. "Yes, I see what you mean. But what of Megan? How does she feel about you?"

All the anger drained from Nicholas. He shook his head, then revealed everything that had happened since the day he met her. "Before Julian's arrival," he finished, "I know she was starting to love me. But now… I really don't know how she feels."

"What can I do?"

He snapped his head up. "You wish to help? I thought you wanted to marry her."

Jeremy cracked a smile. "Nick, my friend, I never put my fingers in someone else's pie, no matter how tasty it might be."

Nicholas blew out a sigh. "I am sorry I lost my temper."

"Yes, well you are notorious for doing that."

"What does that mean?"

"Come on, Nick. You and Julian would still be friends if you hadn't lost your head all those years ago."

His anger swelled. "So Julian seducing Emily was my fault?"

"No, old friend, I just don't believe it happened." When he opened his mouth to argue, Jeremy held up his hands and continued. "When I left Julian at Havenshire's that night, Julian was so bloody into his cups he could hardly stand."

Nicholas remained silent. That did not prove a thing.

"Do you know what I think?" his friend added. "I think it was easier to blame Julian than to believe Emily was a trollop."

"You know Julian's reputation," Nicholas said. "Damn it, you'd even placed bets on whether he could seduce certain ladies." His face flushed hot. "He never lost those bets."

"Nicholas," Jeremy said quietly. "I told you before, we never bet on Emily."

"You've seen Emily's letter. She blamed Julian. How do you explain that?"

Jeremy sighed. "It all comes down the fact that one of them lied. You just need to search your heart and memory to find the right answer."

Nicholas picked up his forgotten drink and took a generous gulp. He stared at his desk, knowing the letter Emily had written all those years ago still resided in the top drawer. Why would she have lied? The answer came easy for Julian. He didn't want to marry and have a child.

He thought back to Emily. She had married some country fellow and that was the last he heard of her. He narrowed his eyes. For the first time, he considered the matter from the other direction. What if he had been wrong about her? What if Julian had spoken the truth? After all, would she really have taken no for an answer if Julian had seduced her and gotten her with child? And why hadn't her father demanded Julian's head over the matter?

He staggered to the nearest chair, then lowered his head into his hands. "Do you know what the funny thing about all this is?"

"What?" Jeremy asked while he sank onto the opposite chair.

He slowly raised his head. "The feelings I had for Emily were a drop of water compared to the ocean's worth I have for Megan. And Julian is doing everything he can to keep us apart. But as it happens, our separation might just be *my* fault."

"Then why in God's name aren't you out there every night fighting for her, Nick?"

He crackled a humorless laugh. "Because, believe it or not, I made an agreement with Julian." He explained the details.

"Give me a little time to think on this, Nick. You know my specialty is how to bend the rules without breaking them," Jeremy said with a wink. "But I don't think we have much time."

"What do you mean?"

"Well, from what I see, many are interested in your ladylove, but it seems that Julian wishes her to become the Duchess of Huntington."

He swore out loud, his heart melting in grief. "Do you know anything of her feelings for Huntington?" he asked. If she began to care for another... He wouldn't allow himself to finish that thought.

Jeremy shook his head. "Now that I think on it, she doesn't seem excited by all of the attention she receives. In fact, she's quite aloof. She doesn't favor any one gentleman, either." He smiled suddenly. "Including Daniel. That's why I thought I had a chance."

The crushing weight upon Nicholas's chest eased, and he prayed that Megan was distancing herself from possible suitors because of him.

After a heavy sigh, Jeremy stood. "I've got to leave now. I'll let you know my plan when I think on it. Oh, and by the by, if you talk to Phyllis, tell her absolutely nothing of any of this. If the old girl knew I was helping you get another...well, I can't even begin to imagine her reaction." His friend shuddered. "I can see how she managed to become a widow after only three months of marriage."

"Thank you, my friend, for helping me. I need you to be my eyes and ears. Watch over Megan, and keep me informed of her actions, all right?"

"I will, Nick," Jeremy agreed.

Nicholas rose from the chair and gazed out the window. Jeremy would watch Megan from within and he would continue to watch her outside. But how much longer could he go on this way, sneaking in the bushes to watch her dance till dawn? He should be the one dancing and courting her, not a bunch of milksop dandies. He gnashed his teeth. By God, he would have Megan's hand in marriage, even if he had to—A knock curtailed his thoughts. He turned to the door. "Enter."

His footman-informant rushed forward, out of breath. "Your Grace, they've departed."

"Who has departed? What are you saying?"

"I just learned from my cousin that Lord Amersleigh has taken Lady Megan away."

"Away? Where?"

"The Duke of Huntington's estate."

Nicholas clenched his fists, his heart freezing to a block of ice. As soon as they returned, he would end the so-called arrangement and would procure a special license. Julian be damned. Megan would be his bride.

CHAPTER 12

"Please, accept this token of my affection and make me the happiest man alive. Marry me."

Megan turned from examining a book and could only gape as the Duke of Huntington reached for her hand and slipped the ring onto her finger. This was the reason he had asked her to accompany him to the library? She stared at him for several seconds, then lowered her gaze to the beautiful sapphire and diamond ring. Marry Huntington? Her mind whirled with images of Nicholas and what could have been. But he didn't want her. He had never wanted her.

"I knew you would be speechless, Megan, but I didn't think it would last this long." He shuffled from one foot to the other.

She snapped her head up. "I'm sorry, Your Grace..."

"Daniel," he insisted, "and don't apologize, just say yes. Then we can marry when I return from Scotland."

"That's wonderful news, congratulations. I know the two of you will be very happy together," Julian said, walking toward them with a large, satisfied smile.

Just as she opened her mouth to inform her brother that she hadn't yet agreed to Daniel's proposal, the two men began discussing the wedding. And before she realized it, they were moving for the door. How dare they treat her this way? She could make her own decisions, especially one as significant as marriage.

Daniel must have sensed she hadn't joined

them. He stopped and turned. "Coming, darling?" he asked, stretching out his hand.

Megan bit her lip until a salty, metallic taste filled her mouth. She cut her eyes to her brother and observed his obvious delight. This was her chance to decline Daniel's marriage offer. Thoughts of Nicholas raced through her mind again. *Why, Nicholas? Why couldn't you have loved me?* The knot of dread that had been in her stomach for weeks now rose up her throat, threatening to spill out. She had to face the fact that Nicholas would not be a part of her future.

She looked back at Daniel and swallowed her tears. Nicholas no longer wanted her. His absence and the way he avoided her made that abundantly clear. She must accept that and move on. Slowly, she nodded and reached for his hand.

When they reached Daniel's study, he sat behind the large mahogany desk. "I will announce the impending nuptials tonight at dinner. Tomorrow, however, I must leave for Scotland to minister to some pressing business."

Julian shifted in his chair. "How long will you be gone?"

A flicker of regret crossed Daniel's features. He kept his eyes on her, even though he answered her brother. "I'm not entirely certain. But I assure you, it won't be overlong."

"Then I would like to give you this for the journey," Julian said as he pulled a palm-sized object from his pocket and handed it to Daniel.

She watched Daniel take her tiny portrait and smile as he moved his finger over the painted surface. He looked back at her brother. "Thank you, Julian. I shall always cherish this," His eyes skidded over to her, "as I will your sister."

A finger of disquiet ran along her spine. Helplessness engulfed her. She could barely breathe.

Rising from his chair, Daniel rounded the desk.

He helped her to her feet. "I'm sorry to be leaving you so soon, darling, but I cannot delay this journey."

She had to squeeze words from her constricted throat. "I understand, Daniel." Although she liked him very much, she would never love him with the passionate intensity she had for Nicholas.

She didn't miss Daniel's smile when she called him by his given name for the first time. She bit her lip when he gathered her close. Her breath caught as he lowered his head. Oh no, he was going to kiss her! Slowly, his lips settled over hers. They lingered, then they were gone. She kept her eyes closed for several seconds so Daniel wouldn't read the disappointment in them. She'd felt nothing.

She opened her eyes. Daniel's brows rose, clearly expecting her to have been blown away by the kiss. She forced her lips to curve up, even though that small action nearly killed her, and ignored her brother, who sported a well-pleased grin.

What had she just gotten herself into?

****

Later at dinner, Megan forced down a few bites of food. Daniel's grandmother and brother had arrived earlier, and she wondered what their reaction would be to the betrothal. She knew that Victoria and Evie would be ecstatic, but she couldn't be sure of anyone else. She also thought of Nicholas's reaction. No doubt he would feel relief.

Sadness enveloped her. She moved the asparagus around her plate with her fork, her stomach rebelling at the idea of any more food. She pressed her eyes shut. Why couldn't she just forget about Nicholas? Was she doomed to spend the rest of her life thinking 'if only?'

When the men joined the women in the drawing room after their ritualistic glass of port, Daniel walked directly to her side. "I have an announcement," he said to the room.

Her stomach knotted and she swallowed hard. Everyone fell silent.

Daniel continued. "As everyone is aware, I am leaving tomorrow for Scotland. But what you don't know is that I wanted...no, I needed to have a certain beautiful woman waiting for me upon my return. Otherwise, there is no doubt she will be taken from me. So, it is my extreme pleasure to announce to all of you that Lady Megan Westland has agreed to become my wife."

The room's quietness lasted about two seconds before everyone began talking at once. Congratulations and well wishes were rained on them. Megan's throat closed up. She wanted to run from the room, from the estate, and never look back. She closed her eyes. She wanted to run to Nicholas.

"You couldn't have made a finer choice, Daniel," she heard his grandmother say. "Have you decided when you shall wed?"

He grinned. "I should hope very quickly after my return, Grandmother."

Megan almost choked.

"My goodness, Daniel, that gives me—I mean us," his grandmother corrected, "very little time to arrange things. Most engagements last a year—"

"Absolutely not," he interrupted. "Three months."

The bottom of Megan's stomach fell away. Three months?

"That will not do," the dowager sputtered. "Planning a wedding takes a lot of time." She raised her brows. "Lady Megan deserves the best, does she not?"

Daniel sighed and nodded. "Indeed. Six months."

"Late November?" his grandmother croaked. "Why, that simply isn't done."

"I'm sure you will think of something," he

indicated, leading his grandmother to the sofa.

The numbness Megan had been feeling since Daniel's proposal started to lift a bit. She gripped her hands together before her. What had she done?

She turned and found Victoria and Evie standing before her with hands on hips. "All right, Megan. Why didn't you tell us?" Evie demanded.

She shifted her gaze to Daniel. He was laughing at something her brother was saying. "Because I wasn't aware of it, either," she replied softly. Why couldn't things have been different? Why couldn't Nicholas have loved her just a little? For a while, she'd thought it possible. His eyes would turn soft and sparkly as he looked at her. No one had ever looked at her like that. Had it all been an illusion? Had Nicholas been acting, as Julian suggested, for revenge? Megan had no answers. But she did know that her love for Nicholas had been true and real. And would be there forever.

****

"How are you feeling, Mother?"

"Quite a lot better, Nicholas." She set her teacup on the table before them.

"You should have stayed with me—"

"And given you influenza?" Genny shook her head. "I think not. A terrible malady, that. Besides, I was quite comfortable staying with Charles."

His young uncle hadn't come with his mother. He glanced around his drawing room. "Where is Charles, by the way? I haven't seen him in some time."

"Oh," she replied with a wave of her hand, "he went hawking with some friends. I am not certain when he'll return. What of Megan, darling, any progress?" she asked, then sniffed a handkerchief doused in camphor oil.

"Julian and I have made an arrangement of sorts," he replied.

Her brows furrowed and she lowered the scented fabric. "What arrangement?"

He sighed. "I must not see or speak to Megan until she decides to wed. And if I am the one she chooses, Julian will not oppose the union."

"Well, that's wonderful, Nicholas. I'll speak to her right away about this, you shan't have to—"

"No, Mother, there's more." He shook his head. "Julian also stipulated that Megan can know nothing of this agreement."

"Oh, dear. She may think that you are staying away by choice."

The drawing room doors burst open. Jeremy hurried inside ahead of the flustered butler with a newspaper clutched in his fist. "Have you seen this? No, you haven't, or you wouldn't be sitting there so bloody calmly."

Nicholas waved his angry butler away and rose from the sofa. "Sorry, Mother. Jeremy, what in God's name are you referring to?"

Jeremy turned, the angry lines easing from his face. "Pray, forgive me, Your Grace. I did not see you there." He shoved the paper into Nicholas's hands.

"What is this?" Nicholas asked. He read the headline and his blood boiled. Megan would wed Huntington?

"Darling, what is it?" His mother's voice sounded far away.

A red haze filled his vision. Someone was speaking to him, but the blood pounding in his ears made it difficult to hear. He could only focus on getting his hands around Julian Westland's bloody neck. "I'm going to kill him!" he roared as he spun around and bolted from the room.

****

"My lady, come quick," Lucy said on the other side of her bedroom door.

Megan frowned at the closed door. She set aside

her volume of Catullus's poetry and rose from the chair in her sitting room. Calmly, she opened the door. If it was another man threatening suicide because she hadn't agreed to marry him...

Julian's furious voice rang through the house. She gasped and ran down the stairs.

Wentworth bowed and opened the drawing room door, as if he'd been expecting her.

Her heart took a crazy leap at the sight of him standing there. Nicholas. She glanced at her brother and grew worried. The two stood face to face with their fists balled and ready to strike.

As Julian moved forward, she flew between them. Her blood pounded hard in her ears. She stood so close to Nicholas, she could feel the heat of his body. She yearned to step into his arms. Had he come to see her? "What are you doing?" she demanded, looking from one wrathful face to the other.

"Leave, Claremont, now," her brother said.

"Not until I have some answers concerning this." Nicholas threw a crumpled newspaper down. "Damn you, Julian, you had no right." Then his gaze shifted to her. Her heart surged up in her throat. He looked flushed with anguish. "How could you do this, Meg? Why didn't you choose me?" His voice grew hoarse, full of pain. Then he went still. "Or did you choose me and your brother did not honor our agreement?" He jerked his head up and nailed Julian with a glare.

Confusion boiled within her. "What agreement?"

A muscle ticked in Nicholas's cheek as he kept his eyes on her brother. "Tell her," he demanded.

She turned to her brother and caught the unease in his eyes. "Julian?"

He heaved a sigh. "Moppet—"

"Don't you dare call me that, Julian!" She poked a finger into his chest. "Tell me everything. Now!"

With a sigh, he nodded at Nicholas. "He was not to see or speak to you until you selected a husband. And I would not oppose your decision."

She kept her eyes locked on her brother. "Even if I had named Nicholas?"

"Yes," he said.

She wanted to kill Julian.

"Your brother also insisted that you were to know nothing of this agreement," Nicholas added.

A sick knot of despair rose up from the depths of her stomach. She started to tremble. Her hands fell limply to her sides. "Are you telling me," She turned to Nicholas, "that the only reason you've been ignoring me is because of a pact you made with Julian?"

His brows were drawn and his eyes filled with pain. He lifted his hand to touch her but halted and lowered his arm.

"Yes, love."

Her eyes prickled as she turned to her brother. "I cannot believe you did this."

"Megan, I did it for you—"

"No, Julian. You did it for you." Oh, God, she had been so wrong about everything. Nicholas. Her brother. Everything. She trembled in earnest now.

Nicholas moved closer. He reached out as if to steady her, but didn't touch her. "Are you all right, Megan?"

She glanced up, her vision swimming. "You were trying to find a way for us to marry?"

"Yes, my little nymph."

A tear skidded down her cheek. "I-I can't. I'm betrothed to another," she whispered, fighting for control.

"The betrothal can be broken, my love." He wiped the tears from her cheeks. His hand trembled as his fingertips connected with her warm, soft skin. "Will be broken."

She closed her eyes. He could touch her forever. "How?"

He hesitated, his hand sliding away. "It will be difficult for you," he warned.

"What is it?" she demanded, determined to do anything for the man she loved.

"You will probably have to inform Huntington that you're no longer a virgin."

"That is a filthy lie, Claremont. How dare you besmirch my sister's good name?" Julian bellowed. Fury distorted his face and his eyes sparked malice.

Megan rushed to her brother and flattened her palms against his chest.

He looked down at her. "Tell me that wasn't the truth," he pleaded.

Swallowing hard, she sent up a silent prayer. "It is," she said, keeping her palms firmly in place.

He shook with anger, his heartbeat thundering under her hands.

Julian's head snapped up. His lips twisted in wrath. "You bastard, I swear I am going to kill you."

"What in the hell is going on here?" a familiar voice boomed from the doorway.

Megan turned. Her parents stood with Nicholas's mother just inside the doorway. "Father!" she sobbed and ran into his arms.

She heard her mother speak. "Oh, Julian, we were so worried when we thought you'd been injured."

With a deep breath, Megan stepped out of her father's comforting embrace. She scrubbed the wetness from her cheeks and looked up. "I am so very glad that you and Mother have returned. What took you so long?"

"The questions concerning our trip can wait. I wish to know what this is about," he ordered, his gaze sweeping the room.

As she started to answer, so did Nicholas and

Julian. Chaos erupted. Her father demanded silence, then told everyone to sit and waved the footmen away.

When only the clock on the mantle could be heard, her mother turned to the dowager duchess. "Genny, do you know what this is about?"

"Indeed I do, Margaret."

Megan twisted her hands in her lap.

"Father—" Julian started, but Joseph silenced him again.

Father turned back to Nicholas's mother. "Tell us, Genny," he said.

Megan's nervousness changed to alarm when the dowager began with how she had met Nicholas at the stream. Dear Christ, what did Nicholas's mother know?

"Pardon me, Genny," Father interrupted. "Megan, I'm sure you were outfitted like Clancy— Yes, I do know about that," he added when her eyes went round, "but why didn't you tell Nicholas who you were?"

"I...uh..." She paused to clear her throat, "I was afraid of being ostracized from Society, Father. If Nicholas knew who I was, he might have told all of London." As her father's gaze moved away, she relaxed until he asked, "Is that all, Genny?"

"I should explain," Nicholas said.

Megan dug her nails into the palms of her hands. She knew exactly what he was about to tell her parents. She wanted to scream for him to stop but heart pounded on the tip of her tongue.

Keeping her head bowed, she listened as Nicholas explained his return from an evening at White's to find her in one of his guestrooms.

"Why did you venture into Megan's room?" Julian interrupted.

She squeezed her eyes shut. Dread grabbed hold of her body. She couldn't move, couldn't breathe. She could only sit there and wait for her parents to learn their only daughter was ruined.

"I told you, I didn't know it was her," Nicholas explained.

"And why is that?" Julian questioned. "Your mother's note explained everything."

A brief hesitation hung in the air before Nicholas answered. "I didn't read the note. I thought it had been a fabrication, a ruse to gain entrance into my home."

"Then what happened?" Julian asked.

She bit her lip and prayed something would happen to stop further discussion. A carriage overturned in the street, the house on fire, anything. When Nicholas didn't answer right away, she glanced up and found him staring murderously at Julian. Her brother, curse his rotten soul, leaned back in the chair and crossed his hands over his chest. Surely he wasn't enjoying this!

"Nicholas?"

Her father's voice exploded through the silence. Megan felt the blood drain from her face. Oh, God, please let her swoon. Please, please, *please* let her swoon. She couldn't take much more of this.

Nicholas shifted his gaze to her father. He looked years older than he had just moments ago, she thought. "When I found Megan in the guestroom, I was incredibly happy and...well, I kissed her."

"But that's not all you did, is it Claremont?" Julian taunted.

Megan closed her eyes, wanting to crawl under the sofa. "No, that's not all," Nicholas admitted quietly.

When she felt her father tense beside her, she lifted her gaze. He was staring at Nicholas, comprehension dawning. His brows snapped together and his eyes shot white-hot sparks.

From her position beside her father, Megan

could almost feel the building force of his savagery. His face flushed with rage. When she placed her hand on his arm, she felt his muscles bunch. Dear God, he was going to kill Nicholas. "Please don't, Papa," she whispered, her vision blurring with tears.

"Father, surely you realize that he intentionally seduced Megan out of revenge against me?" Julian asked.

Megan clamped onto her father's arm. "No, no, that isn't true."

Her father swung his lethal gaze back to Nicholas as if he hadn't heard her. "Is that true?" he snarled.

Nicholas didn't even blink. "Absolutely not, Joseph. I love Megan and wish her to be my wife."

Open-mouthed, Megan stared at Nicholas. As he glanced down at her, his expression grew tender and love filled his eyes. She felt like weeping.

"Well, that's not going to happen, Claremont. Megan has already agreed to marry Daniel Claiborne," Julian replied, sounding quite satisfied with himself.

"What?" her parents asked in unison.

Genny intervened, informing them of Julian's guardianship, and how he had chaperoned Megan to the various galas. She also explained about the arrangement between Julian and her son.

Megan felt her father's warm hand cover her icy fists still clamped onto his coat. "Why did you agree to marry Daniel Claiborne, darling?" he asked.

She released her father's sleeve and took a deep breath. "I thought that Nicholas had come to regret his marriage proposal and no longer cared for me. I had no idea that he and Julian had made that agreement."

"Do you care for Daniel Claiborne?"

Megan considered that. "Well, he's very nice."

"Hmmm. And Nicholas?"

Megan turned her gaze to the sole owner of her heart. Her own heart lurched and began to pump faster. She couldn't look away.

No one made a sound for several seconds. Tension filled the room. Megan held her breath.

"Megan will wed Nicholas after banns are posted," her father said.

Nicholas sat up straighter and a huge smile split his face. Her heart flooded with joy. She would be married to the most wonderful man in the world, the man she had always loved.

"Father, I don't think..." Julian started to say.

Father silenced him with a look. "You, son, have never been in love, or you would have been able to recognize it. And I feel, even if you did recognize it, your animosity for Nicholas has polluted your judgment in this matter."

"But what of her current betrothal?"

"It can be broken."

"That may be difficult, sir. Daniel left two days ago for Scotland," her brother explained.

"It seems to me that if Daniel Claiborne really wanted to marry my daughter, he would have cancelled his trip. For now, I shall have a visit with his grandmother, Anne."

Megan worried her bottom lip between her teeth. She didn't want Daniel to be hurt by the news of her marriage to Nicholas. He had seemed so hopeful after proposing. She picked at the string of pearls around her neck. Would Daniel and his sister come to hate her?

CHAPTER 13

Megan could not believe she was married. The weeks went by so quickly and the ceremony had been a blur. She glanced around the opulent Claremont townhouse foyer, and her vision settled on the stairs. She closed her eyes, recalling the last time she had seen those stairs, when Nicholas accused her of trying to force him into marriage. A sharp pang sliced through her middle at the memory.

"Megan?"

Opening her eyes, she followed Nicholas into the parlor. She sat on the sofa while her husband spoke quietly to Carson at the door. After the brief conversation with his butler, he strode to the liquor cart and poured two drinks. His movements were stiff as he crossed the room and handed her one of the wineglasses. His eyes were troubled and a small frown curved his lips. Had Carson given him bad news?

As the silence stretched out, she grew uneasy. She took a sip of the wine, wondering if she should ask what had happened.

"Come, love," he said huskily and took her wineglass.

She placed her hand in his, ashamed to admit how anxious she was to make love with her husband. She wanted his hands all over her body, then much, much more. A shudder of anticipation raced down her spine.

After they'd ascended the stairs, Nicholas stopped at the door next to his chambers. He brought her hand to his lips, gave it a warm and lingering kiss, then turned and stepped into his room and closed his door.

She stood like a statue for a few minutes, staring at the polished wood. She couldn't even draw a proper breath. Had he just dismissed her for the night?

"Is there something in your bedchamber not to your liking, Your Grace?"

She whirled around. "Oh, Carson, I did not hear you approach." She quickly assured the butler that her chambers were fine and hurried inside. Her hands shook as she closed the door. Her heart pounded with her confusion.

She ran her fingers along the rose and cream bed cover and sighed. Diverting her mind from the bed and thoughts of Nicholas, she sat at the window seat. Taking a thick cushion, she held it tight to her chest. She gazed at the rest of the room. A washstand and full-length mirror stood next to an ornately carved writing desk and chair. On the opposite wall stood the fireplace, topped with an elegant white marble mantle.

She walked into the dressing room and stopped short. Her gowns had been unpacked. Tears filled her eyes. Her parents didn't have separate rooms with separate beds. Her parents loved each other completely, and it showed with every action, every word and every look that they gave one another. And that was precisely the kind of marriage she longed for. The kind she'd thought she would have.

An unladylike snort escaped her lips. She stomped toward the door that appeared to join to Nicholas's room and pulled it open.

The valet started when he noticed her. He stood paralyzed for several seconds, his face aflame, before he bowed and spun around. She smiled at his retreating back, watching him carry her husband's sleep garments with him from the bedroom.

Scanning the empty room, she wondered where Nicholas had gone. Then a sound came from Nicholas's dressing room. Straightening her shoulders, she marched forward.

****

Nicholas had just removed his waistcoat when he felt eyes on him. He knew it wasn't his valet since he'd just dismissed the man for the night. He turned and thought his heart would stop when he saw Megan, standing still with her hands clasped tightly before her. He lifted his gaze and saw wariness in her eyes. Fear squeezed his heart. He cleared his throat. "Is something wrong?"

"Yes, something is very wrong," she replied.

Her words struck him like a fist and he swallowed hard. Oh, God, had she decided marrying him had been a mistake? He noticed the tears in her eyes. "Meg," he began, "What is it, love?"

She let out a small cry and ran to him.

He wrapped his arms around her. He inhaled a shuddering breath and laid his cheek on top of her head. His eyes slid shut and his heart began to mend back together, one tiny stitch at a time.

"Nicholas, why do we have separate bedrooms?" Her question sounded muffled against the front of his shirt.

He jerked his eyes open and eased back to look down at her. "You want to share a room?"

She nodded and he pulled her back to him. "Do you wish to share a room?" she said against his chest.

"Of course," he said, "but on the way here you were so quiet." He moved his hands up and down her back. "I just didn't want to frighten you."

"I'm not afraid."

His wife smiled a slow, seductive smile, and he quickly dropped his mouth down onto hers. He slid his tongue in between her parted lips. In less than a heartbeat, he was hard and ready.

She touched her tongue to his. With a low growl, he wrapped his arms around her. She shivered when he brought her snugly against his fevered body. His manhood strained within his pants and thrust against her. She melted against him. God, she felt good.

When he lifted her skirt and found the silky skin beneath, he heard her moan. Placing his hand between her thighs, he parted her with his finger and stroked the heated little bud within. He smiled when her breath caught.

His smile didn't last long.

She lowered her hands and freed his engorged member. The feel of those soft hands wrapped around him nearly undid him. He went completely still. Sweat ran down the side of his face as he fought for control. Pulling his lips from hers, he scooped Megan into his arms and stormed to the chaise inside the dressing room. There was no way in bloody hell he could wait until they removed their clothes. He sat, then lifted her dress and the frilly undergarment, and gently lowered her onto his shaft. As her body melted around him, he had to bite down hard on his lip to keep from a premature release.

Her eyes flew open. Within their purple depths, he saw intense pleasure mingled with an even deeper passion. He gripped her hips and slowly lifted her, then brought her back down. She parted her lips as the pleasure in her eyes magnified, then began to move to the rhythm he set. His own release drew near, and it took every ounce of his willpower not to let it go. Just one more minute...

She threw her head back and cried out, her muscles contracting around him.

With one final thrust, his loins burst. He

expelled a long groan. His body shuddered with the most intense release of his life.

She laid her head on his chest and sighed. "See how much fun we would have if we shared a bedroom?" she whispered.

Chuckling, he tightened his arms around her. Grazing his lips over her forehead, he lifted her and carried her into the bedroom. Their bedroom. He lowered her onto the bed, undressed her, then himself, and slipped under the covers beside her. After engulfing her within his arms, he yawned like a bear and closed his eyes.

Megan. His wife. His forever. A strong sense of satisfaction overcame him. He inhaled her warm, jasmine-scented skin and pulled her close. He'd been so sure she had wanted a room of her own. What a foolish thought. Megan wasn't the typical virgin bride, frightened of her own shadow. He grinned to himself. Thank God. He kissed her warm skin and listened to her deep, even breathing for several seconds. Who would have guessed that married life could be so damn good?

****

He watched the bedroom light go out and he gnashed his teeth together. Damn it, Megan should have been his! He twisted his ring on his little finger, thinking what to do next. He had managed to raise some money at the gaming table. It wasn't much, but enough to hire a couple of ruffians. That meant another letter to the pirate.

He hated to take Megan by force, but he had no choice. His back was against a wall. Both her father and her new husband would pay a king's ransom to get her back. He rubbed his hands together. Yes, a king's ransom would do nicely.

CHAPTER 14

Nicholas rubbed his pounding temples and resisted the urge to pour a gin. Not a wise thing to do in the bloody morning. He sighed and looked down at the stack of papers before him. His attorney thought him mad and damn near refused his request. Imagine an attorney refusing a duke? He glanced over at the gin decanter.

A knock drew his attention. "Enter."

Megan stepped into the room. Dear God, her beauty could still amaze him. He shot to his feet and rounded the desk. Pulling her into his arms, he kissed her long and hard. He kissed her deep. They had just made love a couple of hours ago and he wanted more. He always wanted more of Megan.

"Goodness, Nicholas," she said with a laugh when they broke free. "Have you missed me that much?"

He was breathless and out of sorts. "Sorry," he replied and took a step back, ashamed for his brutish behavior.

"What is it?" She came forward with worry in her eyes.

"Nothing at all." He turned to the table where Carson had placed the invitations he'd delivered earlier. "Which of these would you like to attend?"

"Nicholas, what is this about?"

The erotic image of taking his wife on the sofa ceased when Nicholas turned and found Megan reading the papers on his desk. Sighing, he plucked the documents from her hands, then placed them face down on the wood with a thud. "This is nothing for you to concern yourself with," he said.

"But my dowry—"

"I do not need your money, nor will I take it."

"That's absurd, Nicholas" she said. "Every husband spends his wife's dowry."

"Not this husband," he said.

"Why not?"

"I will not have it believed that I married you for your dowry."

Her brows snapped together. "Who would think such a..." She stopped as understanding sprang into her eyes. Then anger. Julian, of course.

Grasping for a diversion, he remembered the reason he'd summoned her. "Do you ride sidesaddle?"

She blinked rapidly. The anger in her eyes subsided.

"A little," she answered.

An hour later, they were astride a pair of his finest horses, taking a stroll through Hyde Park. Nicholas lifted his face to the sun and inhaled. Birds took flight as they approached the Serpentine. He slid his gaze to his wife and grinned. Even sidesaddle, she commanded the spirited mare with magnificent ease. A little, indeed. He led Megan into the woods a short distance outside London and stopped at a grassy area under a canopy of trees. As she unpacked the basket, he tethered the horses.

"Tell me, what else are you 'a little' good at?" he asked, then took a bite of his cold chicken. Birds chirped overhead and two grey squirrels raced each other up and down a tree trunk.

Nibbling on a plump strawberry, his wife arched an eyebrow. "Guess," she said. A slow smile spread over her lips.

He returned the smile, liking this playful side of her. "Let me see." He paused and looked at the small patch of sky visible through the trees. "Ah, yes, you can sew a fancy ball gown in one hour's time with your eyes shut."

Megan shook her head. "I couldn't sew two straight stitches with both eyes wide open, even if I had all the time in the world. It drives my mother to distraction. Try again."

"All right, with your lovely voice, you can sing like a sparrow."

She poured him more wine. "Perhaps if the sparrow were being drowned while it sang," she said.

"Oh, I've got it. You are an expert on the pianoforte."

She placed a hand over her mouth and closed her eyes. Her shoulders shook. "G-Goodness no," she gasped. "Poor Mr. Whittle would turn a sickly shade of green every time I placed my fingers on the keys."

Nicholas felt his lips twitch. "I give up," he said. "What else are you good at?"

Her smile turned into a seductive leer. Saucy and sensual. Nicholas tensed, his blood flowing south. She raised a finger and traced his lips. "Chess," she said.

The thought of her pulling off her clothes and having her way with him came to a sudden halt. "You can play chess?"

"Do you?"

"Actually, it's one of my best games," he said. "I'll show you a few of my techniques if you would like." A vision entered his mind of other "techniques." His body quickened with desire. When Megan spoke, he had to concentrate to understand her words. "That is all I'm going to impart for now. You'll have to learn the rest of my talents on your own."

He cocked a brow. "Is that so? Well, I know something else that you're very good at," he purred. He leaned over and whispered, "You play very well at bed sport," into her ear. She flushed a deep, enticing red.

He smiled wickedly and began raining kisses over her jaw and neck. Then he traced the tip of his tongue along the outside of her ear. She shuddered, and when she turned her mouth to his, he eagerly complied. When Megan began to pull him down, Nicholas groaned in complete surrender and followed her. His tongue swept every ridge and curve inside her berry-tasting mouth before he slid it against hers in a sensual rhythm. He kissed her deep and hot, and the bulge within his riding breeches swelled painfully. He closed his hand over her well-formed breast. Through the fabric, her nipple distended, and he longed to lave the sweet pebble with his tongue. But that was just the start of what he would do to her....

The wind rustled through the trees overhead. Megan popped her eyes open. She broke contact with her husband's mouth and sucked in a few deep breaths. When he reached for her, she pushed at his shoulders. "Nicholas, we must not."

"Oh, but we must, my love," he said, then nibbled at her neck.

"But someone might see...Nicholas," she said when he released one of her breasts. As his lips closed over her bare nipple, waves of longing pooled between her thighs. She closed her eyes to find the strength to call a halt to the marvelous sensations engulfing her entire being.

Placing her trembling hands on either side of his smooth face, she lifted his head. His blue eyes were dark and full of hunger. She licked her lips and forced the necessary words from her mouth. "We must stop." She hoped that he would heed her because she wouldn't have the strength to halt him again.

He laid his forehead against hers and closed his eyes. His chest heaved. Poor Nicholas, she thought as he opened his eyes and used unsteady hands to repair her disheveled gown. She would just have to make this up to him later.

He assisted her to her feet. "You, my dear, are an expert temptress of the highest order," he chided as they packed away their picnic basket.

She placed a hand on her chest and gave him what she hoped was an innocent look. "Me?"

His eyes roved over her, a wicked gleam in their blue depths.

She took a step back, laughing. "Nicholas."

With a sigh, he picked up the blanket and secured it to his horse.

Megan gripped her hands together as she watched him work. "Nicholas, about my dowry—"

"I have told you already, I will not take it." He finished tightening the straps and turned to face her, his jaw set in a stubborn fashion. "You need not worry about this any longer."

She resisted the urge to stomp her foot. "I still do not understand why—"

"Let it go, love." He stepped before her and cupped her cheek in his hand. "I will not change my mind."

She placed her hand over his, now regretting the missive she had sent earlier to her father. Her message had asked for help in convincing Nicholas to receive her dowry. Oh, dear. How would her father react to a direct refusal?

"I've been meaning to discuss where you would like to go for our honeymoon. We can leave as soon... What?"

"Oh, Nicholas." She shook her head with sorrow. "My parents haven't been back long. Can't we postpone our trip?"

His shoulders slumped. "Of course."

A church bell chimed in the distance. Oh, no. Her parents! "Nicholas, what is the time?"

With a frown, he glanced at his gold watch. "Almost four."

"Come, we must hurry." She mounted her horse and raced away.

As they arrived, she noticed the Kenbrook carriage already in the drive. She squelched a groan as she handed the footman her reins. Sliding a glance to Nicholas, she noticed his frown at the vehicle as they walked by. She knew he had wanted to spend the rest of the day alone with her, but this was important.

They entered the drawing room. Megan stopped short when she saw her parents and Julian. What on earth was her brother doing here? She looked to Nicholas to gauge his reaction and almost groaned. His rust-colored short coat was mussed, with only one of the four gold buttons fastened and on the wrong hole. The left lapel gaped open. His snug, cream breeches sported a couple of grass stains, and his hair looked suspiciously as if someone had raked her hands through it in a moment of passion.

She brought her hands up to her hair, hoping she looked somewhat better, and grimaced when she found some stray strands of grass poking out of her hastily repaired twist. "Mother, Father, I'm sorry that we were not here to greet you. Nicholas and I went on a picnic and the time got away from us," she said, unable to meet her parents' eyes.

"Come, have some tea," her mother said.

As the servants brought the cart forward, she motioned for Nicholas to fix his clothes and took her seat. Goodness, what must her mother think?

Once all the cups were filled, her father spoke. "Nicholas, my little girl tells me that you won't receive her dowry," he said, sounding as if Nicholas had robbed some poor orphan and widow fund.

She dared a quick look at her husband. Nicholas swallowed his tea with a gulp and cut his gaze to her. She smiled an apology, but he'd already turned back to her father.

"That's right, Joseph."

"And why not? When you inherited your father's titles and fortune, did you refuse it?" he asked as he lifted his cup to his lips.

"Of course not," Nicholas said.

"All right, Nicholas, I can't force you to take it. But I shall have my solicitor place the hundred thousand pounds into a trust under Megan's name and in her complete control."

"Yes, a trust would be acceptable—" Nicholas blinked and lifted his eyebrows. "How much?"

"One hundred thousand pounds," her father repeated.

"My God, that's a bloody fortune," Nicholas said. He turned to her. "You must have had marriage proposals from every eligible man in Europe." He lowered his head and pressed a brief kiss to her lips.

Turning to her parents, she said, "I am ever so grateful to have you back. Tell me about your journey to America. I want to know every detail."

Her father chuckled. "As soon as we learned that the *Sweet Siren* had left America and that Julian hadn't sustained any injuries there, we began the journey back to England immediately. En route, Master Taylor hailed us with the news that Julian was, indeed, safe."

"So the letter you received was made in error?" she asked.

Her father's eyes darkened, and he shook his head. "We think it was a forgery. Mr. Williams couldn't have written the letter because he was with Julian aboard the ship."

Megan turned to Julian, concerned for the man who had saved her from being attacked in the alley. "What happened to Mr. Williams?"

"I'm sure Stuart simply missed them along the

way," Julian said.

"Why would someone pen a false message and scare us so?" she asked, raising her teacup.

"People do such things for different reasons," Julian said from his chair, then looked at her husband. "But it's almost always for self-gain."

She choked on her tea and dared a glance at Nicholas. He shook his head and smiled, which amazed her. She thought he would have thrown Julian out. "So, my motive for marrying your sister has gone from revenge to greed?" Nicholas asked.

The fibers that held her patience together begin to wear thin. "Julian, that's ludicrous. Nicholas has just given up my bridal gift," she said.

"And I'll wager that he is sick with regret now that he knows its worth."

"Julian." Mother's voice rang out in the silence. "Have you already forgotten how it feels to be falsely accused?" she asked, then leveled him with a need-I-say-more look.

Nicholas watched Julian closely. He noticed the stiff spine, the clenched fingers about to break his teacup, but most of all, he noticed his eyes, and the pain there. At that moment, he knew. Julian was innocent.

He closed his eyes, wishing every rotten word said to Julian could be taken back in an instant. Regret filled his heart. "Julian, may I have a private word with you?" he asked.

After a brief pause, Julian nodded. "Please excuse us," Nicholas said as he stood and walked to his study. He poured two tumblers of whiskey and nodded toward the chairs before his desk as Julian entered the room. "Have a seat."

"When I returned home after our fight nine years ago," Nicholas began, pressing the glass into Julian's hand, "I was already regretting the way I had treated you. I felt that neither you nor Emily would have lied, but it was obvious that one of you had. Therefore, the next day I set out to find Emily and to hear what had happened from her own lips."

He paused, recalling the events vividly even after all these years. "I was stunned to learn she had married Arthur Wakefield. And after traveling to his cottage, Emily refused to see me. Instead, she gave me a written message. It was those words that made me sure you had lied to me."

"What did the message say?" Julian asked.

Nicholas opened a small drawer in his desk and retrieved a folded parchment, then slid it across the wooden surface.

Lifting the note, Julian unfolded it carefully. The paper was discolored and tattered from age. The feminine handwriting had been scribbled in great haste, but the tear stains drew his attention. And so did the words.

Lord Hamilton,
You dare come here after what Julian Westland, Lord Amersleigh, has done to me? Go away and don't ever return. Any friend of his is an enemy of mine.
Lady Emily Wakefield

Nicholas cleared his throat. "I was wrong to have accused you of seducing her."

"What made you change your mind?"

Nicholas took a large gulp of his drink. "Megan insists on your innocence. You see, Julian," he added, "until I met your sister, I wouldn't allow anyone to speak to me about any of this. I was too bloody stubborn to hear the truth, I'm afraid. But deep within me, I have always regretted what happened."

Nicholas watched Julian digest his words. They had been like brothers once. And it was his fault that their friendship had ended. "I know that repairing our friendship will be a difficult task, but I would like to give it one hell of a go." He walked around the desk and stuck out his hand. "Friends?"

Finally, Julian rose and set his glass aside. Slowly, he extended his hand. Their palms met. "Friends," he agreed.

CHAPTER 15

The soft sounds of the waltz began. Megan trembled as she slipped into Nicholas's arms. Her first dance with him. She prayed she wouldn't be a goose and miss a step or forget the steps all together. He held her close, much closer than he probably should have.

"I used to watch you dance," he said.

She pulled back to look up at him. "When was that?"

He shrugged. "Huntington's masque, Camdon's fete, Hatfield's ball. And others."

"But how is that possible? You never attended those parties."

He brought her satin-clad hand up to his lips for a lingering kiss. His warm mouth made her insides liquefy. "I was there, love. Watching outside the windows. Watching the most beautiful woman in the world." He pulled her close once again. "Wishing with all my heart I was the one dancing with you."

She closed her eyes and breathed him in.

****

He watched them through the window. The sight sickened him. He should have had Megan by now, definitely before she married. That complicated things. Fortunately, he had been able to alter his plans. Not to the seaman's likings, but the ruddy seaman could go hang.

Tossing back his drink, he poured himself another, damn glad he'd filched the decanter earlier. The night air had turned cold. His eyes followed Megan. Damn! Why couldn't he have been her choice? He had given her every opportunity, even proposed marriage. That incredible dowry would have solved all his problems. He wouldn't have had to go through with the plan.

Taking another gulp of his drink, his thoughts returned to what he had to do. Somehow, he had to get Megan back to Kenbrook. As soon as she returned there, the next phase of the plan would be complete.

****

Megan sighed as she watched her husband slip into the crowd to find her a glass of champagne. She grinned at her parents on the dance floor. They danced beautifully together. Her gaze skidded to her brother talking to Lord Fielding, and she frowned. She turned away, not wishing to look at that rogue.

"Hello, you must be Megan."

Hearing her name, Megan turned to the pretty blonde woman and smiled. "Why, yes I am," she answered.

"I'm Lady Phyllis Granger, a friend of Nicky's," the woman said.

Nicky. Hadn't that been the same voice she had heard outside the theater box? Megan kept her smile firmly in place, even though she wanted to rip that husky voice right out of the woman's throat. "Well, any friend of my husband's is a friend of mine," she said lightly.

The woman lifted her chin and widened her smile. "Then you must be a friend of Angela Cooper's as well," she said. "Nicky's paramour? She recently moved back into his townhouse in Bond Street." Her smile turned malicious. "Surely you know about his *other* townhouse?"

Megan's heart pounded. Each beat felt like a whip cracking over her body. With a great effort, she kept her smile from slipping. "I am confident now that Nicholas and I are married," she said, proud of the steadiness in her voice, "he will have no further need of his *other* townhouse."

Phyllis widened her eyes, bade her a clipped *adieu* and marched back across the room.

"I do believe, dear sister," Julian said as he approached, "you took the wind right out of her sails." His eyes danced.

Megan turned away from the woman's hateful glare and back to her brother. Just beyond him, she caught sight of her husband. Outfitted in his perfectly tailored evening black, Nicholas made her heart flutter. He held a couple of glasses of champagne and smiled as he approached. She would not, under any circumstances, judge and convict her husband based on the ramblings of a jealous woman.

"Here you are, my love," he said as he handed her a drink. His smile melted away. "Darling, what's wrong?"

"Only a dose of Phyllis, Nick," Julian responded before she could open her mouth.

Nicholas jerked his head up. He scanned the crowded room and approached Phyllis.

Megan watched her husband lead Phyllis to one of the room's marble pillars. He smiled and nodded politely, but she wasn't fooled. His words had Phyllis pale and trembling.

Phyllis placed her hand on the nearby column for support while suffering the encounter. Then he spun around and marched back, his jerky movements revealing how furious he truly was.

Phyllis's eyes were full of tears as they watched Nicholas. Then they cut straight to her. Pure hatred washed over the woman's face before she turned and ran from the room.

Julian leaned down and whispered, "Watch your back, dear sister. That one is vindictive."

The next day, while waiting for Nicholas to return from Gentleman Jackson's, Megan sat reading a book in the colorful garden. The sweet scent of roses wafted on the gentle breeze and the sun warmed her face. Hearing someone approach, she glanced up. Carson bowed and held out a silver salver with an envelope on top. Curious, she took the message and broke the seal. Her good mood evaporated as she read the almost illegible script.

She gnashed her teeth together against the flood of anger that poured into her body and entered the house. A string of swear words bubbled up in her throat. She marched up the stairs and quickly changed into a riding habit. After proving Phyllis Granger wrong about Nicholas keeping a mistress, she was going to have a visit with the woman.

The visit would not be a pleasant one.

Thirty minutes later, Megan raised her fist and rapped on the painted wood.

The door opened. The housekeeper's eyes rounded in surprise. "Why, hello, Your Grace," she said.

"Hello, Mae."

"Who is it, Mae?" demanded a female voice from behind the housekeeper.

Megan somehow kept the gasp within her parted lips and watched Mae's features turn dreadfully apprehensive. "Your Grace, now really is an unsuitable time. Could you come back in a few days?" Mae's hands wrung the little white apron tied around her generous waist.

"Tea, Mae," the stern voice ordered.

Mae scuttled away.

The woman stepped forward. Megan surveyed the tall, voluptuous body, sparkling jade eyes, and glorious head of red hair. Angela Cooper was beautiful. But Nicholas would not have an ugly mistress. Megan forced her face to remain a blank mask. The woman froze. Her eyes went round and she released a small gasp. Snapping her mouth closed, Angela smiled without a hint of warmth. "Please, do come in," she said with a sweep of her arm.

With her head high, Megan walked into the salon. She sat primly on the pale-green silk sofa. Her movements were graceful, her posture was perfect, and she kept her expression pleasant. She epitomized the very height of social decorum. Her mother would be stunned.

Moments later, the flustered housekeeper brought in the tea. Just as Mae started to pour the hot brew into the two dainty cups, Angela waved her away. "I would rather do it myself than to have you drizzle it everywhere," she said. Mae scurried from the room. Megan took the offered cup. "I don't believe we have been properly introduced. I am Megan Westland Bradshaw, the Duchess of Claremont." Angela looked up sharply. "And I know who you are," Megan continued, stirring a bit of honey into her cup. "You are Angela Cooper." She watched a cloud of uncertainty pass over the woman's green eyes.

Angela cleared her throat. "Then you know why I'm here?"

Raising an autocratic brow as she'd seen Julian do on many occasions, Megan answered, "Of course."

All politeness vanished from Angela's demeanor. "Then would you mind informing me as to why *you* are here?"

Sipping the last of her tea, Megan allowed Angela's temper to simmer before she continued. Her voice rang flat with boredom. "Miss Cooper, you know as well as I that your visit here is temporary. But I am prepared to expedite your departure by offering you this." She reached into her reticule and retrieved a diamond brooch she'd taken from her jewelry case.

Angela's eyes widened. She gazed for several

seconds at the jewel before looking up. "All right, we have an agreement."

Megan shook her head and moved the brooch out of Angela's reach. "You may have this once your bags are packed and you step outside that front door, never to return. Agreed?"

Angela's eyes flashed with malice. Slowly, she rose from the sofa, calling for Mae.

Megan released her pent up breath and forced back the stabbing pain. Nicholas had a kept woman. After all they been through, he must not be content. Megan closed her eyes and resisted the tears threatening. She would never be good enough for him. He didn't want a girl who rode a horse in breeches and who didn't care anything about the latest fashions. He wanted a polished, sophisticated lady. Someone who painted and played the pianoforte. She opened her eyes and blinked back the tears. How could she face him after this?

CHAPTER 16

Nicholas stood at the windows, eyeing the dark clouds rolling in. Where in the deuce was his wife? She wasn't visiting friends or in any of the ladies' shops. His heart kicked as he recalled the time she had been attacked at the dock. He pressed a hand to the window glass. *Please, let her be all right.*

He watched Julian's carriage pull into the drive. "This had better be good, Nick," Julian said as he walked through the door. "I was up two hundred pounds—"

"Do you know where Megan is? Carson said she received a missive while I was at Gentleman Jackson's, and left soon after."

"Well, then, she was probably invited to..."

Nicholas shook his head. "She's been gone three hours, Julian." He sighed, mopping a hand down his face. "Carson said she was upset when she left."

"Have you contacted Mother and Father?"

He nodded. "They left for their townhouse a little while ago in case she shows up there."

"You don't have any idea what this is about?"

"No." Nicholas glanced back to the window. "My mind keeps recalling what had happened to her at the dock. Julian, you don't think—" He couldn't finish the sentence. He could not put words to the terrible thoughts racing through his mind.

Julian cupped his shoulder. "She wouldn't go back there, Nick."

"Then where is she?"

****

The streets were almost vacant as Megan, numb

with grief, maneuvered her horse through Mayfair. She had no idea how long she'd been riding through the park. Three, four hours? The sky had darkened. A cold wind, thick with the scent of rain, rose and fell, then stopped and changed direction. Thunder rumbled in the distance. The ominous surroundings were a mirror to her melancholy.

She handed the reins to the footman just as the heavens opened. Frigid drops descended from sooty clouds and pelted the ground. As she shuffled to the door of her family's townhouse, she wondered how many people knew about Nicholas's inamorata. How many of them snickered behind their hands as she strolled by? Oh, how they must have made a game of it. And even though the thought of people laughing behind her back sickened her, she could not stand the thought of her mother's reaction. And her father...she closed her eyes. What would he do to Nicholas if he learned of this?

Grief crashed down on Megan with the awareness that Nicholas needed more than she could give.

"Your Grace, do come inside before you are soaked to the bone. Your parents will be relieved to see you," Wentworth said.

She had been in the process of peeling away her rain-soaked hat when the butler's tone caught her attention. "Why?"

"Come, they are in the lavender parlor."

Megan walked into the room and saw the somber faces of her mother, father and mother-in-law. When they noticed her, they stood and rushed forward. Her parents embraced her tightly.

"Father, what is this about?" she asked.

He hugged her once more. "We have been terribly worried about you, sweetheart," he answered, then nodded to Wentworth to dispatch a message to Nicholas.

Megan groaned.

"What is it, darling?" her mother asked.

She shook her head. "I'm fatigued, Mother, and would like to go rest in my room. Will you please see to it that I'm not disturbed? By anyone." She turned before her mother could detect the tears in her eyes. Each time she looked at Nicholas, she would know she wasn't good enough. And that she could not bear.

Megan woke with a start an hour later. She rubbed the salty remnants of tears from her swollen eyes and looked around. The lamp on the nearby table burned low. The warm fire blazing in the fireplace ate away the room's chill but could not warm the cold growing inside her. A movement in the shadows and the rustle of clothing alerted her that someone stood in her bedchamber. Lucy stepped into the light. "I do hope I didn't wake you, Your Grace. I was just checking the fire," Lucy stammered.

"It's all right. Inform Julian that I would like a word with him, please."

"Yes, Your Grace." The maid curtsied and left the room.

Within minutes, Julian appeared in her sitting room. He closed the door and walked to the sofa. "All right, Megan, what's wrong?"

"What makes you believe something is wrong?" She picked at a string on her gown, unable to look him in the eye.

"I know you," he answered, then sat down beside her.

She traced the sofa's rose pattern with a finger. "Why was everyone so worried about me?"

"I should have known you were summoning me to an inquest."

"Julian," she prodded.

He sighed. "We know you received a missive that upset you. Then you disappeared for almost four hours. What happened?"

Megan started to turn away, but Julian brought her head back around with insistent fingers. "What happened?" he repeated.

She bit her lip. "Promise not to say a word to Mother and Father."

"You have my word."

Somehow she managed to explain about the letter she'd received from Phyllis Granger. She added that she had set out to prove that jealous twit wrong, but had confirmed Angela Cooper's existence. She could not manage to tell Julian how she didn't measure up to Nicholas's expectations.

God, it still made her sick to think about that.

Julian scratched at the stubble shadowing his chin. "You're certain about this?"

She closed her eyes, seeing Angela Cooper in her mind. "I'm certain."

Julian smiled. "Did it ever occur to you that Nick hasn't yet had the opportunity to dismiss the woman?"

Megan knew better. The little house had been empty when she first arrived in London. And that could mean only one thing. Nicholas had moved the woman in while he was supposedly finding a way for them to wed. Had it all been a farce?

Examining the rosy glow of the room, she released a sigh. "I think I would like to go home now."

"Good. Nick will be very happy to hear that," Julian said.

She frowned. "I meant to Kenbrook."

His eyes filled with sorrow. "Give him a chance to explain before you do anything rash. Promise me you will."

She bit her bottom lip with indecision. "I don't know, Jules." Tears blurred her vision. "What should I do if the woman returns and Nicholas allows her to stay?"

"He won't, dear heart."

"How can you know that for certain?"

"I'll make sure of it."

****

Nicholas looked up when the door opened and focused his bleary vision on Julian. Noticing the grave expression, he sprang from his chair. "How is she?"

"Madder than hell," Julian replied as he splashed an ample sum of whisky into a glass. "She has discovered Angela Cooper living in your townhouse."

"Dear God." Nicholas downed the remainder of his gin. He closed his eyes and felt the muscles at the back of his neck tense.

"I should really like to hear about this mistress of yours, Nick," Julian said after he'd refilled their drinks.

Taking the offered glass, Nicholas nodded. He sensed Julian's anger, but was damn glad the man wanted to hear an explanation.

Fortifying himself with a large dose of gin, he closed his eyes and told of finding Angela years ago after she had escaped her abusive father.

Julian leaned back in his chair. "Then why didn't you terminate your association?"

"As soon as I returned to London after meeting your sister, I did."

"Don't tell me you asked Angela Cooper back?" Julian sounded amazed and a little angry.

He shook his head. "I didn't want her back. But she called on me a little over a month ago with no where else to go. She couldn't return to her father when her funds were depleted. God, Julian, I felt so bloody torn apart. I couldn't send her back to that monster, and I couldn't explain it to Megan because of our agreement." He downed the remaining contents of his glass, then looked Julian straight in the eye. "But I vow, since meeting your sister, she has been the only one in my bed. The only one I have wanted in my bed. The only one."

Julian nodded. "In the morning, I'll explain it all to Megan. Don't worry, Nick, things will be set right before you know it."

Nicholas lifted the glass to his lips, praying it would be that simple. Something told him nothing would ever be that simple concerning Megan.

CHAPTER 17

Megan woke before dawn the following morning and dressed quickly. She had remained awake most of the night and concluded that she would not stay another night in London. None of the servants were awake as she padded to the master bedchambers and opened the door. She placed her candle on the table beside the enormous bed and tied back the curtain on one side. With a deep breath, she reached out her trembling hand and shook her father's shoulder. "Papa."

He woke instantly. "What is it, darling?"

"Please, come with me into the sitting room," she whispered.

He followed her out a moment later, tying his robe. "What is this about?"

"I wish to go to Kenbrook."

He smiled indulgently. "Of course. Your marriage hasn't made Kenbrook off limits to you."

She closed her eyes and expelled a breath. "Could you be ready in ten minutes?"

Her father stared down at her for two heartbeats. "What did he do?" he demanded with dangerous undertones.

She tried a smile, but it wouldn't stay. "Now, Father, I-I have been away from my horses much too long. I miss them dreadfully."

He hesitated. "Give me a few minutes to dress. I'm sure Nicholas won't object and shall be along as well."

As she opened her mouth to protest, he shook his head. "I cannot legally keep your husband from you, child, unless he has done something in order to warrant it." His expression turned murderous. "Has he?"

She shook her head, wishing that keeping a mistress were that sort of offense.

With gentle fingers, her father raised her chin. "Megan, all newly married couples have a difficult time adjusting. But I think it is a good idea that you visit Kenbrook. Ask Wentworth to have our horses ready. I'll be but a few moments."

She left the room as silently as she entered. If she had to suffer Nicholas's presence, it would help to do so at Kenbrook.

She couldn't wait to be in breeches and astride one of her horses again.

Upon arriving at Kenbrook, Megan visited the stables. All of her beloved horses nickered a greeting. She acknowledged every one with a special treat and promised to saddle each of them on the morrow for a long ride.

She sighed and straightened her shoulders as she neared the house. She had to keep her distance from Nicholas, even eat her meals in her room if necessary. And after a few days, she thought with a bitter smile, her husband would surely tire of her neglect, if he even bothered coming to Kenbrook at all.

By mid-morning the next day, Megan had given each horse a brisk run. She hadn't been able to race across the meadow as she usually did. She had no idea where her maid had placed the new breeches she'd purchased and her riding habit did not allow such freedom. She closed her eyes, feeling the sun's warmth on her skin, then took in the familiar surroundings. A line of fir trees stood on her right, the stream a little way beyond.

Hearing the approach of a rider, she turned and groaned. Nicholas galloped toward her on another of her horses. Blast. She had managed to avoid him yesterday and thought she had sneaked from the house unnoticed.

"He's magnificent," Nicholas praised as he rubbed the thoroughbred's silky brown neck.

"Yes, d'Artagnan is splendid."

He grinned at her. Enchanted with his smile, she berated herself that it took just a trivial thing to yearn for his touch. Oh, God, how long could she continue to resist him?

"Who trained them?" he asked as he moved alongside her.

She sighed. Her gaze skidded across the grassy field before she answered. "I did." The admission made her painfully aware of how unacceptable she was for Nicholas.

"Alone?"

She turned from the familiar landscape and looked at her husband. "Why is that so difficult to believe?"

His surprise melted into a cool glare. "You're right, Megan. We do seem to have difficulty believing one another. It must stop. Follow me." Then he flanked d'Artagnan and began to race away.

She swore and commanded her mount to move. Even riding sidesaddle, she kept close behind. When she neared Nicholas, she called out to his horse. "Halt, d'Artagnan, and stay."

The horse came to a skidding stop. Nicholas lurched in the saddle, narrowly avoiding a nasty tumble. Megan hid a smile behind her gloved hand.

Nicholas bade the horse to move, but all four hooves stayed rooted to the ground. Nothing worked, as she knew it wouldn't. He tried stern commands, but after several minutes he gave up and coaxed softly. And still the horse remained stationary.

Megan closed her eyes. His silky baritone voice slid over her body. She turned away and moved beyond the trees toward a familiar meadow. She approached the azure belt of water that spilled into a deep pool. The grass had turned a deep green, dotted with buttercups, red clover, and creeping thistle. She slid from her horse, paying little attention to the lovely surroundings. What she saw was Nicholas Bradshaw, the Duke of Claremont, tenderly kissing a wet, bedraggled young girl wearing breeches. Unshed tears stung the backs of her eyes. Why would he allow that woman back into his townhouse? Megan shook her head in bitter resentment. Did he love her?

Strong arms closed around her and eased her back against a solid chest. "My love, I know why you're upset with me," Nicholas said quietly. "But darling, I promise you are mistaken."

She dried her eyes at once. How dared he tell her that she was wrong? She'd seen Angela Cooper with her own eyes.

When she tried to draw away, his arms tightened around her. "Don't, Meg. Please, just listen," he implored.

She turned in the circle of his arms and forced her gaze to his. Gritting her teeth to keep from reacting to the pain she saw in his eyes, she pushed away from him. She would never be able to say what had to be said within the circle of his embrace. She forced the words from her mouth. "I would like to speak first, and then I shall listen to you."

He reached out to touch her, but halted and fisted his hand instead. "As you will."

"I have arrived at a decision," she said in a rush.

He stiffened, but remained silent. She licked her dry lips and pressed on. "I-I would like you to return to London as soon as possible. Alone. I shall remain here at Kenbrook." She put her hand up and shook her head when he opened his mouth. "I know what you're about to say and I have thought of that as well. However, since we have already caused enough of a scandal with our hasty marriage, I feel a divorce would be too much for our parents. Therefore, I have resigned myself to stay married to you. And since you are a duke, you will require an heir." She paused, her next words stuck in her throat. With a deep breath, she pried them out. "Perhaps in a year or two..." her words trailed off as a traitorous tear ran down her cheek. She swiped it away. "Damn you, Nicholas." She pounded her fists against his chest. "How could you do this to us?"

When he took her wrists in a firm but gentle grip, Megan fell silent. His eyes softened. He was going to kiss her. Tears glazed her eyes when she realized she wouldn't stop him. Nicholas had won. Oh, dear God, she was going to fall apart. Hysterical sobs rose up in her throat.

She chanced a glance over her shoulder and found that the stream blocked any retreat. When she turned back, her husband's lips came down on hers. She went rigid. Nicholas was easy to resist when he showed his anger. But the kind and charming man she married, the man tenderly kissing her, she couldn't resist. And she loved him with her heart and soul.

A few minutes later, Nicholas lifted his head. She opened her eyes and noticed the stubborn set to his jaw and the determination in his steady gaze. "I pray you mark me well, madam, because I shall say this only once. And, as God is my witness, it is the truth."

He explained circumstances in which he'd met Angela and the events that led to her dismissal and return to the townhouse. His voice never wavered. Megan felt numb. She glanced down at the kid gloves she'd twisted in her hands and grew sick with remorse. Dear Lord, instead of believing in her husband, in his love, she'd chosen to brand him an adulterer and flee. A tremor ran through her. This served to prove how unworthy she really was of him. Tears raced down her cheeks. "Oh, Nicholas," she whispered, "what have I done?"

He gathered her into his arms. "Don't cry, love." His voice grew raw and gravelly, making her cry even harder. She did not deserve him.

His arms tightened around her. He leaned down and pressed a kiss to her temple. "Darling, you are forgiven."

She squeezed her eyes shut, trying to suppress the pain. He deserved someone better. Her sobs tore at her throat. She had to find a way to tell him now before she lost the courage.

Scrubbing at her eyes, she pulled back. For several moments, she couldn't get her voice to work. She looked up at him. His eyes held tenderness, his lips a loving smile. Fresh tears sprang forth. He swiped them away with gentle fingers.

She had to set him free. Now. Or she never would. "Nicholas, we can't—"

He kissed her, long and slow. She raised her hands and wove her fingers through his hair. Just one kiss, and then she would tell him. Then she would set him free.

Passion licked every inch of her body, searing her very soul. She opened up for his seeking tongue and drank all of him in. Every outside sound fell away. Her blood roared thick in her ears, rushing from all parts of her body toward her throbbing core. Nicholas opened the front of her dress and pressed a palm to her breast. She moaned and moved closer, aching for his touch.

He lowered them to the soft grass. Wasn't there something she needed to tell him? He worked open her dress and she couldn't think. She could only feel the pleasure coursing through her body. When he captured a nipple in his mouth, she gasped and lightning exploded within her. His hand slid up her thigh and Megan knew she was going to die from pleasure.

She moaned in ecstasy. Her body pulsated to the rhythmic lunges he set with his finger. He continued to suckle her breast, shooting sparks down to her core and back. She raced to the edge of blissful completion, the tremors seizing her womb.

Her eyes flew open. After a deep breath, she captured his stone-solid erection in the palm of her hand. Hot silk over a marble rod. Her lips curved up when she heard his groan. She moved her hand to the tip of his engorged member and he went completely still. Instinctively, she stroked him. He shuddered and a faint snarl escaped his lips. Megan marveled at the power she wielded over him, and with a tiny movement of her hand, she used that power to return the pleasure he poured onto her.

Spewing out a hiss, Nicholas moved away. She started to smile until she felt his lips, soft and wet, against her stomach. Her breath hitched. The wet trail left a burning ache as he moved downward. He hesitated at the edge of the curls covering her most private area. She ceased to breathe. She bucked at the first contact of his mouth. Nothing could have prepared her for the delicious melting sensations his touch produced. Her thoughts reeled. She grasped the thick grass with both hands to anchor her body, else she was certain she'd lift into the sky and fly away.

Within seconds, tremors assailed her. They intensified with each dip of his tongue. But she fought the urge to succumb to the overpowering release. She wanted her husband with her on this trip to heaven. With shaking hands, she lifted his head so that he had to stop and look at her. "Not without you, my love. I never want do anything without you again," she whispered. He gazed at her with such reverence and love, her eyes grew misty. He moved above her and tenderly took her lips. Then he slipped into her, joining his soul to hers.

When he paused, she opened her heavy lids and saw him watching her intently. She could not break contact with his powerful gaze. She placed her arms around his neck and locked her ankles over his lower back. Then she rocked her hips forward. His eyes darkened and a low growl sounded deep in his throat.

He moved his hips slowly back and forth. She whimpered, unraveling as she watched every intriguing emotion spread across his face and knew that his release also hovered near.

When his strokes increased in speed, Megan could no longer hold back. She shattered like a pane of glass struck by a rock.

Nicholas took one last deep lunge, then spilled his seed. Lowering his head beside hers, he savored the feeling of her pulsating around him while he saturated her quivering womb.

When he could catch his breath, he rose on his elbows and looked down at his wife. His heart swelled with love. She smiled and lifted her head for a kiss. Her arms came around his neck when their lips touched, and she plunged her tongue into his mouth. She squeezed her legs in blatant suggestion. That pleased him. Without further prompting, he grew hard again.

After an hour, he sighed and gathered Megan close to him. The sun sinking into the western tree line drew his attention and he frowned. Was it truly so late? His wife slept. He hated to wake her, so he dressed himself, then pulled her gown on as carefully as possible without rousing her. When he carried her to their mounts, however, he found himself at an impasse. His horse remained as motionless as a statue. "Megan," he groused, "you must wake and tell this obstinate beast to take us home, love."

He heaved a sigh when she mumbled an incoherent word. "Megan, tell this damn horse of yours to take us home," he repeated.

She opened her eyes and smiled. He almost reached down for another kiss but halted just in time. They would never make it home. Instead, he scrambled up the saddle, then helped her into his lap.

"D'Artagnan, take us home."

The horse complied and Nicholas frowned when Megan laughed at his exasperation. She snuggled closer to him and yawned, then her breathing grew deep and even. She relaxed against his shoulder.

When Nicholas reached the stables, Julian was striding from the house. His grin extended from one ear to the other. "Mother and Father were wondering where the two of you had disappeared to all day. Here, I'll take her."

Reluctantly, he transferred his wife to her brother's arms. Then he dismounted and handed the reins to the waiting stable boy.

"Put me down, Julian. I can walk," Megan said.

When Julian did so, Nicholas slid his arm around her waist. He drew her against his side as they entered the palatial manor, needing to feel her as much as she needed the support.

****

He pushed the branch aside and watched them walk into the house. His heart pounded with excitement. Megan was back at Kenbrook. Just in time, too. He was almost out of money. He settled back against the thick tree trunk and opened his snuffbox. All was finally going as planned. He had even heard from the pirate. He looked back at the enormous estate, taking in the beautiful gardens and perfectly tailored lawns, and narrowed his eyes.

Nothing was going to hold him back this time. This time, he would have her. Perhaps he would keep her after they paid the ransom.

He smiled. Now, the second phase of the plan could begin.

CHAPTER 18

The next day, Megan was in the blue salon playing chess with her husband. She watched him move his knight, a cunning glint in his eyes. He released the ruby-encrusted piece from his fingertips, then leaned back against the chair's navy velvet covering. A smug smile formed on his lips. "Your turn."

She masked her features, studied the board, and pretended to ponder her next move. Not wanting Nicholas to realize the trap she'd set for him, she let her hand hover over a piece. He leaned forward, his smile widening. She shook her head. Silly man. She moved her queen and captured his rook. Checkmate. "Did I do it right?" she asked innocently.

Nicholas opened his mouth. He shook his head. She had beaten him for the fourth time in as many games. She couldn't prevent the grin from spreading over her lips.

Julian sauntered into the room. He laughed as he stopped before the chessboard. "Don't look so glum, Nick." He slapped her husband on the back. "I won't even play with her any longer."

"Jules, why don't you restore my husband's ego and have a go with him?" she asked, rising from her seat.

Nicholas stood and shook his head. "I really haven't the time." He explained about an impending meeting with his estate manager at Claremont. "You can come with me if you wish, my love," he offered in a husky voice, pulling her into his arms.

Julian rolled his eyes and shook his head.

Innocence Lost

****

After Nicholas's meeting, Megan looked over Claremont as they waited for their horses, wondering why she never noticed how beautiful it was. She had visited Genny many times with her mother, but now looked upon the magnificent estate with new eyes. The expanse of rolling grassland revealed stunning dandelion and white clover, mingled between the precisely-trimmed oak trees spread across the park. In the center of this enchanted wood stood the palatial one-hundred-sixty-six-room mansion of grey brick. Claremont was not as large as Kenbrook, but it certainly was as lovely. "You know, I fell in love with you here," she said.

Nicholas looked at her, puzzled. She nodded. "When I was ten, I stumbled onto your portrait in the gallery. It was love at first sight."

With a wicked gleam in his eye, he pulled her into his arms. "I always knew you were a smart girl." He nuzzled her neck. "Would you like to visit the gallery before we leave? Perhaps you can show me all your fantasies." He kissed just below her ear.

Megan's body shook with need. "I always knew you were a smart boy."

"Ahem."

Megan pulled away, her face probably as red as the poor groom before them.

"Your horses, Your Grace."

"We'll just finish this later," Nicholas stated softly as he helped her mount the horse.

She certainly hoped so.

They started back to Kenbrook. "Hobbs thinks there might be poachers about."

Megan turned to Nicholas, surprised he discussed the particulars of his meeting. Surprised and pleased. "Why does he think that?"

Nicholas maneuvered his horse around a puddle

in the road. "He found a deer carcass and remnants of a recent fire."

"What are you going to do?" She imagined someone had to be desperate to poach on a duke's land. What if the person had a family?

He shrugged. "I'll talk to your father. Perhaps he has had the same trouble. I would also like to find out who the poacher is. There might be a good reason for his actions."

His words nearly mirrored her thoughts. She smiled. Her husband quite surprised her. She fiddled with the leather strap in her hands, knowing she had been putting off a conversation she had to have with him. Nicholas deserved someone much more worthy. She turned to him, about to speak, when he spoke first.

"Could you be happy living part of the year in London and the other part at Claremont?" he asked.

"I would be happy living in a hole in a tree, as long as I was with you." The words were out of her mouth before she thought better of it. But they were the truth.

He stopped their horses and pulled her onto his lap. "I love you," he whispered.

She swallowed. Could there be hope for them? God, she didn't want to ruin his life, but living without him would be the worst kind of hell. "Nicholas, I—" She stopped when two riders emerged from the surrounding trees, pointing pistols at them. She gasped. Fear speared her right through the middle.

Nicholas tightened his hold on her. "Turn and depart at once or face the consequences," he ordered.

The one with the eye patch spoke. "As I sees it, chum, ye ain't in no position t'be giving the orders." He waved his weapon for emphasis.

"What do you want?" her husband demanded in a low snarl.

The vile man leered, exposing four black, rotted teeth. "We come fer yer wife."

Megan pressed a hand to her chest, feeling her heart pound. She heard Nicholas's swift intake of breath as the bandit nudged his horse forward. Oh, God, she couldn't think!

The man stopped his horse just a few feet before them. "Git down real slow an' come 'ere," he ordered.

"No," Nicholas bellowed. Aramis sidestepped nervously.

The burly brute shrugged his meaty shoulders. He raised his weapon. "I'll jes' shoot ye a'tween the eyes. Either way, I gets the lady."

Megan froze with fear. But when the big oaf raised his gun to her husband, she cried, "No, wait," forcing him to jerk the weapon back onto her.

Nicholas's arm tightened like an iron band. She spoke softly to him without taking her eyes from the barbarian. "Let me go, Nicholas. We have no choice."

"Come 'ere, ye wee tart, or I'll blow yer man's 'ead arf," the ruffian said.

"Nicholas," she whispered, "how can you help me if you're dead?" Knowing her words and harsh tone had stung him, she felt his hold slacken. She slid quickly to the ground.

"No, Meg." He grabbed for her, but she had already moved out of his reach.

She walked to the left so that the insufferable oaf before her was forced into the other ruffian's line of fire. Then, with a silent prayer, she approached the repulsive barbarian. She swallowed the knot in her throat and looked up.

He appraised her with one lecherous, beady eye. Then he smiled wide. "Come 'ere," he said, reaching for her.

"Don't do it, Megan."

The quiver in her husband's voice broke her heart. She bit down on her lower lip and took the final step. Nicholas would die trying to keep her safe. She had no other alternative. The man's meaty arm hauled her onto his lap, forcing a startled shriek from her lips. Regaining her wits, she grabbed the man's armed hand while she called out a command to her horse.

"Aramis, home. NOW!"

"Megan, no!" Nicholas shouted. But the horse had already wheeled around and lunged forward. He swore and pulled on the reins, but the beast would not obey.

He hunched his shoulders, preparing to leap from the saddle, when an explosion roared from behind. He pitched hard against the horse's neck. Searing pain erupted in his left shoulder, making him cry out, and a warm wetness rolled down his back and chest.

He blinked, trying to focus. He still clung to Aramis as the horse thundered toward Kenbrook. Blackness filled his vision. Tremors wracked his chilled body. He fought to stay conscious.

Aramis finally halted near the stables in a cloud of dust. The world spun.

Gritting his teeth, he tried lifting from the horse's neck. Pain pierced his left side. Nausea filled his stomach and large, black blotches danced before his vision. He heard voices and sagged with relief. His father-in-law urged him to dismount. "No," he slurred. "We have...to save...Megan." He started to fall from the horse as a swell of dizziness crashed over him, but he caught himself.

"What? Where is she?" Julian demanded.

"Main road...near bridge...two men with pistols..." His eyes rolled back and the world went silent.

CHAPTER 19

Megan woke to insistent pounding in the back of her head. She blinked and tried to rise.

Moving, even slightly, intensified the ache within her skull. Stars danced before her blurred vision. She tried again to lift up from where she lay and realized her wrists and ankles were bound. Everything that had happened on the road to Kenbrook came rushing back into her mind. She recalled Aramis wheeling around to take Nicholas to safety as a sharp pain exploded at the back of her head. After that, everything was black.

She prayed with all her might that Nicholas had escaped.

The reality of her situation assailed her. Those vile men had abducted her. Oh, God, what were they going to do to her? Tears pooled in her eyes, but she blinked them away and tried and stay calm. Her vision started to clear and she surveyed her dim surroundings. If the room had windows, they were either boarded or shuttered. A single candle on a nearby table was her only source of light. She lay on a straw mattress in a shabby little room that reeked of mold and stale air.

Megan licked her parched lips and closed her eyes. Exhaustion overwhelmed her. The horrible ache in her skull lessened with each second that she succumbed to the peaceful slumber hovering just under the surface. Then the dark void totally engulfed her.

Megan was jarred awake by someone shaking her shoulder. She gasped at the abrupt change from blissful oblivion to painful consciousness. Strong hands sat her up on the edge of the bed. The room spun.

A cup containing some foul-smelling liquid was thrust under her nose. "Drink it."

A woman's voice. She lifted her head in surprise. The newcomer remained obscured within the room's deep shadows. But the hands holding the cup were not female. That meant there were at least two of them in the room. What did they want? She shivered as she recalled the brute with the eye patch.

Megan felt cool wetness against her dry lips. Fighting fear, she took a generous swallow and almost gagged. The putrid beverage tasted worse than it smelled.

"What was that?" she croaked when the cup was taken away.

The woman chuckled. "Water. Not fresh like you're used to, Your Grace."

Lifting her chin, Megan asked, "Who are you, and what do you want from me?"

The woman ignored the questions. "How is Nicholas?"

Megan closed her eyes as her husband's smiling face flashed into her mind. Relief nearly overwhelmed her. He must have gotten away. "How do you know my husband?"

"I knew him a long time ago," the woman answered in a low, sorrowful voice.

"Then why have you accosted me?"

"You will understand all in due time," the woman said, turning toward the door.

Megan struggled against her bindings. "Wait! Where are you going?"

"Worry not, Your Grace, you shall see me again soon."

When the woman left the room, a shuffle sounded behind Megan. Her heart leaped into her throat and she twisted around.

She saw only a vague silhouette within the shadows. But the tall, muscular form allowed her a small measure of relief. He wasn't one of the scoundrels who had taken her from Kenbrook.

"Do not be alarmed. I will not hurt you unless you force me to," he said, so softly she had to strain to hear him.

She swallowed hard. "What is it you want?"

"You," he whispered.

She could not stop shaking. Fear held her in steel claws. She struggled against her bonds, and knew that she could not keep him from taking her.

The door crashed open. Megan swiveled around. The movement dispatched a blinding bolt of pain through her head and wetness sprang into her eyes. She winced, but remained focused on the woman entering the room.

This one didn't stay within the shadows. She sauntered into the light and smiled a triumphant sneer. Her green eyes glistened with vengeance. "Oh, how the mighty have fallen," Angela taunted as she perched her fists on her hips. Megan sat there gaping at the spiteful face of Nicholas's ex-mistress, uncomprehending.

"What's the matter? Someone finally slice off that sharp tongue of yours?" Angela scoffed and took a step forward. She raised her hand.

"Angie," the man's voice rang out in warning.

Angela looked up. She sighed and took a step back, her scornful eyes exuding a promise that she'd not be thwarted again.

Megan knew she had heard the man's voice before, but she couldn't identify when or where. The back of her head started to pound again and she drooped. The room tilted. She vaguely heard the man swear before she felt his arms close gently around her. Megan forced her eyes back open.

A strangled gasp caught in her throat as she focused on him. "Mr. Williams?" she whispered, searching his face for an explanation.

He motioned for Angela to leave.

Angela slammed the door on the way out. When the rafters stopped shaking, he said, "I must apologize for Angela. She has a temper the devil wouldn't even own."

Megan had never been more confused. "How do you know her?"

"She is my sister," he replied.

"Your sister?" Good Lord.

"Come, I would like you to eat. Then we will explain." He assisted her to the edge of the bed. "I am going to untie your legs, but you must promise not to run. I assure you that you will not like the consequences if you try. Do we agree?"

With no alternative, she nodded.

"Good." He removed a six-inch blade from his shirt and sliced through the rope around her ankles. "I'll be right outside the door to allow you a moment of privacy before we dine," he replied, indicating the bed with a dip of his head.

Thank God. Her bladder felt close to bursting. Even though her wrists were bound before her, she removed the chamber pot from under the bed and managed quickly. As he led her from the room, she couldn't stop the questions from leaping into her mind. Mr. Williams was Julian's first mate, so what part did he play in this? What would they do to her? Was she being held for ransom?

They entered a tiny dining room, not even one-quarter the size of Kenbrook's larder. The paint on the walls had peeled off in chunks and a large greenish-black stain lingered in one corner of the ceiling. The small house looked to be falling apart. The two windows had been covered with threadbare curtains, the many holes patched, giving her no indication of her location.

Mr. Williams seated her in the chair to his left, then an expressionless, elderly man with a bad stoop served the meager repast. She ate the bland quail and thin brown sauce without speaking. Her hands remained bound. Mr. Williams hadn't allowed her that liberty and she damn sure wasn't about to beg for it. As her shock waned, her anger ignited. And by the time the meal was over, she had invented some of the most gruesome and vile forms of punishment imaginable to inflict upon her captors.

When Mr. Williams escorted her into a dismal drawing room and seated her on the tattered sofa, she had grown livid. How dared they do this to her! He took the cushion beside her. She scooted as far away as she could and turned to the windows. From the amount of sunlight pouring in, it looked to be about midday. She squinted into the brightness, but all she could see were trees. How much time had passed, she wondered? She shook her head, certain she hadn't been gone any longer than a day.

The sound of ripping fabric drew her attention. Near the flagstone fireplace, Angela stood watching her with an intense, cold glare, shredding a handkerchief. No doubt she sought revenge for being thrown out. Megan almost smiled.

A veiled woman dressed in black shuffled into the room. Megan felt her mouth drop open when Angela assisted the newcomer onto the chair across from her. She hadn't thought Angela capable of that sort of kindness.

After she managed to rein in her shock, Megan inspected the new woman. She wore a dark bonnet with an attached black veil that obscured her features, but Megan guessed by the woman's smooth, exposed hands that she was fairly young. "I'm sure you're curious as to why you are here, Your Grace," the woman in black announced.

That was the same female voice that had asked about Nicholas. Megan nodded to the inky shroud.

The woman inclined her head and Mr. Williams began to speak. "An eye shall go for an eye, so the Bible says," he quoted.

She searched his stony face. "I'm afraid I don't understand."

"Many years ago, your brother ruined my sister's life," he answered, vengeance igniting in his eyes.

"Angela?" She didn't think Julian even knew Angela.

"My other sister." Mr. Williams nodded toward the woman wearing the veil.

Were all these people mad?

Angela jumped to her feet. "That lewd brother of yours defiled my sister, and when she told him she was breeding, he threw her to the wolves."

Megan gasped. What a horrible lie!

"When I went to see your brother," the veiled woman began, "he acted in the worst possible way. Then he had a servant escort me home. But it wasn't for polite assistance, I assure you," she said. "Lord Amersleigh had that servant tell my father I was an opportunistic little trollop trying to force marriage on him. He threatened to have my father stripped of his title and shipped to Australia in chains if I ever came near Kenbrook again." She paused and Megan felt the woman's eyes boring into her.

"Father was livid," she continued, "and barely refrained from beating me to death. But what he did was much, much worse."

"What did he do?" Megan asked, unable to conceive of anything worse.

"He found me a husband," the woman answered. "And I quickly learned what a cruel man Arthur Wakefield was." She ripped the bonnet and veil from her head.

The sound that escaped Megan's lips was half gasp, half sob as she gazed upon the disfigured face. The right side of the woman's head looked as if it had been crushed and melted by fire. Her right eyelid remained partially closed and her mouth drooped down at the corner.

"Dear God," Megan rasped, her disbelieving gaze roving over the pitiful sight before her. "You're Emily Wakefield?"

The corner of Emily's mouth lifted. "I discovered the very first night that Arthur Wakefield was a monster. I was so very frightened of him," she said, "but it was nothing compared to when he learned I was not a virgin. Arthur beat me and called me filthy names. I lost consciousness after the first few blows, but when I woke, there was blood everywhere. And the pain was excruciating."

Megan flinched.

"I soon learned that I no longer carried the baby, nor would I ever be allowed to conceive again," she said. "And it was all Lord Amersleigh's fault."

Megan released a shuddering breath. "What are you going to do?"

No one answered. And Megan wondered how they intended to get even.

****

Nicholas stirred and opened his eyes. Everything hurt, including his hair. He blinked until his vision cleared and saw that Julian sat on a nearby chair reading something.

"Megan," he forced through his cracked lips.

Julian looked up and walked to the bed. His brows furrowed. "Nicholas, my friend, how are you feeling?"

"Megan?" he choked out.

His friend could not mask his worry. "I would bargain my soul to know, Nick," he answered.

Nicholas began to rise, but a scorching pain in

his shoulder brought him back down.

"Have you lost all good sense? You were shot yesterday," Julian chided, placing a hand on his uninjured shoulder to keep him from leaving the bed.

"I have... to find her."

"I know. We already have fifty-seven investigators searching for her. Allow us to handle this until you are able to sit a horse, all right?"

A knock sounded at the door.

Nicholas bade the visitor entrance.

Thomas Porter was a mammoth of a man who spoke very little, but he exuded competence and experience.

Nicholas thought him an excellent choice.

"Is there news? A ransom note?" Nicholas asked.

The investigator shook his head. "No note, Your Grace. My men lost the trail at the stream, however they are continuing to search the bank."

Nicholas swallowed hard. "Are there any leads? Any at all?" He looked around the room. Julian's shoulders slumped and he hung his head.

"None," Joseph answered. Dark crescents hung under his haunted eyes and his hair was mussed as though the man had continually raked it through.

"Your Grace, do you know of anyone who would want your wife?" Thomas asked, taking a seat at the small secretary beside the bed to take notes.

"I have no idea who would wish her harmed."

Julian stiffened and rose from his chair. "Nick, what about Jeremy's sister?"

Joseph turned from the window. His hands were clasped behind his back and his eyes seared with smoldering rage. "Be damned, this entire time I've been thinking a man was responsible." A muscle ticked in his cheek.

Nicholas turned his thoughts to Phyllis Granger. He had not been acquainted with her sufficiently enough to deem her guilty of his wife's abduction. He avoided her like rotten fish whenever possible. He shook his head. "I honestly cannot say."

"Who is Jeremy's sister?" Thomas asked.

"Phyllis Longwell Granger, sister to Jeremy Longwell, the Marquess of Fielding," said Julian. "And the chit has been obsessed with Nicholas for years." The sharp, insistent ache in Nicholas's shoulder, the exhaustion and his weakness evaporated. His fury swelled.

"I'll speak to Phyllis and Angela Cooper at once." Thomas paused to scribble in his notes. "Any other questionable incidents prior to Her Grace's abduction?"

Joseph turned to the investigator. "Thomas, the duchess and I were sent a bogus note regarding Julian several months ago."

Thomas glanced up from his notes. "Do you believe it has any bearing on your daughter's disappearance?"

Joseph explained its contents, but all Nicholas heard was a blur of sound while his fury mounted. God, what must Megan be going through? He groaned, unable to stop horrible images from slipping into his mind.

"I shall need to speak with Stuart Williams and obtain a writing sample to determine if it matches the false note," said Thomas.

Julian shook his head. "I'm afraid that will be difficult. I dispatched him and the entire crew of the *Sweet Siren* to retrieve Mother and Father. They haven't returned." Julian frowned. "I have known Stuart for years. I cannot believe he'd be involved. He saved Megan from being attacked at the dock. If he were a part of this, then that would have been the perfect time to take her."

"Unless, my lord, that hadn't been the perfect time to take her," Thomas said. "His Grace,

Claremont, indicated others were involved. This leads me to believe the abduction had been planned."

He snapped his notebook closed.

"And I have every intention of learning who these people are."

CHAPTER 20

Julian still reeled from the investigator's assessment yesterday. Porter had it wrong. Stuart couldn't be involved in Megan's disappearance.

The door opened and Jeremy entered with Phyllis. The chit looked scared. Or was that guilt?

He rose to his feet with his father and Porter.

"His Grace, the Duke of Kenbrook, the Marquess of Amersleigh, and Mr. Thomas Porter," Jeremy said to Phyllis. His voice turned steely. "They are here on a serious matter. Your Grace, Julian, Mr. Porter, my sister, Phyllis Granger."

If Julian hadn't been so bloody mad, he would have laughed. Phyllis gave the shakiest of curtsies, squawking some nonsensical reply, and plopped onto an empty chair.

Once they were all seated, Jeremy said, "Phyllis, you do know what this is about, do you not?"

Phyllis shook her head.

"Do not lie, Phyllis," Jeremy said, his voice soft.

"I-I don't know," she insisted, studying the lacy handkerchief in her hands.

"Perhaps this will refresh your memory." Jeremy showed her the letter she'd sent to Megan, and her eyes widened. "Now, tell us why you wrote this."

"Sh-She, Lady Megan—"

"The Duchess of Claremont," Jeremy corrected.

"The Duchess of Claremont. She wouldn't believe that Nicky—the Duke—has a mistress in residence."

"First of all, Phyllis, the Duke of Claremont's

personal life is none of your business," Jeremy began. "And secondly, Nick no longer has a mistress. He was allowing Angela Cooper the use of the house until she found somewhere else to live."

"I-I swear, I didn't know," Phyllis whispered as tears filled her eyes. Then she looked down at her clasped hands.

From the corner of his eye, Julian watched his father nod to Thomas Porter.

"Do you know where the Duchess of Claremont is, my lady?" Thomas asked.

Phyllis lifted her head, surprise shining in her teary eyes. "She isn't at Kenbrook?"

"No, she isn't," Thomas answered. "Do you know a man named Stuart Williams?"

The area around her mouth tightened and her brows drew together. "No," she answered, "I don't know anyone by that name."

Julian closed his eyes. A dead end.

After leaving Jeremy's house, Julian rode to Bond Street with his father and the investigator. They halted at the address Nick gave them. A plump housekeeper opened the door, surveying them with cautious eyes. "Can I help you?"

"We must be permitted to speak with Angela Cooper immediately," Julian said.

She shook her head. "I-I'm sorry, milord. She left days ago."

As a string of oaths rent the air, the woman gasped. She attempted to slam the door shut, but Thomas held it open with his hand. "You gentlemen must leave. There is no business for you here," she squeaked, trying without success to get the door closed.

"I am Joseph Westland, the Duke of Kenbrook. I understand that my daughter, Megan, was here and conversed with Miss Cooper. We are here because my daughter was abducted two days ago."

The woman blanched. "Oh, no. Please come in, Your Grace. I do so apologize, I didn't know who you were. Please, follow me." She turned and led them into the parlor. "Can I get you some tea, Your Grace, my lords?" she asked when they were seated.

"No, just some answers. Sit," his father said.

The woman looked as if he'd just requested her execution. She perched on the edge of a nearby chair and waited for him to begin.

"I understand that my daughter came here twelve days ago and spoke to Angela Cooper."

The housekeeper's nervousness evaporated. "Indeed she did, Your Grace. Your daughter had that she-devil out on her ear within an hour."

In spite of his worry, Julian's lips twitched at the visual picture of his petite sister, a duchess, evicting her husband's so-called mistress out of the woman's own provided house. "Were you in the room? Did you hear what was said between them?"

Her shoulders slumped forward and she shook her head. "No, sir. I was told to leave. And my hearing ain't what it used to be. But I do know that there was no shouting and somehow Her Grace got that witch to leave. A miracle, indeed, I tell you."

"How long have you, ah, known Miss Cooper?" Julian asked.

"Oh, eight or nine years. If you don't mind my asking, my lord, where is the Duke of Claremont?"

"Nicholas is at the Kenbrook estate, recuperating from a gunshot wound he received when Megan was accosted," Julian answered.

"Oh, thank God he's all right," she mumbled. Drawing her brows together, she asked, "Do you expect Miss Cooper is involved in Her Grace's abduction?"

"We don't know. That is why we have come," Julian answered. "When Nicholas dismissed Miss Cooper in March, do you know where she traveled?"

"I assume she went to her father's."

"And do you know who he is or where he lives?" he asked, resisting the urge to rub his sweaty palms over his riding breeches.

Her face fell. "I'm truly sorry, I don't. The only time she spoke to me was in the form of an order or reprimand."

"Nicholas told us that you were to send the remainder of her things after he'd dismissed her. What location did she give?"

"She didn't, my lord. She had a young lad fetch them."

"Do you know this boy? His name or where he lives?" Julian asked.

"I haven't a clue, my lord."

"Has Ms. Cooper had any other visitors recently?" Thomas asked.

"No. No visitors. But she did receive a message just before she left."

"Do you know what the message said?" Julian asked.

"Sorry, my lord. But I do know the message came from the dock. The lad who delivered it said so."

****

Complete darkness surrounded Megan, enveloping her like a death shroud. The silence rang throughout the room. The smell of burnt candle wax hung heavily in the hot air, almost too thick to inhale.

Megan forced herself to wait another five minutes before she moved.

After talking with Emily the day before, she had been brought back to the small bedroom. She'd fallen asleep and couldn't tell how many hours had passed before the old butler came in with a tray of food. That had been a long time ago. She guessed it was night. The house was too still and silent for it to be otherwise.

She shimmied into a sitting position on the bed. Damn Stuart Williams for retying her ankles. She brought her wrists to her mouth and began to gnaw at the rope that bound them.

While eating dining earlier, she studied the knot and found it to be one of the complicated ties her brother had shown her. She loosened the twine and it slid down her arms. She rubbed her chafed wrists to restore the circulation in her hands. Pain shot clear up to her elbows. Swallowing hard, she kept the useless appendages resting in her lap until she could use them again.

When the ache lessened to a tolerable level, she loosened the knot around her ankles. Her riding boots had protected them so that she felt only a faint discomfort in her feet.

Megan rose from the bed and shuffled toward the door. She prayed there wouldn't be a guard on the other side. Her body shook all over. She had to escape. Every second away from Nicholas was torture. And what if they never intended to return her?

When her seeking fingers found the door, she slid them slowly down to the knob. She twisted and eased the door open. A quick glance in the hall confirmed it to be empty. A low-burning lamp stood on an old, scarred table.

She crept down the hall, her magnified shadow slinking along at her side like a black specter. Her heart pounded. As she moved away from the lamp, she slid further into the blackness before her. Her palms grew moist and she halted. Holding her breath, she listened and heard only the thudding of her heart. She took a step forward, then another. An open entryway stood to her left. She could just make out the windows at the far end of the room.

Footsteps sounded and a door opened. Megan

flew into the room, looking for a place to hide. The footsteps grew louder. Seeing the shadowy form of the sofa, she crouched behind it just as someone halted in the doorway. Her pulse hammered. When the footsteps moved away, she peeked around the corner of the sofa.

The door across the hall swung closed. She exhaled in relief. Then she realized that someone could find her missing.

She scrambled to her feet. With trembling legs, she located the front door and slipped from the house.

She gulped down several deep breaths of cool night air as she scanned her dark surroundings. A dilapidated stable stood a few yards away. She crept toward it.

A shuffle and nicker within told her that a horse resided inside. She stepped inside and murmured to the skittish animal. The mare snorted and flattened its ears but Megan comforted it with a soothing murmur. Within seconds, it calmed enough to be bridled.

Without bothering to saddle it, Megan led the horse outside and mounted.

Which way? No matter. She'd get directions at the first safe-looking inn. She glanced up at the sky, recalling something Julian had taught her. The North Star had a fixed location in the sky. There! She snapped the reins.

An hour later, she halted the horse and frowned. The trail broke off into two different directions. She spied a roof rising above the trees to her right. Faint with exhaustion and apprehension, she jabbed the horse with her heels and trotted in that direction.

She reached a rustic cabin and pounded on the door.

The door flew open. Her mouth parted in readiness to plead for help, but when she recognized

Nicholas's uncle, she flew into his arms and began to sob.

"What's this all about?" he asked as his arms closed around her.

"Oh, Lord Charles!" she cried.

"Come inside, darling, and tell me what has happened," he soothed. He showed her to the sofa and retrieved some water from a little kitchen off the main room.

She threaded her fingers together to keep them from shaking and forced herself to be calm. She was safe now. Charles would take her home.

Taking the water with a grateful smile, she gulped it down. She hadn't realized how hungry and thirsty she was.

An understanding smile crept across his lips and he turned back to the kitchen. Charles returned a few minutes later with a delightful fare of bread, cheese and strong tea. She devoured the meal, thankful to him for refraining from his questions until after she finished.

"Megan, what has happened?"

She took a deep breath. "I've been abducted. I'm not sure how long it's been, I think a couple of days. Oh please, Charles, take me home now," she begged. Tears slipped down her cheeks. A sob escaped and she pressed her face into her hands. Now that this terrible ordeal had ended, she would be returned to Nicholas. Oh, God, she had almost believed she would never see him again. She sobbed harder.

"Of course I shall take you home, darling. But first, rest a while. You are exhausted. Just an hour," he said.

Megan lifted her head and dashed the tears away. What must Nicholas be going through? Was he pacing the floor with her parents at Kenbrook? His face filled her mind. She closed her eyes, remembering every detail.

Voices brought her sluggishly awake. But the attempt to open her eyes proved unsuccessful. Dismay filled her. She tried to rise.

Footsteps clacked on the wooden floor as Charles moved around the tiny structure. The noise stopped directly in front of her.

"It's only been a few minutes. Are you sure she's asleep?"

Again, Megan tried to open her eyes, but lethargy dragged at her. With alarm, she recognized the effects of laudanum.

"I just checked, she's asleep. How much did you give her?"

Her heart skipped a beat when she recognized the second male voice. Stuart.

"Enough. She'll be out for hours. How in the bloody hell did you allow her to escape?" Charles growled.

Surely they could hear how hard her heart was beating? It sounded like a drum in her ears. She tried to move, only to find her arms and legs bound with rope. Her fear intensified, making her dizzy and weak.

"I have no idea how she managed to loosen the rope," Stuart replied. "I don't like this, Charles. Too many things have gone wrong. Maybe we should forget—"

"You owe me, Stuart. If I hadn't arrived at the cottage when I did, Emily would not be alive today." Charles's voice held a bitter edge that Megan had never heard before.

After a few seconds of silence, Charles continued in a kinder tone. "And must I remind you what Julian did to her?"

The room grew quiet. She continued to fight sleep. The drug pulsed through her body and pulled her under. With despair, she realized that Charles and Stuart would never be considered suspects.

CHAPTER 21

The clank of dishes against a tray woke Megan. She opened gritty eyes and struggled to remember what had happened. Her blurry vision sharpened on the dirty smoke rising from a nearby candle. Someone shuffled forward and poured water into a glass. She heard the sound of the liquid and scraped her dry tongue from the roof of her mouth. The person placed the glass on the table beside her, then left the room. A rotten-egg stench wafted to her. When she saw the glass of murky water, her thirst evaporated.

She was back in the drab little cottage. Hopelessness engulfed her. She blinked away fresh tears and commanded herself not to weep like a weak, foolish child. Her family would find her, and she had to stay strong until they arrived.

Her left ankle was shackled with an iron band and a short chain to the bedpost. Her new sapphire-blue riding habit had been replaced with a clean but plain green dress. Someone had removed her clothing *and* given her a bath. Her thoughts shifted to her attempted escape the previous night. Once she was returned to her family, Charles would pay dearly for this ransom.

Someone cleared his throat.

She snapped her head up and found Mr. Williams in the doorway. She rose with her hands balled at her sides. "I demand to be released or there will be hell to pay."

He smiled and shook his head. "Damn, if you aren't lovely when you're mad." When she started to tell him how her husband would track him down, he held up a hand. "Emily bathed you. And a lady ought not to swear," he said lightly.

"You sound like Julian." She plopped her hands onto her hips. "What would your employer say about you holding his sister against her will?"

His smile vanished. "What would your brother have done if what happened to Emily, had happened to you?" he countered.

Her hands slid down her sides. She knew exactly what Julian would have done.

"That's right," he replied. He squashed a thick, black roach with the tip of his boot. Icebergs radiated more heat than his expression.

Her heart nearly stopped. Oh, God, they were going to kill Julian!

She moved to him and placed a trembling hand upon the bare arms he had crossed over his chest. His long shirtsleeves were rolled up to his elbows and his muscles leaped as soon as she touched him. She resisted the urge to snatch her hand away. "Please, Mr. Williams, you can ransom me if you must, but do not harm Julian," she implored. Tears blurred her vision.

When he remained stubbornly mute, she felt her legs grow weak. Nausea threatened. She walked back to the bed, the chain scraping the wooden floor, and sat on the hay mattress. She welcomed the numbness that swallowed her. "I understand your motive, erroneous as it is, but why is Lord Charles involved?"

"I will return soon," he said. Then he was gone.

Several hours crept by before he reappeared. Megan hadn't moved since his departure. She heard the door open and Stuart approached in four heavy strides. The bed dipped. She knew with some intrinsic certainty that he wouldn't harm her. She also knew he did not like the idea of holding her against her will.

During his absence, she tried rationalizing the facts. Nothing made sense. "Are you going to murder Julian?" she demanded, hating the tremor in her voice.

"It wouldn't be murder." He pinned her with a hard stare. "It would be justice."

She felt the color draining from her face. It took her several seconds to find her voice. "Julian didn't seduce Emily," she whispered.

"Yes, he did." Vengeance burned bright in Stuart's eyes.

She took a calming breath. "Stuart, I know this may be difficult to believe, but Emily lied—"

"Emily wouldn't lie," he insisted.

Sensing him near the point of releasing his anger, she decided to alter the direction of their conversation. "Julian manages Kenbrook Shipping. Why did you seek employment there if you hated him so?"

He groaned and shook his head. "Must you always satisfy your curiosity so completely?"

She held her breath, wondering if he was going to answer her. Just as she was about to repeat the question, he spoke.

"I began working at the dock about a week before Emily went to see Julian." His voice turned quiet. Sad. "Loading cargo was the only job I could find at the time. Thanks to my step-father's drinking problem, we were destitute. A rueful smile touched his lips. "Then Henry Bensford died. I returned immediately and found that Emily had married." Hatred filled his face. "God, I wanted to kill Arthur Wakefield. But I didn't have to."

"Why?" she asked.

"Charles beat me to it. He'd been on his way to his hunting cabin when he heard Emily's screams. Arthur was beating her to death and Charles..."

Stuart closed his eyes. "He saved her from that bastard. I owe him for saving my sister's life."

"Why does Charles need money? He's an earl—"

"With a rapacious gambling affliction."

"But he—"

Stuart leaned over. "Charles has lost everything, and he's a desperate man."

A knock sounded at the door. Stuart rose and spoke briefly to the person on the other side.

He turned with a broad smile. "It is time," he stated.

She swallowed hard.

****

Nicholas looked up sharply as a knock sounded at the study door.

"Enter," Joseph ordered.

The door opened and Thomas Porter walked in. "Your Grace, we've found your daughter's horse."

Nicholas rose as fast as his weakened body would allow, ignoring the fiery pain in his shoulder. "What about Megan?" he demanded.

"The horse was found seven miles north of here," Thomas said. "From the condition of the animal, he must have traveled quite a distance. I have already dispatched more riders to search out the area." He paused and gave Joseph an envelope. "This was found tied to the saddle."

Nicholas watched him read the note. He barely refrained from snatching the document away. Finally, his father-in-law looked up, his blue eyes burning with anger and relief.

"It's a ransom note," Joseph declared. "In one month, we are to sail to Dundee, Scotland, with the Kenbrook and Claremont jewels plus twenty crates of gold in exchange for Megan."

"One month?" Nicholas asked. How could he wait that long?

A knock sounded. Dawson opened the door.

"Your Grace, there is a Mr. Jasper here to see Mr. Porter."

Thomas rose from his chair and left the study.

Twenty minutes later, Thomas returned. "The *Sweet Siren* has returned," he said. "One of the men I have positioned at the dock has informed me that he spoke to a Mr. Black."

"Lucas Black is the second mate," Julian said. "Why didn't your man speak directly to Stuart?"

"I'm sorry, my lord, but it seems Stuart Williams is dead. An armed ship overcame the *Sweet Siren* ten days after her departure. Mr. Williams was taken aboard. When the pirates attempted to relieve the vessel of her cargo and found that she had none, Stuart was shot on the pirate ship and thrown overboard. Mr. Black witnessed the execution."

Julian's eyes filled with anguish. "Dear God," he said.

Nicholas shuffled over to the liquor cart and poured his friend a whiskey.

After gulping down the drink, Julian turned back to the investigator. "Why did it take so long for the ship to return?"

"The bandits set fire to her in their attempt to escape. It seemed they wanted to leave no witnesses behind. But the fire was extinguished and the *Sweet Siren* limped to the nearest port."

Another knock came at the study door. Nicholas swallowed back the oath hovering on his lips. "Your Grace, Lord Stenwick has arrived," said Dawson.

Charles marched into the study, his features drawn. "Good Lord, Joseph, I came as soon as I heard. Is there any news?"

"Charles," Joseph greeted as they shook hands. "We've just received a ransom note."

"Please let me know if there is anything I can do," said Charles. "Nick, are you all right?"

Ignoring the urge to rub his throbbing shoulder,

Nicholas gave a stiff nod. The doctor had wished him to stay abed much longer, but Megan needed him. He gritted his teeth. She must be frightened to death. There had to be something more he could do.

"I stopped at the tavern," Charles continued, "and was completely bewildered when I learned that you'd been seriously injured."

"Lord Stenwick, may I ask you a few questions?" Thomas asked.

"Of course," Charles replied in a strained voice, then inhaled his brandy.

"When was the last time you saw your nephew's wife?"

While Nicholas watched his uncle's face turn haggard, he recalled that Charles had known Megan from his visits to Claremont.

"I believe I saw her last at a dinner party," Charles answered, setting the empty snifter on the desk.

"Was that before or after the wedding?"

"Before." Charles went to twist the ring he normally wore, but it was gone. Nicholas wondered if he had lost it. He narrowed his eyes. His usual diamond stick pin was also missing.

Thomas scribbled in his notes for a moment, and then stopped to ask another question. "You didn't attend the ceremony?"

"No. I've been hawking with some friends and wasn't contacted in time to attend."

"How long have you been hawking?"

Charles's features relaxed a degree. "Six, seven weeks," he replied.

"Thank you, my lord. That is all I needed to ask," the investigator said.

"Certainly. If everyone will excuse me, I would like to see my sister," Charles said. He scrambled from his chair and exited the room.

Nicholas ground his teeth. "He's lying."

All eyes turned to him.

"What makes you say so?" Thomas asked.

"I've known him all my life." He gripped the arms of his chair. "I could always tell when he lied. He can't even gamble..." He halted and sucked in a breath. The conversation he'd had with Jeremy a few months ago came to remembrance. "I think he is involved in this."

Joseph stormed forward. "Are you certain?"

Nicholas shook his head. "But I think I can supply a motive."

CHAPTER 22

The tangy sea air filled Megan's nostrils and whipped hard against her face as she held onto the ship's railing. She much preferred being on deck instead of in the dank little cabin she'd been forced to endure. Holding her face up to the sun, she recalled the times Julian had taken her out on a smaller ship, but never on a clipper.

"Every time I am around you, Megan, you amaze me more," Stuart said into her ear.

She jumped. She'd been so deep in thought, she forgot that Stuart stood beside her. Taking a deep breath, she squinted up to him. "How, exactly, have I amazed you this time?"

He chuckled and grazed her cheek with his fingertips. "Emily and Angie are in their cabin, green as peas. But you are positively glowing. Truly, I thought that the sea made all ladies ill."

"The sea has never made me ill," she said, wishing he would remove his hand from her cheek. His lids went heavy and he leaned forward. With a gasp, she stepped back, her backside bumping against the rail. "Who did you say owned this ship?" she asked.

The corners of his mouth dipped down and he straightened. "Pirates," he answered.

She believed that. The crew was rugged and Stuart stayed by her side at all times. They avoided other ships and didn't hoist a flag.

"How in God's name could you stand the sea for so long a time?" came a female voice.

Megan turned and found Angela standing

behind her. The woman's dull red hair hung limply around her pale, greenish face, and she held her stomach as she shuffled forward. "Don't you dare smile at me like that, Stuart," Angela said. "I can't eat or drink a damn thing. I'm going to kill you when we reach land."

"Oh, Angie, you should be feeling better by tomorrow."

"You said that yesterday!" she said. "I do not know how I shall stand making this trip again in a couple of months."

"You do not have to return, Angie," Stuart said. "You can stay with us."

Angela moaned. "I could not live without Nicky."

Megan's delight at observing Angela so sick evaporated. "What?"

"Goddammit, Angie." Stuart leveled his sister a menacing glare.

Ignoring her brother, Angela gave a smug smile.

Megan gnashed her teeth together. Oh, how she was tempted to slap that satisfied smirk from the woman's face. "You really must taste the slimy, green salted-pork and weevil-infested hardtack today. They aren't so bad after the first bite."

Angela's eyes grew wide, and her pallor deepened to the color of seaweed. Her hands flew to her mouth and she spun around to lean over the rail.

With immense satisfaction, Megan crossed her arms and watched the pitiful wretch try to heave the contents of an empty stomach. She noticed one of the crew looking her way. He had long, greasy hair and a beak of a nose. He licked his lips, his eyes hungry. She shivered and turned away. God, she needed off this ship. Perhaps she should return to her cabin.

****

Megan went below deck and approached Emily's cabin. Thankfully, Angela was still above deck. She was not up to hearing the mewling harridan. She hovered at the door for several seconds. This had to be handled in just the right way.

Taking a deep breath, she knocked on the door. Emily had lied to everyone about Julian, and she needed to learn why. It was possible, if not probable, that Stuart would release her if he knew the truth. When Megan received permission to enter, she opened the door and stepped in.

"May I speak to you?"

"As you wish."

Squaring her shoulders, she decided on the direct approach. "Why did you accuse my brother of getting you with child?"

Emily's good eye narrowed. "Lord Amersleigh is getting what he deserves."

"Are you aware that Julian was falsely accused of getting a woman with child three weeks before you came to him?"

Emily remained silent for several seconds. "Why did you tell me that?" she whispered.

"I wanted you to have a precise view into Julian's perspective, not only what you noticed on the surface. Truly, my brother isn't the cruel blackguard you believe. Emily," she continued, softening her voice, "your husband believed the worst of you because he didn't know the truth—"

"Are you suggesting that I am like Arthur?"

"I cannot say, Emily. But from what I have been subjected to thus far, your codes of ethics and honor are somewhat lacking in my estimation."

Silently cursing her sharp tongue, Megan hoped that she hadn't pushed Emily too far. She wanted to be liberated, but not in the direction of a short plank.

Then Emily surprised her by chuckling. "Oh, Megan, I do believe I see why Stuart is acting a lovesick fool and Angela, a jealous nit-wit." She paused and laughed harder. "I daresay, I was astonished when Angie arrived at the cottage. She was supposed to stay in London."

"Nine years is a long time to harbor a lie," Megan said softly.

Emily shook her head. "I have not lied."

Megan took a steadying breath. "Then convince Stuart to let me go. Even when I am returned, my family will continue to pursue you for what you've done. But if you release me now, I shall make certain they never come for any of you."

"Stuart has promised that we shall remain safe," Emily said.

Megan ground her teeth. "Stuart does not know the extent my family will go for retaliation. Do you not realize that my father will do nothing else until he has me returned? And then he shall deliver the most harrowing vengeance imaginable upon all of you."

Emily's eyes widened, then filled with tears. "Please," she whispered, "you mustn't harm my family. They're all I have."

Megan kept from reaching out to her. Pressing her was the only way to learn the truth. The only way to gain leverage over Stuart to keep Julian safe. "Then you must tell the truth. Now. Before my family catches up to us."

After a shaky breath, Emily closed her eyes and hung her head. "I went to your brother right after learning Nicholas was not in residence." She swiped the tears from her cheeks. "I-I needed help."

"What kind of help?"

Emily raised her head, fresh tears spilling down her face. "I was terrified of my father learning his groom had gotten his eldest daughter pregnant. I foolishly thought I could get help." She paused to wipe her tears away. "Lord Julian misunderstood. He thought I was accusing him of fathering my child. Before I could explain properly, he had me escorted home."

Megan recalled what had been told earlier. "That's when your father made you marry Arthur Wakefield?"

"Yes."

"What happened to the groom?" Megan asked.

"Hanged himself. On my wedding night."

Megan gasped. "Oh, Emily." She took the woman's hand. "That's terrible."

Emily nodded. "That night, I began hating your brother." Her shoulders drooped. "I blamed him for everything. That is why I allowed Stuart to believe it was Julian who fathered my child and abandoned me."

"Please, Emily, you must tell Stuart the truth." She gripped Emily's hand tighter. "I can help you. When my family comes for me, I will help you. Please tell Stuart the truth. He means to kill Julian."

Emily took a slow, deep breath, then nodded. "All right, I will. This farce has gone on long enough."

After leaving Emily, Megan stepped into the companionway. She jerked to a halt when she saw the captain disappear into his quarters. She squared her shoulders and approached his cabin.

Gazing uncertainly at the wooden door for several seconds, she raised her knuckles. It jerked open before she made contact. "May I have a word with you, Captain?"

"Of course." He stepped back to allow her entrance.

Hoping that she wasn't making a huge mistake, she stepped into the cabin. She was surprised to find the spacious room so elegant. The captain walked past the stained-glass windows to his carved oak desk. "Please, have a seat," he offered and poured two drinks from the cabinet behind him. "To what do

I owe this very pleasurable visit?" he asked.

She chewed on her lip as she stared at the dark red liquid. He certainly didn't behave like a pirate captain. She lifted her gaze and clashed with his penetrating stare. "Captain..."

"My name's Jackson. Jack, if you please. And how may I address you?"

"You don't know who I am?"

"This is a pirate ship. One of our rules is not to question the cargo." He sipped his wine. "I know that you are very important to Stuart, though he wouldn't part with any information about you." His dark eyes roved over her face and he gave a jaunty grin. "I did ask."

"My name is Megan Westland—"

"Westland?" His smile vanished. "Any relation to Julian Westland, Lord Amersleigh?"

"Julian is my brother."

He leaned back in his chair and laughed. "Oh, dear lady, what fine yarn you spin."

"I am speaking the truth."

Swallowing his wine, he looked steadily at her for a minute. "Then you would know the name of the fastest ship in his fleet," he said.

"The *Sweet Siren*, a Baltimore clipper, very near to this one. He purchased it two years ago. Please, you must help me get back to my fam—"

A knock interrupted her.

The captain's probing stare remained fixed on her as he gave permission to enter.

When the door flew open, Stuart marched in. Relief slid over his face when he saw her. "By God! I have been searching everywhere for you." He slid his gaze to the captain and his lips formed a grim line.

"Stuart," Jack said in a steely tone. "Did the lady board this ship willingly?" Stuart hung his head. Jack's eyes glittered. The vein in his neck throbbed. He was a panther ready to strike. "Is she

Lord Amersleigh's sister?"

Stuart's jaw tightened. He turned away.

"Now I understand why you felt the need to fake your death," Jack said, then drained his glass.

CHAPTER 23

Nicholas slid from the saddle and marched into the Stenwick townhouse. "I need to speak with Raines," he told the butler. Removing his gloves, he glanced around and frowned at the disrepair. Dust covered the floor, there were missing paintings and statuary, and the house smelled stale. Obviously, Charles had a desperate need for blunt.

Charles's secretary scurried forward and bowed low. "Your Grace." His nasal voice grated on Nicholas's nerves. "What can I do for you?"

"You can tell me the location of my wife."

The man took a step back. His trembling hand brushed his brow. "I-I don't know what—"

Nicholas reached out and gripped the man's lapel. "Tell me!" The rat knew something, and Nicholas prepared to rip it out of the man if necessary.

Raines's shoulders slumped. "L-Lord Stenwick owes a great deal of money. Tens of thousands of pounds." His voice dropped. "If he doesn't come up with it soon, it will be debtor's prison for him."

"Where is my wife?"

The man's eyes went round. "P-Please believe me. All I know is she is on some ship."

Nicholas took a menacing step forward.

The little man paled. "Lord Stenwick hired some men to take your wife. I know where they are."

After obtaining the information, he turned to leave, but halted. "Does Charles know a woman named Angela Cooper?"

Raines jerked with surprise. "Yes."

"Is she involved?"

"Yes."

He gritted his teeth. "Tell me everything."

Nicholas rode back to Kenbrook, his energy nearly spent. He pushed the weakness aside as his thoughts settled on Megan. From what he learned from Raines, the bastards who took his wife were close. And they had information. He handed the reins to the groom as Julian hurried forward. "Where have you been?"

"Come." He started for the house. "I have news."

He told Thomas, Joseph, and Julian all he'd learned. "I'm sure we can sneak up on them. Raines said there were only two of them."

"Why aren't there more men?" Julian asked.

Nicholas almost growled. "That's all the bastard could afford." He tamped back the swell of fury about to rob him of good sense and told them of his plan.

They had to strike immediately. Daylight was nearly spent and Nicholas would not wait another day. The villains could disappear any moment. With twenty of Thomas's men, the two within the old tanner's cottage did not stand a chance.

When Nicholas stepped into the cool interior, he found the prisoners bound and seated on wooden stools. He recognized the same men who had taken his wife. His teeth felt near unto cracking as he clenched his jaw. Only the knowledge that they had information concerning Megan's whereabouts prevented him from tearing the scoundrels apart with his bare hands. Joseph sat in the chair before the larger of the two men. "Where is she?" he demanded.

The man glared. His eye patch had gotten lost during the scuffle, exposing a sunken hole. "I dunno what you be talkin' about," he said, exposing his rotted teeth.

"You will tell me, or you will die," Nicholas replied.

A gasp sounded from the other man. He turned and speared the ruffian a look of pure poison. "Lord Stenwick ain't paid us 'alf wot 'e owes us anyway, Spike."

Joseph rose and approached the smaller man. He rested his hands on his hips. "What is your name?"

"Oliver J. Marsh, milord. But I go by Ollie."

"Tell me what you know, Ollie."

"No..." the other roared and began to struggle against his bindings.

Joseph turned to a guard. "Gag that man."

Ollie swallowed hard. "The seaman took the wee missy ter Scotland for a ransom exchange."

Nicholas felt a twinge of relief. A ransom meant she was alive.

Julian stepped forward. "Is this seaman's name Stuart Williams?" he asked then gave a description of his first mate.

"Aye."

A flash of pain crossed Julian's face. "What ship is he using?"

"The *Enigma*," Ollie answered.

Julian's eyes blazed. "The *Enigma* belongs to Jack Townsend."

Panic seized Nicholas. "Wasn't he accused of murdering his father?"

Julian nodded gravely. "He fled soon after his father was found. All attempts at his capture have proved unsuccessful. And the only ship we have as swift as the *Enigma* is the *Sweet Siren*."

Weakness settled into Nicholas's body, as if Julian's words had sucked all the energy from him. He sagged against the wall. They might find Megan, but they couldn't catch her.

"This wasn't a sudden event. It was planned.

And how does Charles know Stuart?" Julian asked.

The little man's eyes grew fearful. "I swear on me dear mum's grave I says all I knows."

All eyes shifted to his companion. Nicholas grabbed the man's shirt and pressed him to the wall. "Tell me everything that you know," he bellowed, ripping the gag from his mouth. He made a fist and pulled it back. "Then I might allow you to live."

Spike shook his head, his eyes round and full of terror. Julian reached for Nicholas's cocked arm, causing Spike to close his eyes and slump forward in relief. "Nick, wait. He may wish to answer a few questions now."

Nicholas threw the man back onto the wooden stool, then leaned against the stone wall, his shoulder on fire. "The game is up. Say what you know," Julian demanded.

Spike spat to remove the woolen fibers and dirt from his tongue. He looked at Ollie. "Fool. Ye can't trust nobles. We're going to swing fer sure."

Nicholas threw his fist back and struck the large man. The thud sounded sickening in the silence. He hardly felt the pain that vibrated up his uninjured arm as he watched the ruffian tumble to the ground. Spike lifted a hand to his cheek. Nicholas took a step forward, but Julian, obviously reading his intent to pounce, grabbed his arm. "Tell us everything, man, or so help me, you will be drawn and quartered," Nicholas said.

Spike spat blood and part of a tooth out before looking around the room. "Lord Stenwick 'ired us to take the lady. She was supposed to be sent ter Claremont while the duke an' duchess were on their way ter America, but she was sent ter Lun'un instead."

Julian narrowed his eyes. "How does Stenwick know Stuart Williams?"

Spike shook his head. "I dunno."

"Where is Stenwick to meet Stuart after the ransom exchange? How is he to get his share of the gold?" Julian demanded, an undercurrent of deadly intent in his voice.

Spike squeezed his eyes shut and shook his head.

Nicholas stepped forward, his fist raised with murder blazing in his eyes. "Tell us!"

"A tavern on the dock. The Neptune."

Nicholas breathed in deeply. "Are you certain they plan to release my wife after the ransom exchange?"

Spike wiped the blood off his chin. "Lord Stenwick fancies the lass. 'E ain't letting 'er go."

****

Nicholas gazed at the huge orange ball of the sun as it lifted from the reflective waters of the sea. The last crate of gold had just been loaded into the hull of the *Wind Song*, and they were off. His hands tightened on the starboard rail. If his wife was harmed in any way... He closed his eyes. Be damned, he wished the ship had wings.

A hand squeezed his shoulder. He popped his eyes open and jerked his head around.

"I'm sorry, I didn't mean to startle you, Nick," Julian said.

He shook his head. "It is I who must apologize. I'm tense." He glanced over at the color-reflective sea. "God, Julian, I miss her," he whispered. "What if she's hurt?"

"I've known Stuart for years." Julian shook his head. "I'm sure he wouldn't harm her."

"How can you know what that bastard is capable of after this?"

Julian paused, his brows drawn. "You're right, my friend. The man I thought I knew doesn't exist."

Nicholas closed his eyes in despair and held tight to the rail with both hands. Dear God, let them find her soon. And let her be unharmed.

****

"How can anyone breathe such air? I swear I'm going to suffocate if we don't leave this cabin soon," Angela said. "And why must we suffer this dreadful darkness?"

Megan glanced up at the lantern swinging from the ceiling beam and shook her head.

"A lit candle aboard a ship during a storm is dangerous, Angie," Emily said.

Angela ignored her sister's comment. "It's unnatural for a ship to rock about so. I don't think that daft captain is paying attention to what he is doing."

Megan closed her eyes and tried to force the nerve-wracking sound of that shrew's voice from her mind. God's truth, Angela would not allow a whole minute to pass without spewing forth a complaint. The women were ordered to one cabin when the storm arose last night, and Megan could not bear Angela's moaning much longer. Perhaps she could stuff a handkerchief in each ear.

"Don't fret, dearest, I'm certain we shall remain safe," Emily said.

"I can no longer stand the sound of the rain pelting down—"

Megan jumped to her feet. "That is truly outside of enough," she exploded and marched to the door.

"Where are you going?" Emily asked.

Megan jerked open the door and held onto the doorframe while the ship tossed again. "I am going to jump overboard."

Emily chuckled. "But you told me you cannot swim."

"Exactly my point," Megan snapped, then slammed the door behind her. She took a step and crashed into the brick wall of a man's chest. The open door of his quarters allowed enough light for her to see Jack staring down at her. He wore a large smile. "You intend to jump overboard? I must warn you, my lady, these are shark-infested waters."

"A vast improvement," she fumed. "I would rather be locked in the hold than to spend one more second in Angela's presence."

Jack inhaled heavily through his nose. She could see his lips clamped together as he struggled to keep from chuckling. "All right, my dear. You may stay in my cabin. The hold is no place for such a lovely lady."

One of Jack's men moved out from the shadows. His shoulders nearly touched both sides of the companionway at once. Megan could not fathom how such a large man could move so silently, especially with all those knives and daggers he carried. "Problems?" he asked Jack softly.

"No problems," Jack said, and walked into his cabin.

As she followed, the man said, "Och, Captain, you canna—"

Jack held up his hand. "You worry too much for naught, Connor," he said, then closed the door on the glowering Scot.

The captain's room was a lot less dim than her tiny cabin, and she could see fatigue clearly etched on Jack's face. He looked as though he hadn't slept in a month. "Captain, you've come to rest. Perhaps I should—"

"It's Jack. And I've come for a glass of wine. Please, sit." He poured the wine and set a goblet before her. "The worst of the storm is over."

She sipped the Madeira and found it as good as any her father kept in his stores. She looked up and found Jack studying her. Dear Lord, what was she doing alone in a pirate's cabin...again?

Her face must have been transparent. "Do not worry, Megan. You are safe with me," he assured her.

"Jack, please return me."

Regret flickered into his eyes. "I can't risk a trip to London, my lady."

"Then allow me to leave this ship once we lay anchor. I shall employ someone to take me home," she said.

"I am sorry, but you will be much safer in my care."

"Will I be returned to my family when they arrive with the gold?"

Anger crossed his face momentarily, and Megan knew that Stuart had kept a great deal from him. What kind of pirate was Jack the Black Heart?

"That is the plan," he answered.

"May I have your word on that, Jack?"

He must have sensed how much his answer meant to her. He pushed a basket of figs in her direction. "You have my word."

She believed him.

****

The cry of a bird startled Megan awake and reminded her that they had anchored in a secluded cove the night before. She quickly dressed in a dark blue silk gown Jack had found for her and scampered up on deck. She looked at the trees in the distance and smiled. How she longed to walk upon solid earth once again! "Ye smell nice." Megan spun around. Beak Nose was leaning against a mast, staring at her. She didn't like the hunger in his eyes. "Like spring flowers." He took a deep breath and stepped in her direction. "I wonder if ye taste as good as ye smell?"

Horrified, Megan ran to the opposite side of the ship. Her heart hammered in her chest. She heard someone approach and turned with a gasp. Stuart and Connor stormed toward her with distressed expressions. "Take her below," said Connor.

"Captain hasna come up yet."

Now that the danger had passed, she didn't want to leave. She crossed her arms over her chest. "I am not returning to that stagnant cabin until I am good and ready."

"I'll remain with her," Stuart replied, his lips twitching.

She watched the gulls play chase in the sky overhead. How she wished she could speak to them and send them to Nicholas with a message. She would tell her husband how much she loved and missed him. And to please hurry up and rescue her.

"You look lovely."

Megan frowned at Stuart. "You must cease this."

"What?"

"Spouting complements and staring at me like that."

He moved closer and lifted his hand to her cheek. "I like spouting complements and staring at you."

Megan jerked away. "I am a married woman and I love my husband." She spun on her heel and marched back to her cabin, much preferring the small, stuffy room to Stuart's advances.

Ten minutes later, the door flew open, cutting off her thoughts. With a start, Megan jerked her head up. Four of the ugliest, most repulsive crewmen filed into her quarters. One of them was Beak Nose. She blinked, but it was no illusion. Her heart surged into her throat. Megan caught a glimpse of Angela in the companionway just before the door swung shut. The shrew had been glowing in satisfaction. Megan cut her eyes back to the men and felt her skin crawl as they advanced forward.

CHAPTER 24

Megan flew to her feet. "None of you have any right to be here. I demand that you leave at once."

"Ow, now luv, 'ave a 'eart. We was told that ye'd be co-operatin'," Beak Nose jeered.

"Obviously, you were misinformed. Now leave," she ordered, trembling so hard that she found it difficult to stand. They raked their eyes up and down her body. She felt exposed, dirty. And terribly frightened. She wrapped her arms around her middle. Oh, Nicholas. Nicholas! *Please, where are you?* "If you don't leave this instant, I will s-scream." Her voice rose with her panic.

"Ain't nobody gunna 'ear ye, luv. 'Specially if yer muzzled."

Before she could release the shriek of horror lodged in her throat, Beak Nose surged for her. He threw her onto the bed and covered her with his bulky body. Her breath left her lungs in a whoosh. He slapped a grimy hand over her mouth and held her wrists above her head with the other. He licked her cheek. "Ye do taste like flowers."

Terror blazed through her. She kicked and thrashed, trying to scream for help. He laughed at her struggle, fanning her face with his sour breath. "Ye like it, ay?" he taunted, rubbing his hardened sex against her.

Oh, God, no. No! Megan sucked back a sob. The others surrounded the bed. Their images blurred as hot, salty tears raced down her face.

The man shoved a dirty piece of linen into her mouth and secured it with twine. It smelled like a chamber pot and tasted of rotten fish. More twine bound her hands above her head. Bile rose from the pit of her stomach when hands covered her breasts. She shook her head and began to fight with all the energy she had left. Their disgusting chants of encouragement rang through the cabin like a death knell. They ripped at her clothes.

She squeezed her eyes shut until pinpricks of light flickered behind her lids. She whimpered when they tugged at the front of her dress. Her heart thudded. The dress tore and cool air rushed over her breasts. The men's cheers grew. Shame washed over her. How would she ever hold her head up after this? Would she even live after this? She struggled to free her wrists and pain seared her flesh.

Their disgusting hands were everywhere. They tore at the material covering her body and pinched her exposed skin with brutal eagerness. She attempted to kick, but someone held her ankles. For the first time in her life, Megan wished she were inclined to swoon. She didn't want to be conscious for this.

Nicholas! The oblivion that she wished for hovered near. Sounds muffled and numbness washed over her. She could feel her body sinking down...down...down... Just before losing consciousness, Megan thought she heard Jack's voice thunder around the room and the men pleading for mercy.

A crash rang through the room. One minute, Megan heard the roar of the men and the feel of their cruel hands, the next minute she felt a soft blanket settle over her. Was it over? Maybe she was dead. She thought she heard her name.

Strong, gentle arms lifted her. Each bruise, each scratch pulsated on her body and she knew that she still lived. Fiery pain licked over her skin. She yearned for the black oblivion once again. She began to struggle in her rescuer's grasp.

"Easy, now. You're safe." Jack's voice. She slipped into the darkness.

****

Megan cracked open her swollen, salt-crusted eyes. A rainbow of light gleamed from stained-glass windows. She looked around and saw that she lay on the enormous bunk in the captain's quarters. Jack's room.

She tried to rise and piercing pain shot through her. She felt bruised and battered all over. Then the horrible memory of those men surfaced, and a choked sob escaped her lips.

"Megan?"

Jack stood nearby, frowning. Dark circles lay under his eyes and his brows dipped low. "How are you feeling?" he asked softly.

She swept her dry lips with a dry tongue. "Jack, did they..." A tear skidded down her cheek.

Jack lifted a cool glass of water to her lips. "Connor and I arrived in time to stop them."

She inhaled a shuddering breath. "How long have I been asleep?"

"Almost eighteen hours," he answered.

A light knock sounded. Jack's cabin boy carried in a bucket of steaming water. Emily followed close behind, her face pale and full of distress. She stopped before the bed and wrung her hands. "Megan, are you all right?"

Megan smiled in reassurance, ignoring the pain it caused her cracked lips. "I'm fine," she said.

Jack dismissed the cabin boy. "Megan, I will send something for you to eat in half an hour." He spun around and left before she could object.

"I will assist you with your bath," Emily explained. "If you're too hurt to move, I can—"

"I think I can manage." She lifted the covering from her bare body and grimaced. Bruises and scratch marks covered her skin.

She heard a gasp and looked up to see Emily's eyes filled with tears. "Oh, Megan, I am so sorry," she sobbed. "And so is Stuart. He wanted to tell you, but the captain wouldn't allow it." She hung her head, tears dripping from her chin. "Forgive us."

"Neither you nor Stuart is responsible for this. Please help me to the tub."

Emily lifted her damp face, revealing red eyes full of grief and surprise, and did as she asked.

Megan eased into the tub, biting her lip until she tasted metallic saltiness. The steamy water stung her scratches as though her flesh was being torn from her bones. She let out a small sigh and began to wash the blood and grit from her body.

After the bath, she felt almost whole again. Her hair was scrubbed clean, and her battered body no longer ached. Salve and new bandages had been applied to the rope burns that marred each wrist and to the deeper scrapes on her body. Jack had found her a beautiful, cream-colored muslin gown embroidered with dark pink roses. She outlined one of the dainty rosebuds with a fingertip and wondered how she would wear something so pretty after... She gritted her teeth, praying the scars to her soul would heal as surely as the scars on her skin.

Megan sat before a large mirror while Emily pinned her hair into a twist. She lifted her gaze to Emily's ashen face and frowned. "Emily? What is it?"

Emily covered her face with her hands and burst into tears.

Megan rose from the chair. Her heart knotted with fear. "What?"

"I-I'm afraid for Angie," Emily sobbed. "The c-captain has announced that there w-will be a trial up on deck before the day's end. Th-Those awful men claim that she put them up to h-hurting you."

Megan sank into one of the chairs before Jack's

desk. Her mind filled with the image of Angela's satisfied features when those men closed the door to her cabin. What kind of punishment would Jack inflict upon a woman?

A tap at the door cut through her musings. When the cabin boy stepped into the room with a tray of food, Jack's voice wafted down to them.

Emily's eyes filled with alarm. "The trial has begun," she wailed, then hurried from the room behind the cabin boy.

Megan stood at the open door and frowned with indecision. Terror sliced through her at the thought of leaving the safety of the cabin. What would happen if Emily tried to interfere with the captain's orders?

Straightening her spine, she stepped out of the room.

"...And that concludes the evidence against these five. What say you, men? What shall their punishment be?" Jack asked his crew.

Megan stayed within the evening's shadows as she reached the deck. Jack stood before the five tied figures—Angela and those four horrible seamen. She shivered and turned away from the sight of them. The remainder of the crew conversed in a huddle several feet away. Then she caught sight of Stuart watching the proceedings near the rail. His shoulders were hunched, his expression despondent.

Connor spoke. "The men will be flogged at dawn. Twenty lashes each."

Jack nodded. "And the woman?"

Connor's gaze never wavered. "She'll stay the entire night in the hold wi' the men."

"No!" Angela tried to scramble forward but Connor held her back. "You can't do this to me." She sobbed hysterically and shook her head.

"Everyone will be tied and a guard will be present," Jack explained.

She glanced back over her shoulder. The men were scowling mercilessly at her. With a gagging sound, Angela turned away and vomited all over Connor's shoes.

Megan shivered and returned to the captain's quarters. Jack returned a short while later. She turned from the books she'd been studying on his shelf and sat on one of the chairs before his desk.

He poured them each a glass of wine, then eased into his own chair. She indicated the bookshelf. "How do you keep them from falling to the floor during a storm?"

With a smile, he leaned over in his chair. She watched in fascination as he pulled a brass handle and a wooden door slid shut over the books. Ingenious. She glanced back down at the book in her hands, surprised by her amusement. After what she just experienced, she never thought to be amused again. Perhaps, she could get past what had happened.

The next morning, Megan woke with a start to the clamor of running feet and shouting men. She rose from the bed and quickly dressed.

When she threw open the door, an enormous blast sounded. The bottom of her stomach fell away. Dear God.

That was cannon fire.

CHAPTER 25

Megan raced up on deck, her blood turning to ice in her veins. Men scrambled about, shouting to each other to prepare the cannons. They were going to war. The ship shuddered as it eased out of the cove. She gave a screech and held on to the rail. She looked out to sea and noticed the other ship. *Royal Navy*. Her knees went weak. The frigate dwarfed the *Enigma* and held almost four times as many cannons. Cannons pointing right at them.

Please, God, let her survive this.

With a ferocious blast and a belch of smoke, the frigate fired. The metal ball whistled through the air. Megan gritted her teeth and steeled herself for the impact. The ship moved just enough and the ball missed by inches. Water spewed up, drenching her and five of the crew. She gasped, nearly losing her balance, and coughed as salt water filled her mouth.

Megan shook uncontrollably. That had been the navy's last warning. There would be a brigade of firing next time. Her stomach clenched. She could see the scuttle of red coats on board as they prepared the cannons.

They went off just as the wind picked up, snapping the sails overhead to attention. A long succession of deafening thunder sounded. She shrieked. Her ears rang. The *Enigma* found speed.

It wasn't fast enough. One of the balls struck the top of the aft mast, raining splinters down on deck. The other ball took out part of the rail just a few feet from Megan. Still more hit the side of the ship out of view. The ship jolted with each blow, the masts swinging side to side. She stood paralyzed with fear.

The rail gave way and she screamed. A hand snaked out and grabbed her just in time. "Can ye no' stay below, woman?" Connor growled and pushed her toward the stairs.

"Are we sinking?" she asked, terrified of the answer. She swiped a wet lock out of her eyes with a trembling hand.

"No' yet." He pointed toward the stairs. "Go. Capt'n's orders."

On shaky legs, she made for the opening. She dodged wood from the mast and pieces of a barrel. A moan caught her attention. Beak Nose lay in a pool of blood, his left leg missing mid-thigh, the jagged white bone poking out of red-black muscle. She clamped a hand over her mouth and turned away. Her heart raced. She leaned back against the mast for support. God help her.

Jack roared orders. The men flew into action. The *Enigma* picked up speed, but it was wounded. It would not get away from the frigate. Her heart sank to her toes. It would overtake the *Enigma* within minutes. Oh, God. She could not stand another round of cannon fire.

"Look," one of the crew yelled, "she's a-reef."

Megan swiveled around and found the navy ship unable to pursue. The men cheered. She put a hand over her heart, her breath choppy. How long until the frigate became dislodged?

One of the crew whistled. "Another ship." He pointed to the east. Megan found a tiny black dot in the distance, heading toward them. Another navy ship? She leaned back against the mast. How much more could she take?

"Come, lass." Connor pulled her along. "Ye be a stubborn one." He escorted her to her cabin. "Yer no' tae come out, aye?" Before waiting for an answer, he closed the door.

She sat on the bunk and willed her heart to stop pounding. She closed her eyes, her hands gripping the bedding in a tight fist. Within an hour, the *Enigma* slowed and came to a halt. Men ran about. She heard pistol fire and shouts. She put her hands over her ears, shaking from head to toe.

The door crashed open. She shrieked then gasped, scooting back against the wall.

Nicholas.

She didn't trust her eyes. She could only sit there with her mouth hanging open.

"Megan?" He moved cautiously toward her, his voice gentle. "It's all right, love, you're safe now."

"Nicholas?" she whispered, then flew into his arms.

She wanted to faint with relief. Tears poured from her eyes, blurring her vision. She held him tight as his warmth seeped into her bones. Oh, God, how she'd missed him. She breathed in his sandalwood scent. Sobs tore from her lips.

He pressed a kiss to her temple. "Don't worry, love. I am taking you home." His words were thick and raw with emotion. He rubbed his hand up and down her back.

Her sobs subsided into shuddering hiccups. When she found a measure of control, she scrubbed the wetness from her cheeks.

Nicholas leaned back. His concerned gaze roved her face. "Are you all right?"

She nodded. "You found me."

He pressed his forehead against hers. "Always."

Megan hovered near tears again, but she swallowed them back. Nicholas took her hand and led her to the door. "Come, let's get you home."

Home. She closed her eyes and sighed, wanting nothing above putting this terrible ordeal behind her.

He led her up on deck. It took a moment for her

eyes to adjust to the blinding sunlight. Julian's crew held Jack's at pistol point. Her numbness began to lift. She was really going home.

Nicholas started for Julian's ship. "Come, love."

Megan turned to follow. A woman screamed. She spun around in time to see Angela running toward her with murder in her eyes. The air left Megan's lungs in a whoosh just as Angela made contact. They toppled over the gap in the rail, straight into the water.

"No!" Nicholas dove in after his wife, fear squeezing his heart. The cold water swallowed him whole. It stung his eyes as he descended into the ocean's frigid depths. Kicking his legs, he released some air from his lungs and sank lower. His pulse pounded in his ears. His chest started to sting, but he continued to swim, hoping, praying...

Hair grazed his hand. Nicholas grabbed it and pulled the body to his, praying with all his might. With no air left, he worked his way to the surface.

His chest constricted like a knife had been jammed into his heart.

Dear God, she was so still.

He climbed the ladder, then lowered his wife's inert form onto the polished wood. He searched her blue-tinted features and found no sign of life. Closing his eyes, he crashed to his knees and held her tight. Fat, scalding drops ran down his cheeks as he began to rock back and forth.

"God, please, no!" The words tore from his throat.

He was barely aware of Julian's hand clamping his shoulder. "Don't you do this to me, Megan. Don't you dare!" He paused to give her a shake as anger welled up within him. "Do you hear me?"

He halted.

Had she just made a noise? He kept his eyes riveted to her blue lips.

They parted and seawater spilled out. She began to choke and cough.

Unable to move or breathe, he watched her eyelids flutter open. Her violet eyes stood out against her snowy skin. He released a sob as he hugged her tiny body to his.

Joy engulfed him. He scrubbed the dampness from his cheeks. His love was alive, in his arms...and he was never going to let her go.

EPILOGUE

London, three months later

Megan stood before the parlor window, stiff with anticipation. She worried her bottom lip in her teeth as she eyed the dark clouds billowing in from the north. The wind rattled the window. Behind her, the room rumbled with conversation and occasional bursts of laughter. Megan smiled when she discerned Emily's happy chatter and Torie's friendly response. Both Evie and Torie's ready acceptance of Emily flooded her with joy.

A carriage turned the corner and her heart lurched. She kept her eyes on the black vehicle as it approached and willed it to stop before the townhouse. When it passed, she swallowed back her disappointment. Her fear grew. Where was he? He should have arrived hours ago.

Movement in the reflection of the glass pane caught her eye. She looked up and found her husband directly behind her. His eyes gleamed with love, and he smiled. She returned the smile and felt his warm body close the distance between them. His arms crept around her waist, and he settled a hand protectively over her middle, where their child grew. She placed her hands on top of his and rested against him.

"How are you feeling?" he asked.

She squelched a sigh and turned in his arms. "I am perfectly fit."

"Come sit on the sofa, love. You've been standing too long."

She allowed him to lead her to the sofa. "Would you like something to drink?" he asked.

"Yes, please."

As soon as Nicholas crossed the room, the door to the parlor opened.

Megan stood and rushed to her brother. Julian gave her a warm embrace, then pulled away and looked her over from top to bottom. "Ah, darling sister, you're glowing. Being with child certainly agrees with you."

Megan felt like she would burst with pride. Then she sobered. "Did you find him?"

The joyous light within Julian's eyes went out. "Yes."

Nicholas returned and she took the drink he offered. "And?"

"Jack released Charles into my care without any difficulties," Julian said. "That's why I'm late. I took him straightway to Newgate."

She smiled up at her brother and held out her hand. "You owe me one hundred pounds." She wiggled her fingers. "And not a word of this to Mother. You'd be in as much trouble as I."

Julian sighed as he reached into his pocket.

"I told you Jack would give the swine over," she said smugly, stuffing the notes into her wrist bag. "If you'll recall, he did send you quite a bit of gold to repair the *Sweet Siren*. Jack only takes from those who deserve it." She refused to acknowledge Nicholas's grunt of jealousy.

"Have you forgotten about the pending murder charge against him, dear sister?"

Megan lifted her chin. "He did not murder his father." She was not about to add that she had hired Thomas Porter to find the real murderer of Jack's father. "Have you talked to Father about being a ship's captain?"

"Master," Julian corrected. "A merchant ship's

commander is called 'Master.'"

"Well, then, have you?"

"Didn't have to. I'm leaving the sea."

"Oh, Julian." Megan hugged her brother. "That's wonderful news. I shall like having you around more often."

"Yes, well... I think I need a drink."

Megan watched him leave. Maybe now he would find a wife and be as happy as she was.

"Come, love. Sit and rest a while," Nicholas insisted.

Megan sat on the sofa beside her husband and watched her friends. How she wished that they would all find the love and happiness she had. After all, she shouldn't be the only one of them so fortunate. Ideas began forming in her head.

"You look like the cat that ate the cream."

"That's because I feel like it." She snuggled closer to him. "Oh, Nicholas, you make me so happy."

His expression softened with tenderness. "We make each other happy, my love," he replied, then he leaned forward and sealed his words with a kiss.

A word about the author...

From the first moment I saved the knight in shining armor at age eight, I fell in love with romance. Since then, I have conjured many stories, and now I am excited to bring the best of them to you.

My main love is the Regency historical, but don't be surprised if you find some medieval and western romances show up.

I am a native Texan and have deep roots in the small Texas town in which I live. My husband is incredibly wonderful and supportive and I have one awesome teenage son. Going back to school for my MBA is keeping me busy, but has not stopped me from my first love—creating exciting new worlds and interesting characters to fill them.

I hope you enjoy my books!

Visit Tiffany at: *http://www.tiffanygreen.net*

Thank you for purchasing
this Wild Rose Press publication.
For other wonderful stories of romance,
please visit our on-line bookstore at
www.thewildrosepress.com

For questions or more information,
contact us at
info@thewildrosepress.com

The Wild Rose Press
www.TheWildRosePress.com

Other suspense-filled Roses to enjoy from The Wild Rose Press

DON'T CALL ME DARLIN' by Fleeta Cunningham. Texas, 1957: Carole faces not only censorship but mysterious threats and a fire-setting assailant. Will the County Judge who's dating her protect or accuse her?
~from *Vintage Rose (historical 1900s)*

SECRETS IN THE SHADOWS by Sheridon Smythe. Lovely widow Lacy had taken in two young children—and the rambunctious little angels wasted no time getting her into trouble with Shadow City's new sheriff...
~from *Cactus Rose (historical Western)*

SOLDIER FOR LOVE by Brenda Gale—An award-winning novel set on a lush Caribbean island. As CO of the American peacekeeping force, Julie has her hands full dealing with voodoo signs and a handsome subordinate.
~from *Last Rose of Summer (older heroines)*

TASMANIAN RAINBOW by Pinkie Paranya. A concert violinist grapples with remote ranch life, intrigue and the mystery of a missing diary, the peril of a flood in which all could be lost, and the undeniable attraction of the man who would do anything to protect his son.
~from *Champagne Rose (contemporary)*

THAT MONTANA SUMMER by Sloan Seymour. Samantha has everything but love. Dalton has only one thing on his mind: land. Neither wants to be a summer fling or be stalked by a mysterious attacker.
~from *Yellow Rose (contemporary Western)*

A CHANGE OF HEART by Marianne Arkins. Jake Langley returns to Wyoming to find more than changes at the family ranch. Discovery of a well-kept secret sets duty against heart's desire, changing hearts and lives forever.
~from *Yellow Rose (contemporary Western)*

DRAKE'S RETREAT, by Wendy Davy. Maggie needs a place to hide. Drake's Retreat, deep in the Sierra Nevada Mountains, is the perfect solution. But she has to convince the intimidating resort owner to let her stay.
~from *White Rose (inspirational)*